THE CHILDREN OF AETERNITAS

E. J. Myatt

Copyright © 2024 Edward Myatt

All rights reserved

The right of Edward Myatt to be identified as the Author of the Work has been asserted by him in accordance with the Copyright, Designs and Patents Act 1988. All characters – other than the obvious historical figures – in this publication are fictitious and any resemblance to real persons, living or dead, is purely coincidental.

No part of this book may be reproduced, or stored in a retrieval system, or transmitted in any form or by any means, electronic, mechanical, photocopying, recording, or otherwise, without express written permission of the publisher.

For my parents.

ACKNOWLEDGMENTS

Firstly, thank you to my parents for encouraging me to just have a go, and backing me when I actually did. A big thank you to everyone who read through early versions and gave their feedback. Thank you to everyone who heard what I was doing and didn't laugh. And thank you for reading this book, I really hope you enjoy it.

"Everyone sees what you appear to be, few experience what you really are"

NICCOLÒ MACHIAVELLI, THE PRINCE

PROLOGUE

London
Spring, 1666

The city stank. An unusually warm spring had followed the intense rainfall of the months before, leaving the city smothered in festering waste. The vast numbers of people daily walking the streets only added to the filth left piling at every roadside and street corner. In the deserting light of the early evening, every step was a lottery. Only faint candlelight, creeping through cracks around shuttered windows, provided any guidance away from the squelch of a misplaced foot.

Moving with any stealth was almost impossible. The choice was either stick to the shadows or bring a lantern and keep your feet unsoiled. He had chosen the former. A decision he cursed under his breath as his boots slipped, forcing an attempt to regain his balance by scrabbling at the uneven walls that lined the street.

This part of the city was unfamiliar to him. He had only agreed to the meeting place so he could be away from familiar, prying eyes that were the habit of his usual residence. Looking over his shoulder to make sure no one had noticed his blunder, he continued, skirting along the side of the streets, away from the worst of whatever waste it was that sucked at his boots.

On leaving the house he had forgone his usual attire, opting for clothing that would not stand out. The aim was to be as forgettable as possible if the meeting was to go without a hitch. Although it had been a long time in the planning, with any luck this would be the only time the two of them would ever meet. After today, everything would change, his position elevated as one of the heralds of a new age.

The heavy splash of someone's misplaced foot from close behind him brought his wandering mind back to the task at hand. Nothing of any importance could happen if he was followed. No one could possibly know that the meeting had taken place. Slipping down a side street he waited in darkness for a group of three men to pass by. Two of them were propping up the third as they staggered into a nearby public house, greeted by a friendly cheering from inside. Clearly they were expected. Checking that the way was once again clear, he continued along the main street, upping the pace to make sure he wasn't late.

Reaching the square, he pulled his thin travelling cloak closer around his body; an automatic reaction to finding himself in open space for the first time that evening. This was the place he had been told to find. Once here the contact would make themselves known. After a quick scan of his new surroundings he was sure he was alone. Settling into a leaning position against the nearest wall, he waited. Waiting hadn't been part of the plan.

Ears pricking at the slightest sound, he started as an animal yowled, only able to relax as a scruffy looking cat sauntered across the square from another side street.

He watched as it found a dry spot on the cobbles near a doorway, plopping itself down to give its hindquarters a quick clean.

"Been to the market this week?"

He stumbled sideways, almost falling to the filthy street in surprise. A decrepit looking man sidled up next to him. He must have been at least sixty, broad shoulders hunched like many of the men who earned a living labouring across the city, but still, his giant frame was evident. Grey hair poked like thatch from beneath his hood as he stared down, waiting for an answer.

"I'm sorry...what?"

"Have you been to the market this week?" The man repeated slowly.

"Oh. No, I only go on the second week of the month."

He responded with the agreed reply, arranged to ensure they would know each other at the rendezvous. Waiting had made him uneasy, but he had certainly not expected to meet a grizzled old man. His gut felt like it was starting to twist. Though he appeared to have seen better days, it was evidently clear this man was not to be trifled with.

"That's probably for the best. That's always when they bring their best produce."

He almost missed the expected answer, preoccupied with wondering whether he too should have used an agent for this exchange. This man knew the correct signals, but the agreement had been to meet in person.

"Right, do you have it?" The old man asked.

"Well, yes. But I had rather thought it would be someone else I was meeting this evening. We had agreed that for a subject of this importance it would be prudent to meet for the exchange."

"Sorry sir, just doing my job. So if you wouldn't mind handing it over, then we can both be on our way."

Something was definitely wrong. This was not the person he had agreed to meet. They were rushing it. Where was the feeling of triumph? Another exchange would have to be arranged. Even if the old man was bigger than him, he was pretty sure he could outrun him.

"I think actually I do mind. This was not the situation that I agreed to. I will be in contact to arrange another meeting."

With that, he turned his back on the old man and began walking toward the street he had come down. He barely made it two steps. In a flash a hand clamped over his mouth as the blade swept across his throat, sending him crumpling into a heap on the cobbled floor.

"You fool. All you had to do was play along." The old man reached down to remove the letter from inside the jacket of the gurgling mess on the floor. Standing to reveal his full height he removed his hood to reveal a dark mop of hair, the ends tinged grey with soot. He turned to the shadows and presented the letter to the person standing there.

"Thank you. Now go and clean up, that muck on your face is ridiculous and there's blood everywhere. And, in future, make sure you have secured the item before disposing of someone – they tend to be less useful if they can't talk. The river should do for him."

1

Oxford
Early Summer, 1666

William la Penne lay back in a warm bed of grass, his eyes fixed on the skies, as the early morning sun bathed his face in its glow. Though still early summer, the dew of the night before had already evaporated, leaving the ground dry. A light breeze drifting across the meadow from the nearby river provided welcome respite from a heat that later in the day would become stifling. For years this had been his favourite place to escape the noise of the nearby city.

Above him a bird of prey rode the gentle winds, wheeling this way and that. He likened the movement to that of driftwood controlled by the lolling tides. Except, he mused, unlike a piece of flotsam, this magnificent bird was entirely in control. Each change of direction appeared completely effortless, just the slightest tilt of a giant wing. It was not much more than a dark speck in the sky but he thought he could just make out a fork in the tail; marking it out as a puttock.

Sitting by the banks of the river had always been a

rewarding experience for William. There was something about the sounds of moving water and the presence of wildlife that calmed him. Clear blue skies and the warming sun only added to his relaxation.

It had been in a similar spot on the riverbank, almost exactly a year before, that his mind now wandered to. He had been equally lost in contemplation then. It seemed like an age ago. Back then he had company. His wife had been tucked under his right arm as they lay back against one of the many tall trees. While his attention had been fixed on her, a gaggle of unwanted guests had gathered, attracted by generous handouts from the woman next to him. An overexcited honk from one of their feathered companions had made him aware of the growing numbers of geese and ducks. He had been forced to shoo them away before they could deprive him of the bread and cheese that made up the picnic lunch.

He smiled at the memory. Bittersweet.

An awareness of figures approaching his spot tore him reluctantly from his daydream. It was probably a blessing. More often than not such trails of thought led to days avoiding interaction with, or even sight of, another human being. Nowadays self-inflicted solitude was the norm for him. He jokingly told himself that one cannot wallow in self-pity and melancholy in quite the same way when around friends - they have the upsetting habit of providing comfort and occasionally even allowing enjoyment in their company. Perish the thought that they might detract from his sullen mood. With a grimace he looked over to the approaching figures, readying himself for the inevitable encounter.

As the figures drew closer, emerging as silhouettes against the low-lying sun, William was able to pick out three individuals. Only one was identifiable, but instantly recognisable. Standing a good foot taller than the other two, it could only be his close friend, and former colleague, Stephen Berry. He found his sullen mood easing as the tall man walked over.

William and Stephen had met whilst studying at university in Oxford several years ago, forming an unlikely friendship. At first, neither had paid particular attention to the other - William had thought Stephen unnecessarily loud, overly prone to brash outbursts. He had preferred the quieter company of his own thoughts. Stephen had, in turn, thought William extremely arrogant, mistaking his introverted nature for one of contempt for others, a haughtiness that caused him to shun any he considered lower than himself. Though at the same college, it hadn't been until a few weeks into their first winter term that they had been brought together. A chance encounter when a group of mutual acquaintances had invited both men to enjoy a festive meal had resulted in a change of opinion on both sides. Drinks had certainly played their part, flowing freely, as was the habit of young men with nothing better to do than study. Since that day, the two had been virtually inseparable. They had stuck together through the rest of their time at university and had even ventured into the same line of work when called to serve the King. It was only the death of William's wife that had lead to any great length of time spent apart. William had chosen to remain in Oxford, while Stephen continued his work in the capital.

Slowly working his way onto his feet, he waved a welcome, brushing himself down. Stephen flashed a broad smile, greeting his friend as the other two men hung back.

"Hello Will, I thought we might find you here. Lost in your daydreams, as always."

"Ha! Well, someone has to dream them I suppose. How did you know I would be here? Thought I had escaped the notice of anyone this morning." he replied, drawing the large man into an embrace, his solitary mood evaporating.

"Oh I remember the spot well. You are nothing if not a creature of habit. I couldn't begin to count the number of times I've found you here musing after lectures, pondering who knows what."

"How are you? It's wonderful to see you back in this neck of the woods, I haven't seen you in an age. What on Earth are you doing here? Is London not proving enough to keep you busy?"

Stephen's face dropped slightly, the smile of delight turning to more of a grimace, "You know how London consumes a man. I've been trying to get out to see you but something always comes up. And yes, the goings-on in London is actually why I'm here. You see there has been a spot of bother."

"There's always a spot of bother Stephen, that's why you're there to deal with it. I'd have thought that was apparent by now." William laughed, his hand still planted on his friend's shoulder.

"Whilst I appreciate the great sympathy Will," Stephen replied with heavy sarcasm, "But this is rather different."

"Different how?" It was clear to William the direction the conversation was going. He had been reluctant to ask, but his friend's undertone of urgency had pricked his interest. The two men had worked together in the service of the King before the great tragedy that had befallen William; removing him from work and public life. Though he had not gone back since, he had enjoyed their work as protectors of the King's secrets. As part of the network of intelligence gatherers they had been through a lot together. Stephen's unannounced arrival, accompanied by two men, could only mean he was going to be asked to return.

"I can't really say much now, but I'd have thought the fact that I'm here talking to you about work might indicate what I'm about to ask."

"I'd thought as much. So, I suppose His Lordship has sent you to bring me back? Has he really not been able to find anyone to take my place? There must be hundreds working for him across the country, not to mention overseas. I suppose these two are back up in case I refuse?"

"Don't be ridiculous, they were sent to show me where you might be found – not that I needed much help in the end.

And yes, there are many working for His Lordship, but not with quite the same talents as yours. I like to think that I have most cases covered, but I could really do with your help on this one. You see one of the men that worked for me recently washed up at the docks in London. His throat had been sliced open. These things happen in the capital all the time, especially in this line of work, I know, but the problem is, he had a letter…"

"Seriously?" William snorted a laugh, "Let me guess, it's important and has gone missing? How is it that confidential information like that always manages to mysteriously disappear?"

"You don't know the half of it," came the grave reply, "Apparently this letter was no laughing matter. His

Lordship will explain. Doubt he'll say it, but he needs you back, requested you personally."

William sighed. It had been a while since he had worked. After taking leave to mourn the passing of his wife he had not returned. With senses dulled by a numbness that engulfed him, it had been easy to walk away. Nothing seemed worth much anymore and he had not gone back. However, he had not reckoned on Stephen's appearance having such an immediate impact on him. William found he had missed the sense of comradeship. Though he had committed his time to literary studies and the pursuit of academic interests, there was nothing quite like the thrill of a real chase; the result of a puzzle that could mean life or death. He had been itching for something more. Perhaps getting back to work would allow some rest from the demons that too often crawled out from the darkest corners of his mind. He had feigned disinterest as best he could for as long as possible, but his decision had not taken long to make.

"Right. Let me pack everything up, we'll have supper and be away in the morning." Decision made - best not to think about it too long, else he would undoubtedly change his mind. He might not be ready, or even completely willing, but he was good at this work and something was needed to occupy his mind.

"Sorry old boy, time is of the essence with this one. We'll have to go now. These two," Stephen motioned to the others he had approached with, "will follow behind with your things later. Just pack the essentials and we'll be on our way."

"Alright." William conceded, "I'm based at the Bear Inn just down from the Swindlestock Tavern and St. Martin's Tower. Let me jot a quick note to the landlord to keep the room open for me. That shouldn't be a problem."

Ignoring Stephen's questioning look he set off back across the meadow with the others in tow. So, he thought, back to London it is; and back to work.

∞

William's lodgings at the Bear were far from lavish. The rooms were ordinarily rented for only a few days at most. The owners relied on the constant, quick turnover of custom to make their money. His continual residence was therefore highly unusual, but he paid premium rates and the innkeepers had grown accustomed to his presence. He was an easy customer and prompt payment of rent meant his landlords were happy to have him stay for an undefined length of time.

Stepping into his friend's room, Stephen could tell no one else had entered in a long time. The room was not so much dirty as overflowing. Books covered many of the surfaces, with pamphlets and old newspapers filling any remaining space. Their large numbers lent a claustrophobic feel, compounded by the thick, stagnant air hanging around them.

"Would it hurt to open a window once in a while?" Stephen coughed as he tiptoed around the piles of clutter that made up the floor.

"Hmmm?... Is it really that bad?" came the distracted reply as William threw a collection of crumpled items of clothing into a small trunk.

"Yes, it is." Stephen had moved over to the window, wading through a loose collection of papers, to find a layer of accumulated dust and grime so thick that the latch was essentially fused shut.

Finished with throwing clothes into his case, William watched his friend attempt to open the window.

"Are you really not going to tell me more of what's going on until we reach London? What exactly are we dealing with here?"

"Sorry old chap, it's more than my life's worth if His Lordship finds out I told you before he does." With a grunt from the large man, the window was sent flying open. "There, that's better. Oh, you're done. Shall we be off then?"

William accepted the large man's excuse for not revealing more information. His Lordship, the Head of Intelligence, was intimidating at the best of times. It would not do to have him on their case before the mission had even begun.

"After you. No wait, give me a hand with this trunk will you. Oh, and that window should probably be shut, don't want birds nesting in the room and no one else will come in to check."

"I'm not surprised." muttered Stephen, "I doubt they'd find anything anyway."

Between the two of them, they managed to lug the deceptively heavy wooden trunk out to their carriage and began the long journey to the capital.

2

Their carriage jerked along uneven tracks, cut into the dirt of the road through constant use. As the spires of Oxford disappeared into the distance, the city's dense collection of buildings was quickly replaced by yellowing fields of corn that made up much of the county's farmland. Buildings became less and less regular, set further back from the road. Only the occasional inn provided much change in the scenery, dotted along the road to accommodate the needs of weary travellers.

Stephen was still unsure whether it had been wise to involve his friend. For over a year now William had withdrawn almost entirely from all aspects of public life; removing himself from London, he shunned all company. Even Stephen had only seen him on a few, brief instances during this period. Intermittent letters were all that regularly connected his friend with the outside world. On more than one occasion he had thought his friend lost; a deep melancholy driving William further into a darkness he created for himself. But, in the end, His Lordship had made the call; any say Stephen had in the matter had been taken from him.

It was much to Stephen's astonishment that his friend had been so easily persuaded to return to London.

He had written before, asking William if he might return to the capital, from where he could keep a closer watch over him. The answer had always been a gentle but firm "no." His friend had remained occupied with coming to terms with the passing of his beloved wife, and his new focus on academia. But this time William had agreed despite considerably less information than he'd been provided in Stephen's letters. Stephen couldn't begin to understand William's thinking. It was hard enough at the best of times. He supposed the journey would be hard for William; London was where his young wife had so suddenly passed. It would be a long two days on the road with plenty of time to become absorbed in thoughts of a return to the capital. Once there, Stephen hoped work would occupy William's wandering mind. A welcome distraction. Who knew, it may help start the healing. Although, perhaps William's readiness to accept a return to work was a sign that time was starting to work its healing.

Stephen chuckled to himself, thinking of how William and Ana had met. Posing as traders, the two men had been sneaking around the French port of Le Havre. They had been tasked with finding any confirmation of the rumours that the French navy had developed a new build of ship - supposedly it would run rings around the newly founded Royal Navy. They had been caught, red-handed, breaking into the shipyard. But she had inexplicably been there to provide them with an alibi. As the daughter of a prominent, much trusted, Dutch tradesman acting as a private merchant to the head of the French navy, their accusers had no choice but to release them. Only the twinkle in her flashing blue eyes as she looked at William gave any indication of her motives.

The strange encounter had begun a wonderful relationship, William besotted from day one. Ana's bright laughter brought William out of his shell. The usually quiet man had become the soul of the party, made confident in love. It had not taken long for them to be married. Ana had rightfully captured the heart of everyone on that day, leaving the collected friends and family basking in the elegance of the long white dress that - on her tall, slim frame – would have left any of Europe's royalty feeling vastly inadequate. Yet everyone gathered on that day had been made to feel welcome by her easy conversation and amicable nature.

In the three years, they had been married, William and Ana had been a whirlwind of energy; each swept up in the other. Their infectious spirit spread to all they came into contact with.

Her death had been sudden, a terrible, devastating shock. Like many cases across the country, there had been no warning. When the plague struck, it took no care for the devastation it left behind. Within days the physicians had pronounced Ana dead. William had not even been allowed to see the body; the fear of spreading the illness so great that only the plague doctors, in their beaked masks, were permitted access to the dead. Not knowing what else to do, William had fled the capital.

Stephen remembered how, in the weeks following Ana's sudden, terrible death, he had spent a lot of time in Oxford keeping William company. Not much was said between them. There was not much that could be said. William would spend days at a time sitting on the same stone bench outside his ancestral home, just outside the city, staring out into the distance in silence. Stephen would arrive at the house, walk to the rear and simply sit with his friend. He knew there was nothing he could say so soon after such a horrific shock. All attempts at comfort would fall on deaf ears or even trigger an angry outburst that could poison the already sullen mood. He knew that it was best to allow the silence, only hoping that his good friend would appreciate the company. Each visit would end the same way, after spending hours just sitting, Stephen would stand, give an affirming squeeze to his friend's shoulder, receive a pat on the hand in reply, and leave. Except for the occasional brief exchange, it was such silence that dominated the two days in the coach travelling to London.

∞

The two men in the carriage looked an unlikely pairing. Both were tall, but Stephen cast a shadow over everyone he had ever met. The top of William's head came only to the bottom of the taller man's ears. Next to the average man, he was at least a head taller, making him immediately stand out in any crowd. They dressed very differently. William wore no finery. His appearance was markedly sober, dressed predominantly in dark colours. However, if one were to get the opportunity to look closely, they would notice that his dress was of the finest quality. He wore his hair short, in a style close to that favoured by many puritans, completing his understated appearance. His only flamboyance was the close cut and neatly sculpted goatee that exaggerated his jaw, coming to an emphasised point on his chin. Stephen, on the other hand, embraced the fact that he would always stand out. Even the most ostentatious young men considered some of his outfits to have gone too far in their gaudiness.

William felt that this was an altogether generous understatement.

The large man's hair fell in a mass of curls collecting on his shoulders, reflecting the trend of the royal court. Where others spent time achieving this desirable look, even going as far as to wear wigs, Stephen was blessed with the kind of hair that always fell perfectly in place without any effort on his part.

William had not always worn his hair short. When Stephen had first seen his short hair, he had been appalled. That it was less cumbersome and far less hassle was beside the point. It was not fashionable and therefore completely unacceptable. He had, however, eventually come to terms with it. On a few occasions it had even worked to their advantage; people assumed, based on his appearance, that William might be a foreign merchant, which had opened a few doors in the service of the crown.

After a full day juddering along the roads, the carriage had stopped at a conveniently placed inn on the outskirts of Stokenchurch for the night. Approximately halfway between Oxford and the capital, the town had been a commonly used resting place for both Royalist and Parliamentary troops during the Civil War; at least twice it was the site of skirmishes between the opposing forces.

William and Stephen had travelled all day; opting to maximise the distance covered so that they might arrive in London the next day with enough time to meet His Lordship. Passengers and drivers were exhausted. The constant clatter of the wheels provided no opportunity for the passengers to rest, shaken for hours on end by the carriage bumping along the rough roads. Once in the inn, neither man could have fallen asleep any sooner.

They left early the next morning, hoping to stay

on track with their plan of arriving in plenty of time to meet His Lordship that day. It would not do to keep him waiting any longer than absolutely necessary. As they grew closer to the capital, William broke his silence, probing for more details as to why he had been summoned so urgently. What information could have been lost that was so important? The usual inane possibilities had crossed his mind: a love letter to an undesirable lady that had the potential to tear down a great house, an ill-advised opinion that might stir up some underlying civil unrest. Both scenarios were common enough, but neither should be cause for too much concern. Treason then? That would certainly result in heightened activity for the King's men, but unfortunately it was not as unusual as one might suppose. Ever since the plots against Elizabeth and James, they had become increasingly adept in detecting treasonous activity. In such events any sign of threat was quashed privately before any momentum could be gained.

Whatever the situation was, Stephen remained uncharacteristically silent on the subject. It was therefore in a state of intrigue that William arrived in London for the first time since his hasty departure almost a year before.

3

Fingers of late summer sun reached out over the roads of the capital, clinging to the evening sky. Sunset was quickly approaching but the air had remained thick until a light breeze brought relief from the intense heat of what had been a sweltering midday. The drop to a cooler temperature was heartily welcomed by the carriage's passengers and driver alike, close now to entering the city. Hues of pink and deep orange embraced the needle-like spires making up the vast city skyline; each building an intricate silhouette against the vibrant lights. Even from miles away, the tallest spire, that of St. Paul's cathedral, dominated the sky. Despite years of degradation, the cathedral remained one of the highlights of the city – though the Surveyor of the King's works, Christopher Wren, had made public his desire to have the whole thing demolished and rebuilt to his own design.

Passing claustrophobic wooden structures crammed into spaces they had no right to occupy, the carriage wound its way along the roads of the capital. New builds contrasted with scatterings of larger open spaces that announced grander, more solid structures of stone; remnants of previous generations, and the expansion of the formal buildings that made the city the epicentre of legislation and trade.

Continuing their passage through the sprawling streets, William confronted his companion, hoping to glean even a vague idea of what he may have let himself in for.

"Right Stephen," He began, "This is London, so now you can let me know what exactly it is we're doing here."

"All will be revealed my friend." The reply came with a knowing smile, Stephen's focus remained firmly on the passing scenery as it trundled past the window.

"Stop trying to be so damned mysterious. I came with you. So, what is this? What are we dealing with?" William searched his friend's face for any sign of potential weakness on the subject. The large man refused to make eye contact. "Wait a minute," he continued, following Stephen's wayward gaze, "You don't know, do you? You don't actually know what we're doing here at all. For God's sake man, you let me come all the way back without a hint of what's going on. His Lordship could be leading us into anything."

"Well…I…of course…I mean, I know…" Stephen blustered, his gaze shifting to the carriage floor.

"I should have known. There was no way you could have stayed silent on the subject this long if you had known anything. To think, you came all the way to Oxford to bring me back and you don't actually know what for!"

"Now hang on just a minute. That's not fair." Stephen finally recovered his voice, "And not true either. I do know a bit, admittedly not as much as I would like. But it's not nothing."

"Evidently not enough for you to take a guess at

what we might be here for?"

"In truth... no." A guilty smile now adorned the large man's face. "But for a while there you were none the wiser. I completely had you. And let's be honest, you would never have come with me otherwise. His Lordship didn't give me much choice in the matter. Either you came back or I didn't."

"True." William conceded, "You've certainly improved that poker face of yours. So, no idea what we're doing?"

"I have a hunch, nothing more than that though really. I know about the letter of course, I already mentioned that to you, but His Lordship has been keeping the cards pretty close to his chest of late."

"Let's hear the hunch then." William was growing more than a little impatient. He'd never known his friend to be so reluctant to give up information on any subject. He normally had the opposite problem of trying to keep Stephen quiet. There had been one occasion, when on His Lordship's business in northern Italy, they had been walking around a market in the small walled town of Gubbio. Stephen had been talking a little too loudly of their task of acquiring some sensitive material from a prominent local merchant. The town had been part of the Papal states for thirty years, supposedly secure, but rumours of an uprising of the Duchy of Urbino, the old ruling family, against the rule of the Pope were being closely investigated. Stephen had been overheard by the majority of the market and they had only just managed to escape the walls of the city before an angry mob took exception to the invasion of their local privacy.

"Well, I told you we found the dead man in the Thames, and that he had lost possession of a letter."

William nodded, encouraging the other man to continue. "I was instructed by His Lordship to deliver the letter to one of our men in York, but...well, it went missing before I had even left home. The contents are unknown to me, only that it was sensitive state business. It was made clear that it was not for my eyes, but it would appear that it was of great importance. I can't say I was particularly happy about acting as a glorified messenger, but I wasn't in a position to argue with His Lordship."

"Who ever is?" mumbled William.

"Where it gets rather more embarrassing for me is that the man found in the Thames was a newly hired member of my household. We are assuming that he was the one that took the letter, his services no longer required he must have been disposed of. What I can't understand is that he came highly recommended. The man had been with his former employer for years. Other than that, I know next to nothing. He had only been part of my household a short while, I didn't really know him yet.

There has been a lot of talk about France hovering around recently, it could have something to do with them. Or maybe the Dutch, they seem to be arming ships fairly heavily for something – they're still fuming about our possession of what was New Amsterdam two years ago."

William shook his head in exasperation.

"You lost the letter." Stephen's cheeks reddened as the blood rushed to his face in embarrassment. "But why assume the dead man stole the letter? Maybe he died attempting to stop the thief from taking it. And still, how important can a single letter be anyway?"

"You can see why I didn't say anything." His

friend replied, growing slightly agitated, "Same old story. Stephen makes a mess and William comes to the rescue. I don't know what was in the letter. That man was the only one who could have taken it though, no one else knew of its existence. He was actually in the room when it was handed to me. Poor security, I know, but I had no reason to suspect him. His death and the disappearance of the letter can't possibly be a coincidence."

"I wasn't blaming you," William attempted to calm his friend, "I agree, it can't be coincidence. We'll just have to see what His Lordship says."

The clattering of the wheels on the assembled slabs of stone and debris that made up the roads came to a halt as the carriage jerked to a stop. A call from the driver on the front seat confirmed that they had arrived at their destination. He leapt down, opening the door for his two passengers to step out.

"Here we are then, sirs. Back in the capital." He gave them a cheery smile despite the long hours of travel.

Stepping out of the carriage, William readied himself to face London for the first time in many months. Ignoring the building in front of him, he looked out onto the wide stretch of water that was the River Thames and took a deep breath. Reluctantly, he turned to the vast structure of the Palace of Westminster perched on the banks of the winding river. The tall buttresses and ornate stonework couldn't fail to captivate the attention of all but the most self-consumed passers-by. The seat of power in England for so long, it had only increased in importance and influence over the last few decades. Within its walls lay the centre of all the turmoil that had gripped the nation for the better part of the century. Such was its imposing nature that one could be forgiven for entirely failing to notice the relatively simple structure standing next to it.

Unlike its much larger and ornate sister building, there was nothing to draw the eye to the smaller construction. It was, William thought, remarkably unremarkable. As such, it was the perfect place to act as the headquarters for the King's more secretive information gathering projects. No one was aware that it was from this plain-looking building that plans to secure the future, and security, of the nation so often emanated.

"Ready?" Stephen asked, joining William on the riverbank.

"I suppose so."

Together they turned and made the short walk over to the small building where His Lordship waited.

∞

The crossing from Ireland to the north of England was nowhere near as simple as Captain Aldworth had made it sound. As he entered the bustling port a few days before, Valentine Greatrakes had noted the clear blue skies. Their tranquillity only surpassed by the crystal clarity of the calm waters visible out in the Irish Sea. He had spoken to the captain to arrange his passage to England and had been promised these would be the best conditions and easiest journey he had ever undertaken in his life. Captain Aldworth looked like a sailor, face tanned a leathery brown from exposure to sun and wind, his arms and neck thick with cords of muscle from fighting the unpredictable seas. Valentine had been satisfied that this was what a good ship's captain should look like. The crew of The Coral equally fit the stereotype Valentine had fixed in his head. The captain had been so convincing in his confidence that Greatrakes completely disregarded the sight of many smaller fishing vessels, further out to sea, heading back to port. He had managed to persuade himself that they must have fulfilled their catch quota for the day; that they were all heading back at the same time was simply a sign of a particularly successful day.

As the winds picked up and the dark clouds descended upon them, Valentine had maintained confidence that the captain was completely in control. It was only when, as the clouds turned an angry, deep grey colour, and the churning sea began throwing their vessel around, that it dawned on him that actually they were in a large amount of trouble.

Waves taller than great oak trees carried The Coral wherever they pleased. Captain Aldworth and his crew, resigned to their complete lack of control, did all they could just to stay afloat. As Valentine slid along the decking of the small vessel, his misery was only added to by the booming clap of thunder that sounded overhead. As if on cue, the heavens opened, sheets of rain obscuring all sight so that it was near impossible to see where the sky ended and the sea began.

Just as he thought he might have managed to brace against the next crashing wave, the swell would pick them up and throw them in the opposite direction. There was nothing the crew could do. They fought tooth and nail, hour after hour, just to keep the vessel upright.

"Start bailing man, and you better get praying." A wooden bucket was thrown by a member of the crew in his general direction, bouncing off a reel of thickly wound rope near his feet. Still sprawled on the deck, Valentine made a desperate attempt to aid the crew in their bailing.

No sooner had he filled the container than the ship lurched again, sending the icy saltwater into his face. Spluttering he wiped a drenched hand over his eyes in an effort to clear them.

"How much longer can we survive like this?" Valentine cried out, hoping one of the crew had some good news.

"We're already dead men." The man next to him had a crazed look in his eyes. "Shut up and bail."

Valentine's stomach lurched. Everything froze. Looking up he saw crew members hanging onto the rigging for dear life. Though he stood upright, he was actually parallel to the deck, feet braced against the side of the small ship. Above him, the rest of the vessel reeled, completely sideways in the rough sea, before mercifully dropping level into the seething waters.

An ear-piercing scream broke through the thunder, a young man thrown by the sudden movement lost his purchase on the rigging and was catapulted into the air. With a bone-shattering thud he hit the deck, a limp pile of useless splinters, still only for a moment before he was swallowed by the sea. For Valentine it all happened in slow motion, time dragging as the man impacted with the solid deck. He felt the crunch of bones as the life left the crewman's body. He was helpless against his body's reaction, falling on all fours as his stomach heaved up their contents.

As if accepting the life of the sailor as payment, the storm began to show signs of abating. A glimmer of sunlight became visible through the dark clouds. The crew had no energy to dwell on the violent death they had all just witnessed. It was pushed to one side as they continued to fight to survive. The flash of sunlight provided a nervous hope, slowly easing the atmosphere of dejected acceptance. The repercussions of watching their crewmate die would have to be dealt with once they reached dry land.

Valentine had endured the storm for days longer than the journey should have taken, finally England was in reach. As they neared the port it became clear that they would need to wait before docking. He could wait no longer. Jumping from the edge of the deck as soon as he thought he could reach land himself. Ignoring the shouts of alarm from the rest of the crew, he put his large frame to good use; cutting through the water with strong strokes.

Crawling up onto the cobbles of the beach he had aimed for, he dragged his sodden bundle of clothes behind him. Dropping onto his hands and knees, he felt the solid earth below, thanking God that he was once again on dry land. Looking over his shoulder, he could see the crew still watching him. Maybe once they had docked he would seek them out for a drink.

Finally in control of his legs, he would begin his journey to do God's work. He had been called to England for a purpose. The storm had been a reminder of his mortality and his creator's vast power. His survival he took as a sign that his mission was indeed favoured by the Almighty. He set off with renewed vigour, in the knowledge that God was with him.

FROM THE DIARY OF SAMUEL PEPYS.

January 5th 1666 - London is once more returning to normal. The sights and sounds that make the city the greatest on Earth are trickling back onto the streets. Brightly coloured shop fronts, closed and empty this past year, open their doors to trade again. The sounds that accompany them are really what makes the city feel like home again. Without them, the streets have felt deserted, the fragment of the population remaining in the city passing through them like silent wraiths.

I travelled with Lord Bruncker to his residence in Covent Garden, such stares at the coach as we passed through the streets I have not felt before. The four horses drawing the carriage pulling in the eyes; such a rarity has it become to see a nobleman in London.

Yet Westminster remains empty, no court nor gentry ate there. Almost all of my fellow government officials ran scared from the plague. I cannot blame them, what help can they be to people if they are dead. I expect they will follow in their return soon enough.

January 9th 1666 – Woke up, and then to the office.

Meeting for the first time since the plague struck, from which God has preserved us. After dinner, there was much chatter of the favours of Court. Lord Sandwich is thought lost. Though the King remains his friend, everywhere people speak slightly of him. I find this saddening, I hope that he might once more find his place.

January 20th 1666 – At the office I sent my boy off home to fetch my papers. I cannot imagine what took him so long. My temper wore thin and when he returned, I boxed his ears. It hurt my thumb so much that I was unable to move the next day, and the next was still in large amounts of pain.

January 22nd 1666 – I met my fellow members of Gresham College at the Crowne Tavern today. It was our first meeting since the plague saw the flight from London. Now that the gentry are returning, the physicians follow. Though Dr Goddard filled our ears in defence of his colleagues' flight from the capital, all know they are never far from those that will pay for their services.

January 28th 1666 – After dinner this evening, I took the carriage to Court, where I found the King, and Lords, in council. Their business completed, out came the King. I kissed his hand and he grasped me kindly by the hand. He thanked me personally for the service I have provided in the last year, assuring me he was well aware of the good work I am doing.

Lord Sandwich looked awfully melancholy, his beard has grown unsuitably. I asked how I might be of his service, but was told it would be best if we met in private at his lodgings so that we are not seen to be talking together.

January 30th 1666 – I made my return to church today. I left feeling most uncomfortable. All have been well aware of the extent and brutality of the past year's plague, but seeing the many graves packed into the church since last I was there really shocked me. I shall have an extra drink this evening.

4

William and Stephen were shown into the building by a wispy, wraith-like man who appeared from behind the main door. He took them through a large, dusty entrance room which, though once grand, now gave the appearance of having been neglected for years. Both men knew where they were going, but their guide made sure to direct them into a side room which acted as a compact waiting room. One side of the room was lined with chairs, a small row laid out between two large windows at either end of the wall. The layout meant that, if seated, the outside world was not visible. However, each window was fitted with a narrow window seat that could be perched upon if the chairs were occupied. The narrow room held two doors, one of which the two men had just entered through, the other stood filling the space opposite the chairs.

In the window furthest from the entrance sat an old man. He raised his head as the two friends made their way over to the chairs and sat down. The waiting room was sparsely decorated, the kind of room that was entirely functional and as such held little that was remarkable. Still the old man looked over at them. It was the kind of space that demanded silence; in much the same way that, once over a certain age, everyone becomes aware that in certain situations anything above a whisper is completely out of the question.

Such silences are uncomfortable at the best of times but William was becoming increasingly unnerved. The pale eyes of the old man, boring into them from the moment they stepped through the door, were unrelenting. William found himself flitting his eyes over the room, each time returning to the old man whose gaze was unwavering. On every occasion their eyes met, William would quickly change his focus, settling on the door opposite or a suddenly interesting piece of flooring. Eventually he decided, despite seeing it many times before, the door required his undivided attention. He began studying what was, in reality, nothing of any importance. A simply cut wooden door, slightly worn at the edges. It's only peculiarity was that it had no handle so could only be opened from the inside; there must be another entry into the room, but he had never found it.

With relief he noticed the old man stand, walk towards the door, which opened just enough to let him through, and exit the waiting room; finally releasing William from his unblinking eyes. He nudged his friend,

"Who was that?" he asked, "He wouldn't stop staring at us."

Stephen let out a burst of laughter, shattering the silence that hung over the room. William looked over, startled by the response.

"What? What's so funny?"

"That..." Stephen replied, fighting not to choke with laughter, "That was His Lordship's secretary, though I suppose you won't ever have met him before. His name is Thomas."

"So, why is that funny?" he demanded, utterly confused and feeling entirely stupid at his lack of understanding. This only led to further, almost hysterical levels of laughter from the giant man sitting next to him.

"He's blind, Will." Stephen managed to say, before falling back into unseemly fits of mirth.

William's cheeks flushed a deep burgundy as he realised the obviousness of the situation. Of course he was blind. What better way to ruffle the feathers of someone who had been out of the game so long. The old man must have been sent to sit outside by His Lordship.

It was through scenarios such as this that His Lordship undermined the intelligence of those around him; consistently attempting to reassert his authority. Such is the way of power and the egos of insecure men. The childish need to instill a sense of authority by making William look a fool should have been expected. It would probably set the precedent for how this meeting with his employer would go. He was intrigued further. It must be something potentially disastrous to recall him now.

Just as Stephen was managing to regain his composure, the door opposite them opened to reveal the blind old secretary.

"His Lordship will see you now." A thin smile stretched across Thomas' weathered face. He could not have failed to have heard the fits of laughter, even through what was revealed to be a very thick door.

The two men stood, patting off the non-existent dirt and dust that had collected as they were seated, and made their way through the open door.

The layout of the room that greeted them was in

stark contrast to the plain functionality of the waiting room. It was not a large space but held numerous sizable desks, overflowing with paperwork. Along three of the walls ran cases full of books reaching from the floor to the ceiling. The entrance to the room was held within one of these cases, around it the books formed a welcoming arch. The opposite wall was almost entirely taken up by maps. These varied in size, the two most prominent were of western Europe and England. Indistinguishable scribbles obscured many of the country borders giving the impression that a small child had at some point been let loose on them with a bottle of ink. The lack of wall space made the room feel quite enclosed, almost a cave-like claustrophobia that would certainly have made many feel uncomfortable. The only natural light in the room came from a small ovular window high in the wall of maps.

    The largest of the desks was positioned along the map wall so that it was the first thing anyone entering the room would see. Another ran at a diagonal angle across the corner to the left of the entrance. Everywhere was littered with papers. Various odds and ends poked out from beneath the stacks of paper. An old pistol had been recommissioned as a paperweight, though William was almost certain that it could still fulfil its original purpose. He was fairly sure that what looked like a sun-bleached piece of driftwood, partially hidden by a yellowing scroll of paper, was in fact a human finger, stripped of the flesh. He wondered whether the rest of the human remains were also to be found somewhere in the room.

    Stephen's attention was equally absorbed by the room's contents. His eyes had settled upon a small collection of stuffed rodent-like creatures that were strewn across the floor to the right of the door. They had certainly not been there the last time he visited. However, he knew better than to ask what their purpose might be. With new arrivals such as these a regular occurrence, he marvelled at how the blind old man was able to make it around the room without suffering serious accident.

Movement from behind the smallest of the desks refocused the two men to the purpose of their visit.

"Ah gentlemen, so good of you to join me. I trust you had a pleasant journey?" A squat man removed himself from behind the piles of debris in front of him and moved to a corner of the wall of maps where a collection of slightly undersized armchairs stood. "And Mr. la Penne, welcome back. Please do take a seat."

"Good evening Your Lordship." replied William, only just loud enough to cover up Stephen's muttered reply of "since when have we had a choice." If the man by the chairs had heard, which William was fairly sure he had, he chose not to respond. Instead he motioned that the others should join him in being seated. There was an authority in his movement indicating that this was a command rather than a suggestion; he was not about to ask twice for anything.

His Lordship, as the men called him, was in reality not a lord at all. In truth, the two men didn't know his real name. As far as they knew, no one did. This was the title that the man charged with maintaining the King's networks of intelligence gathering had always adopted. William thought it was probably because the original holder of the position might have been a real lord, but this had never been confirmed. Since working for the King, the two men had worked for two men called 'His Lordship' but the current man was by far the longest standing. They had only known the other for a few weeks before he had disappeared. Apparently holders of the position had an uncanny habit of dying in extremely suspicious circumstances. This was perhaps why the post no longer lay with any members of the aristocracy. Of course, there were other networks maintained by members of the royal court, but the real work originated in this cluttered room.

The current 'His Lordship' had held his role for almost five years, bucking the trend of his predecessors. The former title holder had not lasted long after the restoration of the monarchy. It had been a brutal period of political subterfuge but much of it had been kept from the public eye. In those five years, His Lordship's face had aged considerably, but it remained difficult to put a number to. William assumed he must be quite old; his hair was a grey turning to white. The energy that he displayed defied this theory. He never showed any signs of the weakening joints or chronic stiffness that plagued the ageing members of the population, and his mind was still sharper than anyone either man had ever met. As if to defy the colour of his hair, his piercing blue eyes retained the ability to cut right to a person's core. William always made a point of finding any excuse not to hold eye contact for any length of time. It was as if he could reach into the soul, gleaning all one's secrets in the process. A thoroughly unpleasant experience.

As the two companions settled into chairs that were really far too small for them, His Lordship cleared his throat and announced his plan.

"I won't waste your time with unnecessary chit chat or reminiscences. Let's get down to the matter at hand." He paused for breath, as if readying himself for an unpleasant morsel of food. "Gentlemen, I need your help. I'm sure that Stephen has got you up to speed William?"

William nodded his reply, noticing his friend staring at the floor. "Well, you can probably forget most of what he told you. It's almost completely false."

Stephen's eyes snapped up. He began to object, only to be silenced by a wave of His Lordship's hand.

"What I mean is, although the events that Stephen has told you are true, the reasons behind them are not."

The two men exchanged a look of surprise, but said nothing, allowing the older man to continue.

"The letter that was stolen was a fake. We had been keeping an eye on that particular member of Stephen's household for some time now. And yes, obviously we'd known about him for a while before he joined you. The move to Mr Berry's staff provided a perfect opportunity to test him. It appears our suspicions were correct. What we are more concerned by is who now holds this letter. Although the information it contains is harmless, the people who now hold it are most certainly not. My wish is that the two of you will investigate further. No one outside this room must know anything of your real task. Whilst the two of you pursue the letter, thereby confirming its authenticity to those now in possession of it, you will be rooting out the real threat."

A flood of questions filled the room as the two men began to verbally process the information that had just been shared with them. What was in the fake letter? How would that keep their adversaries occupied if it was fake information? How did they know who now had the letter? Was there actually a real threat or just a perceived one? To these Stephen added his objection that His Lordship had allowed a known security threat to remain in his household without alerting him.

The old man leant back in his chair, fixing them with such an icy stare that the questions quickly ceased.

"If you are quite done blabbing, I will enlighten you with the details. The letter is in code. No doubt it will be broken, but as a result, our adversaries will find themselves in possession of some nonsense about the King wishing to resume Dr Dee's conversations with the angels in order to mount a spiritual defence of the kingdom. Nothing more.

However, were the information correct it may allow for a scheme concocted in the guise of some sort of demonic attack, or the appearance of a new prophet – God knows we have enough of those at present. Anyway, it would be a perfect excuse for a smoke and mirrors plot. As such, I do not think it will be discarded. Any attempt to get close to the King is likely to be leapt upon.

I believe that there has been a group responsible for much of the civil unrest in recent years, perhaps even stretching further back. They stir up trouble and melt away before we have any chance of getting near them. As you can appreciate, we would be best rid of such a group, especially as I believe they have the potential to escalate their exploits significantly. The plan is, therefore, to draw them out and put an end to it."

"Escalate significantly?" Stephen interrupted, "Are you thinking war?"

"More than that. Gentlemen, I believe that this group led the country into civil war in order to overthrow the old King. Now that the monarchy is back in the form of his son, I believe they may try again. How - well, that is up to you to find out."

"You think they killed Charles I?" Stephen said. "But

why allow his son to rule for six years before making an attempt on his life?"

The civil war had split the country in two, setting brothers, fathers and sons, on opposite sides. It still sat vivid in the memory of all who had experienced it. It had forced every member of the population to choose a side, turning the country upside down in the process. Even after the restoration of the monarchy, the country was only just beginning to rebuild itself. The huge fatalities of the plague, which swept through the country only a year before, had left the kingdom in a fragile state. Another war of such magnitude was out of the question.

"Some people don't need a reason" replied His Lordship "but I suspect, in this case, they require a specific kind of turmoil in order to sow the seeds of whatever new ideal they wish to force upon us all."

William had remained pensive throughout this exchange, allowing the other two to voice their thoughts, then broke his silence.

"I have heard of this kind of group before, though I must admit, I thought it to be nothing more than a conspiracy dreamt up by wandering minds. If what you suspect is true, then we need to act fast. I for one do not wish to see the nation torn apart only to be replaced by some ill-advised political idealism."

Stephen nodded his agreement,

"Where are you sending us?"

"You will go where I last received any indication that they might be gathering."

"That is wonderfully obscure of you, even by your standards." replied Stephen, starting to let his frustration erode his previous courtesy. "Do you have a specific location for us?"

"Yes, I do." A flicker of a smile played across the older man's face. "Oxford."

The two younger men looked at each other in exasperation.

"You mean to say, that you sent me to Oxford, to tell Will you needed him here, in London, so that you could send us both back to Oxford?" Stephen was barely able to contain his anger, his voice rising even through gritted teeth.

"How very astute of you Stephen." The grinning old man said with heavy sarcasm. "That is exactly what has happened. I could hardly send a letter. You have shown only too well what happens when you have such responsibility. My time is too valuable to spend on the road for so long. I am needed here, close to the King. I need you on top form for this one. We can't afford any mistakes."

They both nodded their acceptance. Behind them the door opened, indicating that this meeting was over. The two friends clambered angrily to their feet, attempting not to lose face whilst struggling to extricate themselves from their chairs. Turning their backs on the collection of maps and assorted oddities, they followed the old secretary as he ushered them under the archway of books and out of the room. Had they looked back they would have seen a heavy look of exhaustion settle on the face of the man they had just left.

The door safely closed behind them, Stephen filled the corridor with an unhealthy stream of expletives, so personal that even William winced.

FROM THE DIARY OF SAMUEL PEPYS.

February 12th 1666 – Mr Caesar, my son's flute-master, visited today. It was the first time I have seen him since the plague, though he remained in the capital all the while. He told tales of how, at the height of the plague, the boldest of people would make sport of going to others' funerals, and how, in spite, those housebound by their illness would lean out of the windows to breathe in the faces of those that were well enough to be passing by on the streets outside. What a state of torment they must have been in to attack their fellows such I cannot imagine.

March 9th 1666 – Travelled by water to Deptford to meet with my Lord Bruncker and Sir W. Batten in order to look over Mr Castle's new ship, named Defyance. I was able to save the King some money, but also gained the experience of learning how ships are measured.

Afterwards, we all made very merry and seeing Mrs. Knipp, God forgive me, I must admit that my nature will place pleasure above all things. Music and women I have no power to resist. Though, truth be told, this is the time of my life to indulge. Most men wait until they receive their estate, but by then are too old to enjoy the pleasures that life might provide.

April 8th 1666 – The Court today was filled with talk of the death of the King's closet-keeper, Tom Cheffin. Last night he was fine and well, and apparently not even unwell this morning at six o'clock, yet dead by seven. People are mightily fearful that his death was caused by an imposthume in his chest. Such is the fear of the plague that conclusions are being drawn all too quickly, though reports of plague cases returning are increasing every day.

5

Stephen Berry still lived and spent the majority of his time in London. Being close to the heartbeat of the country and the goings-on at court was invaluable to keeping on top of his job. When William was last in London, Stephen had been complaining about the location of his apartments. On first arrival in the capital many years before, the large man had been forced to take rooms in an area some considerable distance from the city centre. William had lodged with him for a while. It had made sense. Their work meant a lot of travel, so a base slightly further out made this more manageable; less at the mercy of the potential hold-ups at the busy core of the city. However, for a highly social man such as Stephen, being such a distance from the hustle and bustle equated to solitary confinement. For all the years William had known him, Stephen could never be close enough to the action.

It appeared though, that the last year had seen a reversal of opinion on this perfect location. Although still more central than William would have chosen, Stephen had migrated along the river to the west of the city. The area was home to many large houses belonging to the fashionable aristocracy, the current trend in building spreading out from the city of London so that Westminster was now well connected. Stephen's home was small in comparison to many of the houses that surrounded it, but still much larger than the small apartments available in the nucleus of the city.

The light of early evening had hung on for a while, but they arrived at the front door in darkness. After the meeting with His Lordship, the decision had been made to stay at Steven's home for the night. There was little point in travelling back to Oxford so late. Nothing would be achieved by tiring themselves travelling in the dark, which would be dangerous and slow. They would leave early the next morning having rested well. Besides, they only had a location to work with; arriving a few hours earlier would not make a difference.

During the short journey to the house, William had pointed out that His Lordship had actually provided very little material for them to work with at all. While away from work, he may not have been looking for plots, but William had been living in Oxford, and news travelled fast among the locals. Nothing of any importance had come to his attention in quite some time, certainly not something as potentially ruinous as a plot to kill the King. It was rare that anything of significance took place without a large proportion of the city hearing of it soon afterwards. Even views that were posited in the strictest confidence to a select few would end up common knowledge eventually. Appearances from out-of-towners with potential gossip resulted in a thorough quizzing. In such a close-knit community the walls had ears, and they caught even the faintest whisper. But without even a whisper to work with, the first task for the two friends would be to find a place to start. They needed information before anything could progress. By the time the two men arrived at the house, evening was pushing into night.

"I have to say, Stephen, this is definitely the best place you've been in since you moved to London." William made the observation as he settled into a tall chair positioned next to an ornate fireplace.

The house, though appearing smaller than those surrounding it due to the narrow façade looking out onto the street, opened up into a magnificently spacious residence large enough for Stephen and his assembly of house staff. Each room was modelled slightly differently, taking inspiration from European fashions. It captured a relaxed grandeur somehow different from some of the colder, more formal rooms that he had inhabited in the past. It was certainly still decorated in the style of the grand city buildings, but it had a touch of the rural about it giving it an easier tone.

"Still no one to share it with though, eh?" William knew full well Stephen lived alone. It was one of the few topics that had been a regular theme in their letters. He hoped that what he presented as a light-hearted dig at his old friend might one day reveal a desire to finally settle down with someone.

"You know me," replied Stephen with a grin and a shrug, "I want them all or nothing at all, and all is definitely better than nothing." The reply caused William to tut, maintaining a good-natured smile but disappointed by such a response. He hoped there was more depth behind such a blasé outlook on life. He worried for his friend but knew further comment would not be welcomed. "What about you though?" Stephen asked gently, "Do you think you'll find someone else?

What are the women like in Oxford?"

William stared at him, shocked into silence for a moment, before answering.

"I've given up Stephen. Well, never really started." He said honestly, knowing that such a conversation was bound to occur at some point. It had been over a year since the unexpected death of his wife. At such a young age, it was unfortunately not a rare tragedy and society assumed he would be on the lookout for another bride. Knowing it was coming did not make it any less uncomfortable. "And you know very well what the women in Oxford are like."

"Given up." Stephen laughed off his reply, "Come now, they can't be all that bad."

"You know there's nothing wrong with them Stephen. Some I would even consider attractive, but that's all they are."

"That's all you need isn't it?" came the response. Stephen could tell this was difficult for his friend but no one else could talk like this to him. Keeping the conversation going was the only way he could discover what William was thinking, even if the responses were short enough to drive him crazy. "Some wit might help a bit I suppose, not essential though."

"I'm afraid I can't settle for just an object Stephen. Meaningless rendezvous will always be meaningless. I want my life to be full of meaning. And the truth is, I will always make comparisons in which the past will eternally triumph over any future I might have. I know it's bleak but that's where I am." The words fell from his mouth like a landslide, eyes fixed on the fire.

"Will, are you doing alright?" Stephen's expression betrayed the concern he had been feeling over the last months. He knew that it would take time for William to come to terms with what had happened, but the answer suggested that the healing process was taking much longer than he had hoped.

"I'm tired, but nothing a good night's sleep won't sort out."

"That's not what I meant."

"I know... She was my life. It might not look exciting from the outside, but the knowledge someone really knows you and will stay with you, is what everyone is looking for really. I had that. And it was stolen from me in the most unexpected way. Nothing I could do to stop it. I still don't really know how to process what happened. It's better that I just keep to myself. I have plenty to occupy my time - my writing is coming along and I've been sitting in on some of the discussions at the colleges."

William's withdrawal from the conversation was almost visible. Knowing from past experience that there was not much more he could do, Stephen did not pursue it. He was not surprised when, a few moments later, his friend excused himself for the night; leaving the large man alone by the fire.

Stephen remained sitting alone for a while longer, finishing his glass of wine, before he too turned in for the night. There had been a lot of travelling over the past few days, the morning would only bring more.

6

The journey back to Oxford was, though time-consuming, uneventful. On the second morning, Stephen had risen from the inn bed with a stiffness in his neck, making any turning movement to his right a painful experience. William, with only a pang of guilt, had made a point of sitting to the right of his friend for precisely this reason; the conversation within the carriage restricted as it trundled along. In theory William's plan to achieve silence was a good one, however, despite the lack of eye contact, the large man was, as ever, a fountain of pointless observations on the changing landscape and grumbles about the erratic weather. Any awkwardness left as a result of the conversation at Stephen's house was seemingly unapparent to him, and so the evening remained unmentioned. This suited William perfectly; he had no wish to unpick that particular thread of conversation.

As the journey wore on, William began warming to the inane chatter of his tireless companion. Some comments even managed to bring a smile to his so regularly sullen face. Normally he preferred to travel in silence. No matter the distance, there was something about travelling that created the perfect opportunity to sit peacefully and watch the world pass by. Fortunately for William, Stephen was unable to see that his efforts at cheer were working. If William's companion was to get even the slightest indication his old friend was gaining any amount of enjoyment from his efforts at conversation, he would never hear the end of it. In order to maintain the status quo, William restricted himself to the occasional grunt of affirmation or monosyllabic response.

They approached Oxford, making their way through numerous outlying villages and towns. No one paid them much attention, it was a well-travelled route. Only the occasional inquisitive glance betrayed the locals' notice the carriage passing through at all. Their destination now close, Stephen's ramblings gave way to questioning William about exactly where they would be heading.

"When I came to collect you, you were based in the inn. I didn't press the matter at the time, but why were you staying there and not at home? Where are we going to base ourselves?"

"I was just thinking the same thing actually. It's not a normal situation. We have to appear to be discreet - but, in a way in which whoever it is we are looking for remains aware of our intention to find the letter. I suppose we need to act as normally as possible. I've been splitting my time between the house and the city for a while now, so either wouldn't appear out of the ordinary."

"Let's stay at the house, shall we? It seems a shame to pass up the opportunity. And honestly, the thought of going back to that nest you made for yourself makes me slightly squeamish."

William had thought this might be his friend's decision. Nodding his acceptance, he sighed. In truth, the house had become a torment to him and he had not been back for a long time. It felt unnerving to return to the house in which he and his wife had lived. Every inch of the building held a memory, equal parts comfort and curse. On occasion he would turn a corner, still expecting to find her there, only to be hit once again by the cold reality that he was alone.

Staying in the city was a chance to get away from a home where he felt so alone, but he had to admit to himself it had been too long since he had last been back. He tried to claim that his indefinite relocation to the city was also a chance to reconnect with more scholarly pastimes, but even he knew this was a poor excuse. Occasional opportunities to view and discuss the work of some of the most celebrated minds in the country kept his mind busy. It had also inspired him to write down some of his own musings, quick scribbles that he was sure were of little imagination, but certainly held some truths that he was rather proud of. Not that he was confident enough to ever allow anyone to see them.

"Well, what do you think?" asked Stephen, rotating his entire body so that he could face his companion. William couldn't help but smile at such a ridiculous situation. Forgetting that his friend would not have seen his nod of agreement, he chuckled before vocalising his agreement. Taking this rather too personally, the large man huffed, resuming his previous position in silence. It was not long before his chatter began again.

∞

The main entrance to the La Penne property took the carriage along a worn, old dirt track. Large hazel trees lining either side of the road had overgrown, looming in and whipping their spindly branches along the roof of the carriage. This main route was one of several entrances to William's property and had obviously not been well maintained; visitors from out of town were unheard of recently. Any guests coming to the house from Oxford tended to come along a separate path that wound its way across the fields to the North-East of the city.

Once past the trees, the grounds opened up into an expanse of grassy pastureland through which the track continued. The new view held a stark contrast to the outer approach to the house. Past the dark, unrelenting canopy of trees, the rest of the track was open and light. Many houses with such extensive grounds were framed with grand gardens, a conspicuous display of wealthy extravagance. In keeping with his character, William's land remained undecorated and practical. Throughout the lush green, cattle could be seen grazing. Their long horns and shaggy brown coats held their own elegance, a more rugged beauty. As the carriage trundled past, the two men were met with the gentle lowing of bovine welcome.

The house appeared as they progressed over the knoll, the track began sloping down into a shallow valley. The position of the house meant it was hidden from view until the carriage moved away from the line of trees forming the boundary of William's land. Only by moving further into the stretch of green fields was it revealed. Beyond the building, further seas of green lined the hills, framing the house in emerald. Specks of white in the distance suggested the presence of scattered flocks of sheep.

A long time had passed since William had approached his house from this direction. While he resided in Oxford there was no reason to. Sunlight showed off the intricacies of the sandstone, the magnificent result of hours spent by master masons. He was surprised to find himself looking forward to his return. The building stood two stories high, each level displaying long, thin windows that were the height of architectural fashion. The front left corner of the building was modelled into an octagonal tower, standing roughly six feet taller than the level of the roof. In the centre of the building was a large double door so high that it almost reached the first floor. The entrance was enclosed by a pillared porch, which formed a balcony leading out from a room on the first floor.

Despite its grand appearance, the building was showing signs that the master of the house had been absent for a prolonged period. There was little sign of life. Each of the windows was covered by a large wooden shutter of the French style. They had evidently not been removed for a while; their supporting struts covered in a dirty green moss. Age showed on some, cracked where debris from high winds had been hurled at them during rough weather. Despite such evidence of neglect, it maintained a comfortable elegance rare in large houses. It was clear that the party cutting its way through the sloping fields were not expected. No one had sent any notice ahead that the house should be readied. Regardless, William was surprised by the complete lack of any signs of movement from his family home.

As they pulled into the area directly in front of

the house, he motioned to the driver, sending them on a course past the main door. Rounding the corner, the carriage turned through a stone archway that was cut into a walled courtyard, set back from the house so that it was hidden from view when approaching the front of the house. Here, in the courtyard, the house sprang to life. Various tools leant against the walls, shavings of recently split wood and loose animal feed scattered across the cobbles. Any coldness in the formal approach to the house evaporated completely, giving way to proof that life was very much present here. The wheels of the carriage clacked through the paved courtyard. Stray chickens were scattered, squawking for cover in one of the open stables lining the wall opposite the main house. At the commotion, a young man came running from a small dwelling built into the courtyard walls. Tripping over the long wooden handle of an axe, he scrambled to his feet, approaching the unknown carriage with caution. Seeing the two men within, he visibly relaxed, smoothing down his overcoat as he opened the carriage door, welcoming its occupants.

"Master William, Sir, it's been a while since we last saw you here. We didn't know you were coming." This was more of a question than a statement. In recent times it was unusual that the master of the house was home, but more so that he hadn't allowed them to ready the house. "And Mr Stephen too. You may not remember me but…" he was cut off mid-sentence as the two older men clambered out of the carriage.

"Hello Robert," boomed Stephen, clapping a large hand on his shoulder. "Why, you've really filled out since I last saw you. Where is everyone?"

"Begging your pardon sirs, father is out exercising

the horses. We didn't know you were due to be back." He tried to sound as apologetic as possible, failing entirely to hide his joy at being recognised.

"Not to worry Robert. I will catch up with him later." replied William, "I trust everything is well here?"

Before the boy had an opportunity to answer, William turned toward the house, making his way to the side entrance. He realised that despite himself he had missed his home. It was wrong that he had neglected it for so long. In the weeks after Ana's death it had become tortuous; so many ghosts of past joys that did nothing to comfort him.

Fear had prevented him from returning for months after her death. Fear that it would be an agony he could not face. Even when he had eventually returned, he had not stayed long; choosing to stay in one of the small cottages on the estate. It was a welcome surprise to find his return after months in the city caused excitement. Memories that he had suppressed engulfed him: of his childhood in this place, of days spent in the fields, the life that he had been building with his young wife. Memories that a year ago would have crushed him, now brought great peace. The warmth of these images washed over the frost that had formed over his life in the last year. William had returned to his house, but what he had not bargained on was the feeling that he had returned home.

He made his way slowly around the ground floor. Looking. Remembering. Allowing the flood of memories to swirl around him. Every turn provided countless treasures that had lain dormant since the death of his wife. The way the light broke through a crack in the shutters. The dusty fireplace that had been a favourite childhood hiding place. The familiar creak of the second step on the staircase. The swish of a cloak disappearing through a doorway. A flash of sweeping blonde hair. The click of booted heels on the stone slabs in the hallway. Hysterical shrieks of children's laughter. The light touch of her hand on his as she pulled him into a dance. Teasing eyes, beaming smile.

Why had it taken so long to return? He was alone wherever he was, where had the fear of being alone here come from? Away from everything he was still alone, still trapped by his own thoughts. Running had not been the answer, there was no escaping the demons in his head. It was true that he had found some solace in his writing and had been spending much of his time with members of the university. But why had he not returned sooner? His home was more comfort than distress, he was more home than alone. Could it be that by removing himself from these memories he had prolonged his suffering? They had become clouded, as they faded from memory they lost warmth, leaving only bitterness. He had made himself a hermit, stripping himself of everything that might have sustained him; all of the insecurity and none of the love.

∞

Stephen had followed William into the house, worried by the look he had seen in his friend's eyes. He trailed him, on hand if the return home should prove overwhelming. A glassiness in the eyes as they departed the carriage, and the distracted tone as they were greeted by the young Robert, confirmed the large man's suspicion that, despite William's claims to the contrary, his friend had not spent much time in the house over the last year. Stephen wondered when William actually had last returned. Judging by the figure lost in memories wandering in front of him, it had been too long.

Stephen simply watched for a while, not wanting to interrupt whatever reconciliation was taking place. After a while, he was relieved to see William smiling, even if it was clear from his face that he was in a different place. Eventually, content his friend would be alright, Stephen decided to leave him to his thoughts. They could begin their work later.

Wondering if Robert needed any help outside, Stephen went in search of the young man. Some sort of physical activity would do him the world of good after so long travelling. Turning, he retraced his footsteps to the back door, removing his fine coat and rolling up his shirt sleeves.

7

William woke from his daydream. He found himself seated in a large leather armchair, covered in a burgundy coloured blanket, which stood by the window in the master bedroom. Habit must have taken him there. He had no recollection of moving beyond the hallway. Looking around at the room, he noted everything was as he had left it when last there. From the thick wool fleece thrown across the bed as a blanket, right down to the small collection of books on either bedside table, all was the same. This spot had been one of his favourites as a child. His parents had often found him watching from the window, surveying the goings-on in the green and gold of the fields around the house. In later years it became the perfect viewing platform for spectacular sunsets; the myriad lights, deep purples and burnished oranges, framed by the wide oak window frame. Back in the house, he felt energy returning to him that had been missing for longer than he could remember. Embracing it, he made his way downstairs to find Stephen.

William found no trace of his friend on the ground floor, so sought out Robert to ask if there had been any sign of him outside. Walking through the door to the courtyard he was greeted by the peculiar sight of the giant man wielding an axe. Around him lay decimated chunks of wood, unable to withstand the ferocity of the violent attacks. Next to him, Robert stood, looking unsure how to react to the wild swings. The litter of splintered logs had been hacked into useless chunks, there was no way they would stack properly for storage and seasoning, but the young man was evidently not going to be the one to correct the axe-wielding berserker.

Stephen had not taken the time to change into more suitable attire, he still wore a pair of bright blue trousers, met below the knee by what had once been ivory coloured socks but would probably never recover. The only concession was that his jacket had been removed, his equally unmendable, white shirt billowing out around him. All of his garments were of the finest cut, tassels and all. His outfit was completed by the addition of a pair of elegantly long leather shoes with overly large silver buckles. The entire ensemble now completely ruined. Either Stephen had not realised the damage they would take, or simply did not care.

"I am glad you remembered the dress code, Stephen. Even a stint of manual labour demands one dress with the highest aplomb." Laughing at his friend, William strode across the courtyard.

"I don't mean to alarm you, old boy, but something seems terribly wrong." Stephen called back in mock seriousness, "Your face appears to have contracted some sort of smile. That won't do at all." Leaning his considerable weight on the axe, he accepted a friendly push on the shoulder as William arrived next to him.

"I see you've been butchering my firewood, you oaf." William replied, "It's good to be back, isn't it. I haven't felt like this for a while. I feel more like me again."

"Good to be back, and good to have you back. Long may it continue."

"I was thinking. As we still don't actually have a place to start, what do you say to heading straight into the city? We can see if anyone has any ideas where to begin."

"Sounds like a plan to me." said Stephen, enjoying the display of rekindled energy, "Or at least the beginnings of a plan."

∞

The bright sunshine that had heralded their return to William's family home soon gave way to an overcast day. A blanket of soft white cloud lay across the sky, darkening in the distance and threatening a tempestuous night. A light drizzle could be seen only a few miles away. The air around them already felt heavy with moisture. Despite the impending weather, the decision had been made that a walk to the city was in order. It would allow a stretch of the legs and an opportunity to discuss what might lie ahead. A bit of rain wouldn't do them any harm.

William had already made it clear that he had no leads to follow. This initial journey to the city was an opportunity to immerse themselves in local conversation, pick up on the gossip, and hope they found something to work with. Stephen had his doubts. He knew that, however withdrawn William might have been recently, he was a native of the city. As such, he knew people, and people knew him. He would know exactly where to be and who to seek out about any odd goings-on. Either William knew exactly who to talk to, but for whatever reason wanted to keep their identity hidden, or they really were stabbing in the dark. Stephen sincerely hoped it was the former.

The walk into the city would be short, taking an hour or two depending on the state of the paths, plenty of time for Stephen to air his questions and see what his friend had planned. William's brain was quick, perfectly suited to solving the puzzles that arose in their line of work. However, quick thinking could sometimes cause confusion as everyone else was left behind. He could take giant leaps between topics, failing to explain how they were in any way linked, before having to eventually explain more thoroughly. When in full flow it was very difficult to follow what was happening. Fortunately, Stephen knew exactly how to handle his friend. He knew a lot took place inside William's head that was never spoken, but over the years he had learnt to coax him into conversation. Thought processes that would habitually remain unspoken became more of a discussion between the two of them.

It was with all this on his mind that Stephen began the walk into Oxford. After they had been on their way a few minutes, exchanging only chatter about the incoming weather, he realised that his friend was not going to volunteer any new information. Deciding to be blunt, he went for it.

"What are we doing Will?"

"Err…walking into Oxford. What do you mean?"

"No. I mean, what's the plan? Who are we going to talk to? I know you haven't worked in a while, but you're on home turf. And even when we've been in tricky situations before we've never just gone in blind like this. I can't help if you don't tell me what your thoughts are."

Stephen began to get animated, arms waving as

he gesticulated to emphasise his point. Seeing the clear frustration, William paused, allowing his companion to calm.

"Sorry, Stephen. I know I haven't said anything much up until now, there are always others around. I think it's best we keep as little information as possible from becoming public knowledge. I know we were at home, but it's been a while. I'm not sure how much Robert should know – he's only young, don't want him doing anything stupid."

Relieved that his friend was already thinking ahead, Stephen nodded his agreement, allowing William to continue. "We need to make a bit of a show. Letting whoever it is we're after know we want that letter back is essential. That way we can cause a scene, get noticed, and work from there. Until they've been drawn out and we can identify them, we don't have anything to work with. I do have one contact I want to see, but we'll need to go everywhere, make it look like we're already desperate."

"Shouldn't be too difficult, we are desperate, aren't we?" Stephen replied, flashing a wary grin, "And causing a scene is certainly something I can do."

William chuckled at the large man before continuing.

"I don't think we're desperate just yet. Something of this magnitude can't have gone completely unnoticed. And we're going to see the man who always notices, mainly because most of the time he's somehow involved."

"Huh?...Not B..."

"Yes." Interrupted William, "He'll know anything there is to know."

"Alright. This is starting to sound like a proper plan. I was concerned for a moment that we were going full headless chicken." Stephen was beginning to look forward to this. William seemed to be much closer to his normal self than he had been for a long time. Stephen could see the gleam of excitement back in his friend's eyes. There was just one doubt that stayed with the large man as they approached the city.

"What about this mysterious league though?"

"Oh, come on Stephen. You don't actually believe that do you?"

"But you said in London..." Stephen trailed off.

"I know his Lordship has to be concerned by this type of rumour, but they're only ever rumours. There has never actually been a shadowy group masterminding criminal activity across Europe. It would be absurd."

As they moved down the hill and across the river into the city, Stephen decided to keep his thoughts to himself for now, not wishing to invoke the ridicule of the renewed sarcastic cynicism shown by his colleague.

∞

Valentine had not been in England long before word began to spread of his presence. He had still not managed to make the journey to any major cities, but the trips to smaller market towns had been enough to develop a reputation he hoped would quickly escalate and spread. Large crowds were already beginning to gather, news of his arrival at each destination preceding him. They came from miles around to see for themselves the healing power he was said to be blessed with. His actions in these more sparsely inhabited areas would be the flicker of flame that would spread like wildfire throughout the country. He was sure of it.

Being a vessel of God's will was not a task that he was taking lightly. With each miraculous healing, he was very careful to ensure that the Almighty received all of the praise. People had been easily carried away when they saw the results of his gift. Declarations of messianic power had been bandied about at first, some had even announced the second coming of Christ. He made sure to quash all such claims at every opportunity. That was not the message he wished to spread. He was certainly no messiah, simply a tool of the Lord. He knew his task, it had been made very clear to him before he left his native country. To show the nations that this power was readily available to all, that was his mission. That way he could be of use to the King, a councillor from God to guide the new monarchy away from the influence of men and toward the light.

He would continue his God-given task, slowly making his way to London showing the glory of the Lord. A meeting with the King would surely be granted then.

FROM THE DIARY OF SAMUEL PEPYS.

June 2nd 1666 – News has been brought to the office that a Dutch fleet has been sighted by the Duke of Albemarle as he was sailing to Gunfleet Sand, off the coast of Essex. The letter was dated yesterday, so they are almost certainly engaged in combat now. Orders to hastily send two hundred recruits to the fleet were dispatched. I went down to Blackwall on the north bank of the river to see the soldiers off. It was strange to see the way the poor men kissed their wives and sweethearts in a simple goodbye, letting off their guns as they left.

June 4th 1666 – The Dutch fleet was found at anchor between Dunkirk and Ostend, it is larger than all feared; numbering about ninety. The sound of cannon fire carrying up the river heralded the beginning of the engagement. All are praying for a swift and decisive victory.

8

The first few drinking establishments William and Stephen visited were, as they had predicted, not helpful. The only thing they had gained was local gossip; unfaithful husbands and a particularly fruity scandal concerning two locals who had eloped two weeks previously and not been heard of since. William knew this had to be endured to ensure their presence in the city became public knowledge but it was still tedious. They needed people to know they were asking questions. It was a bore, but a necessary one.

William was surprised to find Stephen was enjoying himself, perhaps a little too much. On several occasions, William had been required to prize his friend away as he became overly comfortable by the bar, the large man's natural affinity for people getting the better of him. At one point he resorted to administering a hasty kick under a table, the attention of his large friend had wavered too long after a barmaid fluttered her eyelashes at him. Stephen couldn't help himself. Like a moth to a flame. All other thought processes failed at the sight of a pretty girl, and he was only further encouraged by the interest she showed in return. William had seen the innkeeper glance over at her, checking her progress. It was an obvious ploy to attract more sales. They must have seen Stephen coming a mile off, not least because of his height, William mused, chuckling to himself. Winding his leg back under the table he had delivered a swift kick to the lower shin, rescuing the jovial giant's rogue attention. A barely stifled yelp sounded from across the table. Solid connection. Should be a good bruise. A little reminder to stay on task. Stephen glared over, eyes watering. Must have been a better connection than he thought. William motioned to the door with his head. About to protest, Stephen's mouth dropped open before submitting with a sigh. The two men wound their way through the mazy tables, leaving a disappointed looking innkeeper to berate his staff for not ensuring the customers spent more money.

Making their way to the centre of the city, they turned onto a cobbled street leading to the corn exchange. On either side of the cobbles rose tall wooden buildings, fronted in dark wood. The prosperity of the owners displayed by the quality and intricacy of the carvings adorning the panels. Those that wished to make certain the outside world knew of their wealth had designed large bay windows, projecting out into the street in a pyramidal design, so that as many window panes as possible could be put in place; taking their cue from the new fashions of France.

Toward the end of the street stood a tall wooden building characteristic of many of the structures in the city. Beams latticed across wattle and daub, whitewashed to contrast with the wood. Delicately intricate woodwork adorned the window bays. It bore a very similar appearance to many buildings on the street but was marked out by the warm glow emanating from the window panes. The good-natured bustle of a well-run meeting place was audible from the street, enticing in further custom.

"Last one." William announced, shuffling his coat closer onto his shoulders. The rain that had threatened was just beginning to fall in full force.

"So…we meet him here?" As the question left Stephen's lips, the door opened and the two friends were swallowed by the atmosphere.

Both men scanned the room as they entered. Conversations stalled, curious eyes flickering up to acknowledge their entrance before returning to their drinks, at which point the tavern returned to full volume. Food was still being served. The rich gamey smell of a stew wafted past as two bowls were placed on a nearby table. Large chunks of bread accompanied them, provided to mop up any leftovers. Nothing smelling that good could go to waste, thought Stephen appreciatively.

They made their way, sliding between the establishment's patrons, to a table recently vacated by the previous inhabitants. As they passed the bar a shoulder bumped into William. The man, evidently there for a while already, span round slurring an earnest apology. William reassured him that he had caused no bother and the two men seated themselves at the table.

Stephen's eyes settled on a table near a dark corner of the room. It was the only area of the room not bathed in the deep orange glow, provided by the many candles scattered around the tables and larger wall fixtures. A thick wooden pillar forced the lone table into shadow. He could just about make out a figure leaning back against the wall. Despite being indoors, whoever it was had chosen to wear a sweeping hood that draped down over the eyes. Long, pale fingertips gripped the bowl of a long pipe protruding from the hood. All other features were lost in a plume of thick pipe smoke collecting in front of the face. What wasn't hidden by the smoke remained bathed in shadow.

Nudging his friend, Stephen whispered, "Burns is here."

"Yes" came the simple reply.

They had been seated for a few minutes, Stephen remained looking intently over his friend's shoulder at the table shrouded in shadow. As the hooded figure inhaled from the pipe, a rush of golden light from the bowl revealed twisted, cracked lips surrounded by a dirty greying beard. There was little movement, smoke drifting up into the rafters of the building.

It was another ten minutes before the hooded man revealed himself. William and Stephen had been sitting in silence, waiting to be approached as they sipped nervously from their tankards. As he stepped out from the shadows, the man became bathed in candlelight, his hood no longer obscuring his face. A thick beard fell down past the man's broad chest, almost long enough to tuck into his belt. Though greying, the man was heavy set, his sinewy forearms visible below the sleeves rolled around his elbows. But it was the man's face that had Stephen staring. One cheek was horrifically scarred, the shape of an arrow tip reaching along the cheekbone to his upper lip.

"He fits the description so far...quite terrifying"

"Wait," William turned to look at his companion, a confused look on his face, "Who are you looking at?"

"Don't speak so loud." Stephen hissed, "There.

Coming over from the shadows."

"That's not him." William grinned, watching as the scarred man nodded his thanks to the man behind the bar and, resettling the cloak over his shoulders, walked out into the night. "Burns has already acknowledged us. The man at the bar."

"B...but, he must be our age. Maybe even younger. And he looks normal."

"He is." replied William, "Probably mid-twenties, and a perfectly normal looking man. He realised quite early on that he didn't have the physical presence to run a criminal enterprise. So he invented one. Not wanting to ever dirty his hands with the everyday business of crime, instead he organises, and people answer to him. Few have actually seen him though. It wouldn't do for gang lords to know they were being controlled by a rather weedy looking younger man."

"But the name Burns? I thought he had horrific scarring from being tortured by his own family as a young boy."

"Clearly not, it's all part of the myth he created. His surname is actually just Burns." Sensing his friend's disappointment, William added, "He is just as dangerous as you've heard though. More so in fact. It wouldn't surprise me if the few who do know who he is are all also here, guarding. Keep your wits about you, he may appear harmless, but it is entirely an illusion."

Their hushed conversation hastily ended with the appearance of Burns at their table. Pulling out a stool, he lowered himself slowly before apparently giving up and falling heavily onto the seat. With legs dragged underneath him, he swung one shoulder round so that his arm came to rest on the table. A childlike giggle emanated from his mouth, head lolling from side to side as if too heavy for his neck to support. Wondering whether their efforts would be better spent returning on another occasion, the two friends remained silent, unsure who should make the first move. After a short pause, the swinging head snapped upright, eyes fixed on the two men. With utter clarity, Burns began,

"Hello Billy boy." All traces of his total inebriation were lost, "It's been a while."

Stephen wasn't entirely sure what was happening. Upon entering the public house, he had almost completely failed to register this man. He was still reeling from the revelation that the man opposite them haunted the dreams of many a law-abiding citizen in England. The tales of his exploits were notorious, a criminal phantom capable of striking fear into the hearts of even the most hardened men. As a man used to dealing with securing the country from the wide range of threats it faced, Stephen had come across more than his fair share of dangerous and powerful people. At the realisation Burns appeared to be no more than a reasonably wealthy country gentleman, he had to admit to himself that he was slightly disappointed, but the whole scenario unfolding before him left him on edge.

Burns was dressed well, in simple clothes that had been well cut. Nothing in particular distinguished him from the other patrons of the house. This man was average height, an average build that Stephen judged to be a little overweight. There was really nothing that in any way resembled the troubled character he had heard of in the tales. He was just another rich alcoholic with a slightly wobbling chin. At least that was what he thought before Burns began to speak. With the snap of his head, all pretence of the bumbling fool was lost. A pair of keenly focused eyes cut into him from across the table, awaiting an explanation for their intrusion into his domain.

William shrugged off the shock of the unexpected conversation opener before Stephen. He knew this was no time for pleasantries. Burns was not a pleasant man. Instead, he got straight to the point. In an attempt to keep their complete lack of information hidden, William spoke slowly, keeping the tone as light as possible.

"We need two things, Burns. Two bits of information really, if you have them. We ask this in the strictest confidence."

"What's new?" came the bored reply. Pausing to smooth the point of his beard, William took the time to think of his next move. He needed something to spike Burns' interest. A change in tactics was required.

"This is of national importance." Burns' ears pricked at the whisper before William continued, losing the informal tone, "Firstly, there was a letter stolen in London recently detailing the King's wish to continue Dr Dee's conversations with angels. We need to know who now has it. In addition to this, we think whoever has the letter might be involved in a plot to assassinate the King. There is talk of some link with a group, or person, who has been behind recent civil unrest and previous plots."

"And you think I have something to do with this?" Burns' question was slow and openly hostile.

"No, of course not." replied William, "But we're stuck if you can't help us."

Sensing his potential importance to their mission, Burns puffed his chest like a bird ruffling its feathers.

"You realise that letters go missing in London every day? To limit the search to one would be a fool's errand."

"We understand that, of course. But if anyone was in a position to know where to start it would be you."

"You're too kind." Burns smirked. "I do have many ears to the ground, it's in my interests to know what is happening. Where exactly was the letter taken from? That would be the place to start."

"From the house of Stephen Berry. It was due to be taken up to York but went missing before it had left the house. A member of his household was later discovered in the Thames, throat slit open." William's eyes flicked over to his friend. It did not go unnoticed by Burns.

"Ah yes, I think one of mine found the unfortunate man. You see I keep a close eye on the work of King's men such as Mr Berry." Burns said this without acknowledging the third man sitting at the table. "I may have news of such a letter, though I don't see how such information is limited to a single piece of paper, or even what danger it may bring about. Dr Dee has been dead a long while now, and his work was hardly successful.

I can tell you there has been a power struggle in London recently, money pumped into those that I consider to be my...er...competitors, shall we say. Someone wants me out of the way, more so than before, so my efforts at collecting information have increased somewhat. I believe the letter you speak of is still in the hands of those who took it originally - two individuals who, as it so happens, have made their way to this neck of the woods. I hear neither of them is English, but where they are from, I don't know. One of them, a woman would you believe, is rumoured to be in Oxford.

When I have anything more complete than that I will send word, but for now that's all I have. Are you at home?"

William nodded his reply, not wanting to interrupt the flow of information – besides, he knew the man opposite would already know the answer. Burns continued, "The other matter is, I'm afraid, more guesswork than anything. There have always been rumours, passed among the more shady circles of society, but more recently they seem to have intensified and I have been looking into them with great interest. As you can imagine, if such a group were to exist, they could cause issues with interference in my own... interests. As I said, I have many ears to the ground but nothing has materialised. Only rumours passed down from generation to generation. No witnesses to any of the events they report. And these whispers led nowhere. However, I personally see too many similarities in all this hear-say for it to be entirely coincidence. There is no smoke without fire after all, but for now the smoke is too thick to see clearly.

I believe the same group to be behind many monumental events of the past century, perhaps much longer, all of which have aimed at destabilising countries across Europe: the Gunpowder Plot; playing both sides at La Rochelle; the Bishop's wars in Scotland; that recent sweep of witch hunts; the civil war in France, not to mention the horrific war in this country. Some are saying they are even responsible for this sickness that is sweeping across Europe, a pact with the Devil, that they converse with the dead and curse with the power of the moon. This, at least, is nonsense - if they were that powerful why stay hidden. I know the power that reputation and fear have over logic, and logic is in short supply. Still, rumour has to start somewhere, and people are latching onto it."

"Is that all we have then?" Stephen spoke up for the first time, "Rumour and half-baked ghost stories?"

Burns cocked his head as if noticing the other man for the first time. The look Stephen received was intensely uncomfortable. He shuffled in his seat. Of all the terrible stories he had heard of this man, the look he received gave him a totally different type of fear - the sudden feeling of complete emptiness. The pale grey eyes fixed on him, coupled with unnatural silence, made Stephen feel childish in his doubt of Burns' theory. Burns broke eye contact and continued talking.

"Not quite Mr Berry. A name emerges every so often. Too often for it to be a coincidence. It is a name that even I now feel the chill of; Aeternitas.

My method has always been to follow the money. It reveals the true nature of any enterprise and, though sometimes difficult to trace, comes to light in the end - but in these cases, it has always led to dead ends. The only thing that links the origins of these events is this name."

"So, what is Aeternitas, what do they want? Surely someone knows – no matter how secretive people are the truth will always leak out somehow."

"Aeternitas was a goddess, the personification of eternity. One of the daughters of Jupiter. She was represented by various Roman emperors with a phoenix, for the cyclical nature of time. And holding a globe, the symbol of world domination."

Making a show of resuming his former state of inebriation, Burns stood, signalling that he had deemed the discussion to be over. With a turn back to the two men seated at the table he hissed, "Do not disdain the whispers of evil these people may be capable of. They are likely more real than we know."

With that, he turned his back on them and staggered back to the bar.

A stunned silence fell over the two friends. The need to process the information Burns had provided left the two men sitting wordlessly. After a while, William was again the first to move.

"We should go. We can't talk openly here anymore and won't gain anything from staying here any longer than we already have."

"Are you serious? Have you not seen how dark it is now? We've been walking around all day, it's late. And when are we going to eat? I'm starving. That stew smelled divine on the way in."

William had failed to register that the evening had drawn in, it was now pitch black outside and the storm that had guided them into the inn was yet to pass, not the conditions to be walking home.

"Always thinking of your stomach, eh?" he said before conceding, "We'll eat, lodge here for the night and head home early tomorrow. Truth be told, I'm famished too."

The two men were careful to keep a low profile as the rest of the evening passed. This was no small feat considering the presence of Stephen. They chose not to continue the conversation they had been having with Burns. It seemed prudent not to re-air such information in public so soon after it had come into their hands.

Stephen had only one question for William, so burning that he had to ask it. Why was Burns helping them in the first place? He was a criminal, the name whispered on the lips of those that feared his powerful reach. What was in it for him?

"I met Burns when we had both started out on our

respective life paths," explained William, "I was looking for information on that occasion too. A London crime ring had taken to targeting the royal residences. Nothing serious, but a concern that they seemed to be infiltrating the buildings so easily nonetheless. He came forward with information. It was a strange situation then too. He knew a lot, was able to explain everything in great detail. When I asked why he had given over so much information he told me of his staunch national pride and belief in the monarchy, which led him to help us."

"Wait," Stephen cut in, "a criminal who loves the King? You bought that?"

"I was happy to accept the information at the time, no one else had come forward with anything at all and I didn't know who he was. I certainly didn't guess he was Burns. But he knew names, places and all the details of the operations. As you know, people do sometimes come forward, but not with that level of detail. I decided to follow him to see if I could find out more.

As it turned out, I saw a little too much of his operations to be ignored. Obviously we knew each other and managed to come to an agreement; he would provide information to me on subjects relating to national security or royal welfare, in return I would remain blind to his activities in the knowledge that they would not affect the stability of the country.

Though I was wary of his true intentions at first, he has stuck to his end of the bargain. It seems that his love of the monarchy is more common than you'd think. Though happy to steal and murder from the vast majority of the population, the King's divine appointment lends a certain authority that many are unwilling to challenge. I also keep his identity secret, as must you.

He is undoubtedly dangerous, but he would do nothing to hurt the country he loves. I have been reassured of this countless times. That he fears the mention of this Aeternitas doesn't fill me with confidence. We need to be on our guard at all times."

William ignored the triumphant look Stephen wore at the news his friend was seriously entertaining the idea that there might be some truth to the rumours of a mysterious group manipulating events.

The food arrived just in time, preventing Stephen's smug look from breaking out into full-blown gloating. The gamey stew provided a warmth that took their minds off the task that had been set before them, for the moment at least.

∞

The night at the inn passed without further incident. They spent the remainder of the evening engrossed by the culinary delights supplied by the kitchens. There had been nothing fancy at all about the produce of the inn, it held no graces, only good honest food capable of warming the stomach and the soul.

After eating themselves to the point of exhaustion, they had taken to their rooms, falling into coma-like sleep that lasted until midday. On awakening, they had skipped breakfast, both still full to bursting from the feast the evening before, and began the walk back to the house. Thoughts turned once more to the information Burns had provided.

"It appears, William, that you were wrong" Stephen smirked, "We are, in fact, on the trail of a mysterious group intent on world domination."

Sensing that his friend was attempting to wind him up, William began to calmly explain why Stephen was actually wrong.

"Not quite fact, Stephen, even Burns said all he had heard were rumours. And I doubt there isn't a criminal group out there that wouldn't consider world domination an ideal scenario. It's all just fear, based on the unknown."

Stephen smiled at the response, completely ignoring the counterpoint, he continued.

"Talking of the unknown. What kind of plot does His Lordship think someone will conjure up when they read that the King wants to resume Dr Dee's work? I understand it's another way to potentially get close to the King, but is that it?"

"Dee was very close to Elizabeth though. I suppose someone would want that kind of control and influence. Charles' death disguised as some sort of demonic attack would certainly stir up more than a little trouble."

"Why is it that the villains always get the best names. Aeternitas. You have to admit, that's a good one. And a phoenix as their device. Whoever they are, they've got style."

"They probably don't even exist" replied William adamantly, "It is almost certainly the imagination of some halfwit with their head running wild with stories of the ancients."

Seeing he had achieved the desired ruffling of his friend's feathers, Stephen chuckled, changing the direction of the conversation.

"Alright, alright. What do we do now though? All we have to work with is the name until Burns gets back with more detailed information. We can't just sit around and wait. We may feel quite removed from the issue at hand here, but we need to remember that it's the King's life, and the stability of the country, that's at stake. If we wait around too long it could all be too late."

"We're doing what we can. Burns works fast. Perhaps a visit to the books is in order. We might uncover something about Aeternitas there."

Stephen looked at his friend in surprise. William had only moments before been adamant that this group did not even exist. There must be some cogs at work in that head of his that were not yet ready to reveal their results.

"The books? Won't that appear a bit strange? We still need to work under the façade of looking for that letter. Why would we go to the library?"

"Good point." William had not thought of that. After a brief pause, he continued. "At this point we might need to split for a day. I visit the library fairly regularly, so there is nothing out of character there. At the same time you can ask around for a foreign woman recently arrived from London. We'll need to find out who they are at some point anyway. Burns didn't seem to share His Lordship's view that the two trails are linked, but I suppose we should be as thorough as possible."

"Agreed. I'll have another look around the inns, see if the extra detail yields any results." Looking over at the eternally serious face of his friend he added, "I might even pay that barmaid another visit."

William's head snapped around, jaw dropping. Seeing the huge grin on the larger man's face, he realised he was still the target of his mockery. Setting his mind to a little retribution, he made a lunge toward Stephen. The movement was quickly dodged. Only too late did the giant realise he had acted exactly as William had intended. He found himself missing his step, the grass still sodden from the heavy rain the night before, and tumbling backwards into a small ditch, hidden along most of the road by a tangle of brambles.

Lying in a crumpled heap on the floor, Stephen was left staring up at the sky as the standing water seeped into his clothes. Howls of laughter carried over the edge of the ditch. Picking himself up, he scrambled back up onto the path.

Finding William bent double with fits of amusement, he found the perfect time to respond. So incapacitated by laughter was his unsuspecting victim that he was powerless to prevent Stephen's revenge. In a spattering of thin mud picked up from his fall, Stephen approached his friend. With a huge embrace, he engulfed the laughing man. William's feet wriggled in the air in protest as he was lifted off the ground. With a final squeeze, the large man returned his spluttering friend to the floor. Both men were now covered in thick layers of dank, watery mud left in the ditch from the downpour the night before. Still laughing they continued on the way home.

One mission down, thought Stephen, for the time being at least Will has forgotten how miserable he has kept himself.

"So no running off with strange women then?" he joked.

"I'm sure you'll find time later" came the reply as William attempted to beat some of the muck from his coat sleeves, "Nothing anyone has ever said has stopped you before."

"I told you, all or none at all – and what kind of fun is none at all."

William shook his head in disapproval, he had quite given up trying to tame his friend long ago. There was always hope though.

FROM THE DIARY OF SAMUEL PEPYS.

June 5th 1666 – Even with less than sixty in our fleet, we put them to flight until they were joined by reinforcements. The fight continued until the next morning. Eventually the Dutch made for their own coast, but the consequences of the battle are not yet clear.

It is thought that of the almost one hundred sails the Dutch brought against us, only fifty returned home. So great was the news that the Court was in hubbub, reflecting the joy in the city.

London is aloud with the sounds of victory. Out in the streets the joy is tangible. After the uncertainty of having to wait through the sound of guns, the feeling of relief is glorious.

9

The woman approached the old house, it was almost lost in the murky greyness of an overcast day. The effect did nothing to diminish the imposing nature of the building. In fact, the vast, looming walls blended with the sky, giving the impression of a building on a monstrous scale. Around it, skeletal trees with yellowing leaves, stripped of their green by the heat of the summer, took on the appearance of all manner of monstrous beings. With a shudder she quickened her step, trying not to imagine what might be hidden by their spindly branches.

A lone lamp lit the columned entrance of the house. It flickered in the slight breeze, working hard to penetrate the miserable gloom. Along the top of each column, a grotesque leered out at the surroundings, guarding those inside against any evil spirits that might be wandering restlessly on such a night. The appearance of the building may have inspired fear in others but she knew what lay inside was far more terrible; a power that brought nations to their knees and entire empires crashing and burning.

She checked behind her to make sure no one was following. Content that the coast was clear to continue, she pushed through the front door. It had been left open. She knew she was expected.

Through the door was a well-lit hallway. An elaborate staircase lay directly ahead. The room had six doors leading off it. As per her instructions, she opened the second door to the left and passed into another room, slipping the Venetian-made mask she had concealed in her cloak over her eyes. Held by a thin ribbon of black silk, the mask covered both cheekbones, reaching up over her brows to conceal the majority of her face. Her mask was entirely covered in black feathers, an ebony beak protruding a short distance over her nose so that even the lower portion of her face remained partly hidden.

There was nothing remarkable about the room itself. It was dark. Again only a single, small lamp hanging from the centre of the ceiling provided any illumination. Decorated in wooden panelling and with a beamed roof, the space bore a resemblance to many rooms in large houses across the country. This room though was dominated by an enormous table, one single piece of white marble. It was so large that the seating almost came into contact with the walls. It must have weighed an absolute ton, how someone had managed to get it into the room she could not tell.

Equidistant around its circumference sat figures. Each wore a beaked mask similar to hers, making them unrecognisable. The true identity of all other members in the meeting was unknown to her. She had known the man who had recruited her, but he had died soon after. It was up to her to find a replacement, but the right person had not been found yet. It was not a recruitment process that could be rushed. The system meant everyone around the table was only ever known by name by one other person, except Phoenix, the leader of their meetings, who's name no one knew - though he knew them all.

Chosen at random to serve a lifetime, Phoenix was the only one permitted to monitor the attendees. Any who had known Phoenix's identity before they had filled the role paid for it with their life. A small price to pay to ensure the security of their group. There would be no power struggle among them.

Noticing that the time she had been allocated to arrive had made her the last to take her seat, she made her way over to the only vacant chair, high backed and padded with dark scarlet velvet.

As she sat down a figure directly opposite her stood. Where everyone else's beaked masks were dull colours: black, greys and mottled browns, this mask was fiery colours of deep reds, oranges and flecks of sunburst gold. Phoenix.

With raised arms, the figure looked around the room,

"Welcome, Children of Aeternitas."

∞

On their return to William's house, the two men had been greeted by Robert and his father, Samuel. Concern was etched across their faces at the appearance of the friends as they came through the door. It was only when they saw the amused looks of the returning men that their worries were eased. The childish escapades on the journey home were passed off as slips on the flooded road, the tracks made treacherous by the storm of the night before.

Samuel was a hardy looking man, every inch a

workman. Born and bred in the lands around the city, he held a disdain for the easy life of those living within its walls. He knew the land better than anyone and was well aware that nowhere along the path home should they have encountered any difficulty. The opportunity to 'slip' would not have arisen without provocation. He remained silent on the matter, however, knowing all too well the mischief the two men had been able to get themselves into ever since meeting years before. Instead, he apologised profusely for not being at the house to welcome them home the day before, encouraged them both to wash and change, and went to fetch some food.

Appetites fully restored by the walk home, William and Stephen hurriedly rinsed off the worst of the mud on their hands and faces, changed into clean sets of clothes and rushed back down to eat. Rather than wait for food to be laid out in the formal dining rooms, they made a nuisance of themselves in the kitchens. Joined by the eternally ravenous Robert, the kitchens soon descended into chaos as all the men crammed in to scavenge whatever tasty morsels they could lay their hands on.

William spent the time catching up with Samuel, hearing any important local events that he had missed and reports of how the household was faring. News even a limited distance outside the city held a different focus to the gossip of the Oxford inns. Robert and Stephen amused themselves by taking it in turns to sneak food from the platters that were being prepared. Their takings were limited to a few scraps. Robert's mother, Hannah, kept a vigilant watch over the food she was organizing. With eyes in the back of her head, she would swoop around, scolding the would-be thieves as they made for the selection of cold meats.

William may have been the master of the house, Samuel the head of his family, but in reality Hannah reigned supreme. Like a mother hen, she ruled the roost, not afraid to berate William for his failings. Over the years she had developed a soft spot for her employer's giant friend, but even Stephen could not escape her wrath if caught stealing food. With everyone gathered in the kitchen after so long apart she was visibly content. Her adopted brood once more under her wings.

There was no sign of the attack upon the produce of the kitchen diminishing, leading to Hannah making a show of giving up her defence. She served the food in situ, the four men gathering around the kitchen table to tuck into the array of delights that made up their feast. The highlight was a pie which, sitting in the middle of a work table, was first to disappear. Left to cool in the pantry, it had time to mature in flavour. Rich gamey meat from rabbits, snared in the neighbouring fields, coupled with the sweetness of carrots and leeks, grown in the house gardens, all married together with a thick sauce made from boiling down the bones of previous meals. All four men were in agreement, it was a marvel.

Having once more appeased their appetites, the household fell into a lazy afternoon. A fire was burning in a large stone fireplace dominating the snug, a much less formal living room which, coupled with the kitchen, was one of the most used rooms in the house. William allowed the rest time, he continued to hear from Samuel about events that he had missed during his absence from the house. He was quickly brought up to date on affairs of the estate. At no point had he been concerned about how well Samuel would run things, nevertheless, he was glad to hear that his land was prospering. Hannah sat with her husband, occasionally chiming in her opinions.

Meanwhile, Stephen had found a kindred spirit in young Robert. Besotted by the two men he had idolised as a child, Robert was perfectly content to sit and listen to Stephen's ramblings. The big man needed no encouragement, jumping from topic to topic, a flood of words with no agenda or desired outcome, happy merely to talk and be heard.

The late afternoon passed in a contented haze. The hours had drifted by, the household happy to pass the time in each other's company. Samuel and Hannah came and went, coupling the completion of their duties around the house with time spent in the snug. Before long the fire lulled William into a deep sleep. Despite feeling that he was once more able to call the house his home, and the new lease of life it had injected into him, it was a lot to take in over a short period of time. After all the travelling they had been through, he had been left completely exhausted.

∞

Stephen woke to the sound of raindrops lashing against the window panes. Moving over to the window, he looked up at the array of aggressively darkening clouds. The unseasonably dry weather was looking like it might once again be giving in to a tempestuous assault that would make the rain the night before seem little more than a brief shower. Although not yet heavy enough to prevent the trip back into Oxford from going ahead as planned, the sky did not look promising.

He sought out William. Finding him still asleep, he shook his friend awake, pointing to the window,

"What do you think? It doesn't look like we'll be going back to the city any time soon."

Rousing groggily, the other man stared at the encroaching storm, taking a few moments for sleep to give way to full consciousness.

"No, not really worth getting stuck in that. Burns hasn't been in contact so I don't think we'd gain much by going in this evening anyway. We can stay here today and go in tomorrow. That way we can be sure to spend the whole day gathering any information we can find."

"It will give you more time with the books too."

"Good point. We have quite a collection here anyway. We can both start today. Between us it shouldn't take long to get through them. I'd not heard of Aeternitas before now though, so I can't imagine there'll be much we find here."

"Huh...books. Great." Stephen groaned. "I thought I'd managed to avoid them this time."

"Oh, come now. Where would we be without them? All of the world's greatest thoughts and achievements are recorded in their pages. Imagine the wisdom that would be lost if no one were to keep it written down."

"I suppose." He conceded. But all our weaknesses and downfalls are equally present, he thought, wordlessly.

∞

Burns walked out of the inn where he had spent the evening dining. The arrival of the rain heralded a mighty storm. Though a man of habit, not wanting to get caught when the downpour was at its heaviest, he had left his meal earlier than usual. The normal retinue of watchers and bodyguards had remained behind at his behest. He had urgent work to complete and they sometimes made moving locations a chore. Besides, he would not be travelling far.

The low evening sun glittered off the wet street, reducing sight as it reflected up into his eyes. He could just about make out the outline of a figure approaching from the other end of the street, he looked to be making directly for him, a dark silhouette against the blinding light. Burns brought his hands up to his eyes in an attempt to better see the swirling figures around him. Dark shapes moved past him in a rush to get out of the imminent storm, their footfall skipping along the wet cobbles as they dodged the worst of the growing puddles.

He was now sure that the figure he had noticed at the other end of the street was making for him. Turning to rush to the safety of the warm pub he had just vacated, he glanced over his shoulder. The figure was fast approaching. As they grew closer all he could distinguish was that the shape was incredibly tall and broad in the shoulders. The man, surely no woman could be that tall, must be the largest he had ever seen. Burns was running, but so was the large man. There was little chance of escape now. The distance was too great and he had misjudged the speed of the looming giant. It was not until he was almost on top of him that Burns could pick out any detail.

"You?" was all he could manage before a blow to the head left him face down on the cobbled street. Burns' vision was already spinning as he attempted to crawl away from his aggressor, all the while clutching at his chest pocket, when a second blow to the back of his head left him motionless on the cold cobbled floor.

As the rain continued to fall, the blood pouring from his head swirled around the body before washing away. No one in the street stopped to check the state of the fallen man. Concerned only with rushing from the deluge they might be caught in, no attention was paid to what was just another obstacle to their route. Diluted by the gathering water, it was barely noticeable as his life flowed from him.

FROM THE DIARY OF SAMUEL PEPYS.

June 7th 1666 – There are now confusingly mixed reports arriving back to Westminster concerning the naval battle that has taken place with the Dutch fleet. Lord Brouncker has come to Court with quite contrary news to that which we had heard before.

We are now said to have lost the naval battle against the Dutch. Though our adversaries were prevented from advancing, so many of our ships and men have been lost that we cannot claim a victory.

The outpouring of emotion only two days past is now dampened. Feeling on the streets is very much muted.

10

They were calling him 'The Stroker'. Valentine was not keen on the name, but had decided that the attribution of a nickname was probably a positive thing. He was being talked about, that was what really mattered. It was also difficult to dispute that it summed up his miraculous gift rather well.

More and more people were coming to see him in the hope that his touch would heal them. At first, it had been only sufferers of the King's Evil, the deep bluish growth on the neck that in time ruptured and formed an open gash at the throat. People were left with terrible scarring at best. Traditionally only the King had been able to cure this disfigurement by touch, but God had called Valentine to serve them. Now all kinds of ailments were brought to him, though skin diseases were the most commonly seen. In some of the larger towns there had even been queues waiting for him. And, one by one, he had laid hands on them and seen them walk away praising their healing.

After several weeks of service to the poorer members of society, Valentine had been called to the home of Lord Edward Conway in the hope that his wife,

Lady Anne, might benefit from his gift. His fame had been rising steadily, but this could be the real break through he needed.

The night had set in early, closing gloom accompanied by rising winds which left the flame of Valentine's torch flickering ceaselessly. As he approached the castle that was home to the Conways, he thought of all that he had endured before this point. He had survived the deadly storm on the crossing from his native land and, armed only with the knowledge that he was destined for great things, he had begun his work. Now he would finally receive the recognition he deserved.

Reaching a large gate that guarded the entrance, he stopped to offer up a prayer that the Lord would be with him in this endeavour. He had placed Valentine in this position, success would take him another step toward the King.

"Almighty God, be with me as I meet with this family. May they benefit from Your healing power. In this, as in all things, may Your will be done."

On entering the grand building, he was guided through the thin stone walkways and into a darkened room. Candlelight flickered around the ancient stone walls, picking out distorted shapes in shadow. Bare stone walls were shielded by figures huddling along the edges of the room; hidden by the poor light. Valentine made his way to the centre of the room. Standing there was a woman, dressed in all the finery of the aristocratic elite, she could only be the Lady Anne.

Why did people always assume that the Almighty could only work in eerily darkened rooms? He had been the one to create the Sun after all. There was so much that still lingered of the country's pagan past. Shaking his head at the thought, Valentine approached.

"What ails you my Lady?" he asked calmly, noticing the slight shake of the greying woman's hands. To have been put in such a position was a risk for her. What would it do to her reputation if the Lord deemed her unworthy of healing? This was as much a test for her as it was for Valentine.

"A great pain in the fore of my head, sir." She replied, swishing the dark blue velvet of her dress in a display of her nerves.

Valentine nodded reassuringly as he moved closer.

"All will be well my lady, do not fear. If you will allow me, I will place my hands on the affliction."

Lady Anne nodded her head, her trembling bottom lip further betraying her fear.

Reaching for her, Valentine placed his hands over the woman's ears. Gently moving them in a circular motion, he began muttering a prayer. A command for the pain to leave the body; for every part of her body to return to physical normality and proper function. Feeling the warmth of power flow through him, he maintained his hold for a few seconds longer.

Removing his hands he said,

"Your pain is gone."

The lady stifled a cry, staring at him in disbelief.

"It's gone. Edward, it's gone!" She called to her husband. The figures that had held back in the shadows now moved forward to see for themselves the power on display. Valentine felt a clap on his back as relief settled the barely concealed panic that had held his stomach in knots. He had done it. Thank the Lord.

∞

The storm that plagued the city overnight gave way to a murky early morning. Raindrops swarmed the air. They seeped through even the thickest layers, but William and Stephen had decided the journey back into Oxford could not be delayed any longer. Horses were taken to speed up the journey. They had the added benefit of keeping the riders out of the worst of the mud now making up the path into the city.

Even on horseback, they were slowed in the marshy area around the church of St. Clements. The land at the bottom of the hill would already have been soft under foot; the night's downpour brought their passage to a crawl. In places they were forced to dismount, not wanting to risk breaking a horse's leg. It was only once they reached the bridge next to Magdalen College, which took them over the swollen banks of the river, that more assured footing was found.

Since the journey to and from London, both friends had lost track of time. Carried away by the peculiarities of the task handed to them, trivialities such as the day of the week had slipped their minds. The discovery that the streets of the city were so busy was, therefore, a surprise to both of them. It quickly dawned on them that it must be market day. From towns and villages surrounding the city, the population gathered in an attempt to sell their wares.

Interspersed throughout the crowds, pedlars of various trades were drumming up business with witty tunes and verses. Vendors cries merged with those of the travelling street entertainers, hoping to profit from the goodwill of the masses thronging through the cramped streets of the small city.

With so many people in Oxford, gossip was sure to flow freely. Sure enough, it was not long before news of a murder just inside the North Gate of the city reached William and Stephen. As more details emerged the two friends became increasingly alarmed. It was reported that the murder took place outside the inn where they had met Burns only days before. No one was able to provide any clear information as to who had actually died, but the vague descriptions of the man indicated that it could well have been the criminal turned informer. With the very real concern that Burns might be in some way involved, they began further enquiries.

It had not taken long to locate the physician charged with examining the body. Such a role was common knowledge amongst the locals. Kept by a physician training at the university, acting as a mortician for the local Justice of the Peace, the body lay covered by cloth on a table in one of the many rooms that made up his offices. William, as a local large landowner, was known to the men guarding the mortuary and Stephen, despite not being long in the area, was known by many to be a King's man. He had waved a crumpled piece of writing at the guards and they had allowed the two men in without question.

"What was that?" asked William, "I was expecting to have to argue our way in."

"Oh, new protocol from His Lordship," sighed Stephen, "I have to admit, it did make that much easier, but if anyone were to get hold of a copy it could be easily forged – it doesn't even have a seal."

The young physician, a Dr Lower, known to William for his work on the heart and lungs under the instruction of Thomas Willis, had shown them through to where the body was held. Inside the front door was a room in which he would normally attend visiting patients. Along the walls stood shelves full of an assortment of glassware and porcelain pots. Each was labelled with an ingredient that might be used to treat the human body. Brightly coloured jars boasted of oils, powders, and the extracts of various plants. Next to them, numerous intimidating instruments were collected, far too many metal prongs for Stephen's liking. They looked more like instruments of torture than devices that might cure someone.

They walked through the building being used as Lower's place of work and study, the increasingly sickly putrid smell announcing their proximity to the doctor's makeshift mortuary. William and Stephen attempted to block the worst of the stench with handkerchiefs. As they walked, the young physician made it clear there was no doubt as to the cause of death. He stopped them inside a smaller room in which several long tables were positioned. They had been spaced out to allow free movement around them. Each raised platform held a white sheet through which the undeniable lumps and contours of human bodies were poorly hidden.

Unveiling the nearest body, Dr Lower displayed the crushed back of a man's skull. Shards of bone barely covered the grey matter bidding to burst from the open wound. The victim's nose was also broken to such an extent that it lay flat across the face. Lower pointed out that it appeared to be a secondary injury caused by falling face down with force.

William and Stephen looked at the mutilated head of the dead man in uneasy silence. Though no strangers to death, they were both struck by the brutality of the scene. Taking a step forward, Stephen gave a slight shudder.

"Well, it's certainly him." His voice was muffled by the cloth held over his nose and mouth, "Do you think this is linked to our discussion? In his line of work he must have had other people after him?"

"Can't ask him now." William replied, mouth equally guarded, "Perhaps he gained knowledge of something he wasn't meant to know? Being so close to our meeting can't be a coincidence."

"Have you looked through his pockets?" Stephen asked Lower, who had remained in the room but hung back to give them room to work.

"I'm a physician Sir, not a thief. I do not spend my time rifling through the pockets of the deceased. Besides, you are the first men here, it would seem that last night was a particularly busy one for the local constabulary. The storm appears to have provided ample excuse for many a misdemeanour." The physician, riled by what he considered an accusation, showed obvious affront. Stephen merely shrugged an apology before going through Burns' possessions.

A search of the dead man's pockets provided an array of papers. He must have spent a while lying in heavy rainfall before anyone had moved him, the loose sheets found on his person were all ruined, not much more than mulch. There was however a small leather booklet. It was slightly more intact but mostly empty.

"We'll take it all. The constable can find us later if he has any more information." Asserted William. It was no use to Lower, who would no doubt have discarded it all anyway. Thanking him for being so accommodating with their investigations, they left the young doctor to continue with his day.

On the street, William led the way along the city wall to their old college. One of his friends was still teaching there. William knew he was away for a few weeks; on the continent collecting further materials for his research. He was sure that, whilst away, the professor would not begrudge them the use of his rooms. The porters on the college doors knew William well and, once he had explained the need for a place to talk discreetly, they happily permitted the two friends entry.

Attempting not to dwell too long on the lingering vision of Burns' crushed skull, the two men went straight to task. Searching through the papers recovered from the body, they were able to confirm the assessment that they were mostly useless. Any traces of ink that had once clung to the pages were no more than faintly blurred streaks.

The small leather booklet was of more interest. As they had thought, it was mainly empty, but the leather cover had managed to preserve at least some of the pages. Most of the scribblings were an unintelligible scrawl, a combination of diagrams and random letters filled the majority of the occupied pages. These appeared useless, only providing the two men with the conclusion that Burns was an intelligent man who passed the time on complex mathematical theories.

William, well on his way to giving up any chance of finding a lead amongst the papers, sat back in thoughtful silence. Stephen remained scouring the booklet for anything useful. With Burns dead, their only real lead had disappeared. All they had were the rumours given to them by the dead criminal. Still no known identity for the two they were meant to be looking for. And only the name Aeternitas, which may or may not be linked to a shadowy group acting as puppeteers for discord throughout Europe. Without further intelligence, they were lost. The fake letter may be stumbled upon, but by then it would probably be too late.

Burns' death clearly indicated to William that their investigations were being followed. It was too much of a coincidence to be anything else. Whoever the murderers were had the distinct advantage of knowing their pursuers, whilst William and Stephen had no clear idea of who they were after. For their adversaries to have heard Burns' whispers and acted so quickly was a testament to their organisation and power. What chance did two men have against them? Before too long the King would be dead and they still wouldn't know who was behind it.

William grew increasingly despondent, low for the first time since their arrival back in Oxford. He was pulled from his melancholy by an exclamation by Stephen,

"Look here," he pointed to a messy page in the notebook, "it's not wholly clear, but you can just make out the odd word."

William squinted at the blurs of ink that covered the page. It was hard to work out, but it was true, he could just about make out three words amidst the inky mess.

Souls   recital   Dutch

"Souls...Recital...Dutch," he looked up at Stephen, "What can that mean?"

"I don't know," came the baffled reply, "might be worth asking around to see if there are any recitals that might draw a crowd? Maybe the two we are looking for will be there."

"Good thinking." A thought flashed through William's head. "Burns said the two weren't English, didn't he? So perhaps they are Dutch, or one of them anyway?"

"It could also mean the recital is Dutch though."

"I suppose so. Wouldn't you expect the order to be different though? If it were a Dutch recital, the words would be next to each other."

"I don't know. Can we really read much into the spacing? All we have is three words. I suppose we just keep a look out for both. That way we might find something. It's far from perfect, but at least it's something."

"Definitely. Good find."

Jumping to their feet they made their way back into the busy streets. Eager to make some progress, they began a frantic search for anything taking place in the city that might match their new find. Burns' death had shown their adversaries were close. There was no time to lose.

FROM THE DIARY OF SAMUEL PEPYS.

June 28th 1666 – We are expecting an imminent second attack from the Dutch.

Spurred on by the heavy losses we took earlier in the month, our enemy have doubled their efforts. Though under much pressure, many in Westminster remain confident that our coastal defences are ready for any hostility. All that we are able to do is to wait, and hope that their constant reassurances are grounded in truth.

11

The previous week's meeting at the old house had left her with no doubt that events she had put into action over the previous months were now unstoppable. Everything, meticulously planned before even the smallest move had been made, was in place. Not even the inconvenience of Burns' snooping could do anything to stop them – besides he was no longer in the picture, they had seen to that. William la Penne and Stephen Berry, known to have arrived recently from London, had met with Burns but remained completely unaware of what lay ahead. Of that the Children of Aeternitas were confident. She had to admit Burns' potential to cause them issues had been underestimated. The two King's men had done well to meet with him as soon as they had, but she was confident they were still no closer to the truth. The situation in England was entirely under control, she had made sure of that.

The same could not be said for the rest of Europe. It was ripe for revolution, yet Phoenix insisted that they must bide their time. The failure of the revolution in England earlier in the century had proved that people could be relied on for one thing only; weakness. The monarchy had been overthrown. The country fractured, almost broken. The dawn of a wonderful new republic. The gentry had been so divided that they would easily crumble. The people would rise. Democracy in its purest form would take hold. An opportunity for mankind to reach its highest potential. A success story so perfect the rest of the world would look on in awe. An example that others would strive to replicate.

All this had come so close to realisation in the war that split England. It was the weakness of man that had left their dream lying in the dust, shattered by the ever-burning lust for power. Oliver Cromwell had installed his harsh regime; a Child of Aeternitas gone rogue with the taste of power. Cromwell had caused a schism amongst the Children. It was only recently they had unified once more under the banner of their true purpose. All the Lord Protector had achieved was a reuniting of the people against him and his son. The population had been driven back into the arms of the old monarchy. Now the country was under their grip once more, in the form of that flamboyant fool Charles II. Those close to him held the real power. Parliament was nothing more than a façade. The power of a few suppressed the potential of so many. A people unknowingly kept in check by the agents of government, working in the shadows to maintain their masters' lavish lifestyles.

Well, now the shadows would strike back. All this would change. Soon. Her colleague had been performing his role admirably. Burns was not an easy person to remove. Their journey back to London gathered more and more momentum. A meeting with the King must soon be due. A meeting that would define the age.

∞

It was proving far more difficult to find information on recitals in Oxford than either William or Stephen had first thought. Asking around on the streets was proving to be a useless exploit, and they had been at it for days. Many in the city only travelled in for the markets, so were devoid of any local knowledge. On several occasions, they had been told to visit the Sheldonian. Despite still being under construction, it was the closest many got to anything other than church hymns, street performers, or bawdy tavern chants. The two friends thought looking at a semi-complete building might not be quite what they were searching for, but had thanked them for their advice nonetheless.

Despite their frustration, William and Stephen were able to enjoy the atmosphere of the market days. Several had passed since their visit to Dr Lower's rooms to view the body of Burns. The bustle of the crowds held a welcoming warmth that engulfed all passers-by. Rich smells wafted from some of the stalls. William frequently had to drag Stephen away from street vendors who managed to entice his friend with their freshly cooked wares. Apparently, the sight of Burns' savaged head had done nothing to dampen the larger man's insatiable hunger. Even now, many days later, William pictured with unease the brutal mess made of the man's skull. The image resurfaced unexpectedly from time to time. Months away from this kind of work must have softened him. It took a conscious effort to force himself to ignore the thought. In time he would, like Stephen, become desensitised to such sights.

Cutting through the crowd surrounding a stall manned by a father and son selling freshly roasted chestnuts, Stephen was struck by an unwelcome thought. The day had been long and unproductive, he was tired of the lack of progress. Who was to say that Burns' note had been describing an event in Oxford, or even England, for that matter? They had no way of knowing that the information held within that booklet was even relevant to them. Having only three words to work with was nothing, it could really be about anything. Had they been carried away by their desire to find information? He dearly hoped not, he could not risk William's good mood, in such fine balance, from disintegrating. He feared that one wrong word and it could take days to bring his friend back from the shadows that constantly threatened him.

William seemed so fixated on the task that such glaringly obvious concerns had not even crossed his mind. If they had, they had not been spoken of. Not wanting to dampen the enthusiasm shown by his friend, Stephen was reluctant to bring his concerns into the open. But it really was something that needed to be addressed. At the moment they were making no progress at all.

"This note Will," he said, turning reluctantly to his friend, "are we clutching at straws a bit here? I mean, we have three words. They may not even have been intended for us. And the recital could be anywhere. There was no indication at all that we should be looking in Oxford. We're no further along with this than we were days ago."

"I know," came the reply, "I've been thinking the same thing. But the rest of that booklet was entirely numbers and random letters. There was no sign that

Burns used it for anything else. I have to believe it was information he was recording."

"Oh come on. Listen to yourself. That page could be absolutely anything. We can't get drawn into this so far that we miss the bigger picture. We'll end up chasing shadows, and then there'll be no hope at all. We followed this lead and found nothing. We need to move on."

"To what Stephen?" William snapped, "What else do we have? It's been weeks now since His Lordship summoned us to London, the two we're after could be anywhere by now. This notebook is all we have."

The two men continued pressing through the crowds of the city in silence. Both knew their frustration had got the better of them. And both knew the other man had a valid point. It was a lack of any solid progress that was the cause of the growing defeatism. Eventually, William continued, attempting to rein in his temper. "It can't be a coincidence that Burns was murdered so soon after talking to us. It just can't - which makes me think that he must have been asking questions that were getting somewhere, or he knew something dangerous. They wouldn't have silenced him so efficiently if he didn't know something he shouldn't. And for him to have been disposed of so obviously, it must have been something significant."

"Granted. But the two we are looking for may not have been directly involved. If this mysterious Aeternitas group are so powerful, they'll have people to do their dirty work. Which leaves us with nothing."

"Do you not think though, if it was us and we knew we would be out of Oxford by the time the information came to light, we would just leave it? Even if someone were close to the truth, they wouldn't be able to do anything about it. Why waste time and potential injury?"

"So they killed Burns because they intend to spend more time in the area? Or something important is planned here… I suppose. But why go for Burns and not us? And Will, these people aren't us. They don't care how many people have to die, even if it's entirely unnecessary."

"I have no idea why they wouldn't go for us. It's just a gut feeling, but I still think something is here for us."

"You know I trust your gut, but I think we need a time limit on this. We can't afford to wait. If Charles is in danger, the least we can do is head back to London and guard him."

"His Lordship will have that covered, I'm sure. And he sent us here, he won't be happy if we turn up with nothing. But I share your concern. Just give this a few more days and then we can rethink the plan."

∞

Robert had been looking for William and Stephen all afternoon. They shouldn't have been hard to find, especially as Stephen was literally head and shoulders above the average man. Factor in his customary brightly coloured attire and one would think finding him would take seconds, not the hours he had spent looking.

Tired of what felt like walking round in circles, he had decided to wait by their horses, which he had found soon after entering the city. Passing the time was easy on a market day. He knew many of the vendors were friends of his father, they were usually happy to slip him a few treats. Leaning against the wall nearest to where the horses were tied up, he satisfied his boredom by eating and chatting whenever there was a lull in trade.

On the verge of giving up and going home, Robert looked up at the sound of an unmistakable voice. As was often the way, he had heard Stephen before he saw him. Over the crowd, he could pick out the two tall men wading through the masses of people. As they approached Robert signalled to them. Recognising him, they sped up, wondering what could have brought him into the city after them.

"Good afternoon Sirs," he said smiling, "there was a man came to see you earlier today with a message. I said you were out but that I would deliver it to you personally."

"Who was he?" they asked simultaneously.

"Someone from one of the colleges. I don't know who he was, looked respectable though, an oldish fellow wearing college garb. He said there was going to be some music at a social gathering at the college in three nights' time. The man said the master of the college was pleased to extend an invitation to you as his guests."

"Which college?" asked William, already confident of the answer.

"All Soul's, Sir."

Recital, Souls. So, perhaps Burns had come through for them even in death.

∞

"You managed to find them then?" Samuel asked his son. The three of them had returned not long ago. An almost tangible excitement fizzed between them. It was evident that his son was unaware what had put the two older men in such a state, but he was happy to go along with it, feeding off the atmosphere like a young pup caught up in a game.

"Yes, father. No trouble at all." He lied.

"What has got to them? I've never seen anyone get so excited about being invited to listen to some music. They're like little girls on May Day."

"I don't think it's the music. When I told them about the invitation they seemed more concerned with the college. It was all they talked about on the way home."

"The college? All Souls College?" Samuel was unaware that anything remotely exciting ever happened in any of the colleges, let alone the one that was always closed. "Why? They've been in the colleges plenty of times. They studied at one of them."

"How should I know? It was All Souls that sparked this mood though. They looked quite dour before I told them."

"How strange. Oh well, at least you got the message to them. That's the important thing."

His son turned to make his way back to the company of William and Stephen. Samuel sighed. Although happy that Robert was able to enjoy the influence of the older men, it could not last. He and his family were much lower in social status and though William treated them like members of the family, it did not change the fact that he was the master of the house. Samuel did not want his son dreaming too big, only to be disappointed by the reality of their life. The opportunities available to Robert would just not be the same. It might be time to start reining him in, he mused, that way expectations might be better managed. It was time for his son to start learning how the world worked.

Before Robert got too far, Samuel called him back. There was work to be done and it was their job to do it. Reluctantly his son walked back down the passageway, glancing longingly behind him. Noting this, Samuel placed a hand of support on his son's shoulder, remembering the day when it had dawned on him that not all men were born equal. It was a difficult lesson to learn, but a necessary one. Life in their household was a down sight better than most, William may be master but they had a lot to be thankful for.

Stephen caught sight of father and son walking out into the courtyard. Observing the sag of the young man's shoulders, the flicker of a frown appeared on the large man's face.

∞

Back in the main room of the house, William and Stephen were piecing together a plan for the upcoming evening recital. On arriving back at the house, Hannah had been able to provide them with some detail missing from Robert's version of the message. It turned out she had been the one to receive the messenger and had sent her son to find them. The invitation, though verbal, had been sent from the warden of the college. A staunch supporter of the King, he had been removed from his position during the rule but was now back.

"The man from the college was very apologetic not to provide a written note, but said that his employer had thought you'd understand. The Warden of All Souls heard from a close mutual acquaintance that the two of you were here in the service of the Crown. He extended a warm invitation for you to join a small gathering he's putting together. A young violinist will provide entertainment for the evening. He said that some of the other guests might be worth introducing yourselves to.

I didn't recognise him, but then I don't have much reason to spend time around the colleges. It was all rather cryptic if you ask me, but I suppose it makes sense to you?"

"Thank you Hannah. Yes, we were expecting to hear from him, so no need to worry about the lack of note." William lied. Both men had listened intently to everything she had to say.

Sensing that this was important, although, with no idea why, Hannah left the two friends alone. It was evident that they had much to discuss, itching to talk but not wishing to involve her. Wondering what could be so important, she made her way upstairs to ready the rooms for the night. It was probably nothing more trivial than some scandal Stephen had caused. She loved him like a son but was well aware he had a habit of attracting unwanted attention. Either that, or he had managed to rope William into another of his hare-brained schemes. It wouldn't be the first time the large man had needed William to bail him out of a tricky situation. She only prayed that they were careful. The last year without them had been hard, she couldn't lose them so soon after their return.

"Burns?" Stephen asked once Hannah was out of earshot.

"I think it has to be."

"So, you were right. I'm sorry."

"I appreciate the apology Stephen, but let's not count our chickens before they've hatched. We still have to attend this thing and see what Burns was steering us towards."

Stephen nodded, accepting that it was too early to get carried away. "Well, we can arrive early and scout the place out – make sure there are no nasty surprises – and I'm sure all will become clear."

12

The day of the recital was almost upon them. William and Stephen had returned to Oxford twice, making sure to remain conspicuous in their search without allowing anyone to know they had made any progress. The constable had asked to see them about their search of Burns' body. He'd had no actual interest in anything they had to say, content to allow the record to show he had pursued the line of questioning – but not wanting to make more work for himself.

The tail end of last week's storm was blowing. It had remained dry, but winds outside were picking up, whistling under the doors and leaving the fire in the snug dancing even more vigorously than normal. All manner of twisted shadows were thrown onto the walls. To protect the windows from any debris in the wild winds, the shutters around the house had all been securely fastened down. The dying light outside could not force its way through these barriers, leaving the house lit only by candles and fire.

Stephen couldn't help but play with the fire. Each time he poked at it, bright sparks were sent spitting across the flagstones. He had to act quickly to flick them back into the fireplace, and away from the rugs that helped to warm the room. Sensing disapproving looks, he placed the iron spike down to reduce the chances of spreading the fire. To resist temptation he moved to sit on one of the elegant wingback chairs they had moved close to the warmth of the fire.

William had not spoken for a while. His initial excitement over the invitation had worn off over the last two days. The wait for progress began to take its toll. Stephen looked over at him, his friend lost in thought, eyes transfixed by the flickering of the flames.

"What are you thinking? You look troubled?"

The question hung in the air. Stephen left it there for a few seconds before trying again. "Will?...William."

"Eh? Oh, beg pardon. What did you say?" came the eventual reply, groggy as if just woken from a deep sleep.

"I said, what are you thinking? You look troubled. I don't want to lose you to your thoughts. Who knows how long it will take to get you back again."

"Ha, I wasn't thinking much to be honest, certainly nothing to concern yourself with." The look on Stephen's face told him his attempt at deflecting the question hadn't worked, so William continued. "Fine. I was just thinking about Burns' notes again. It would appear we are on the right lines - if 'soul' is All Souls and 'recital' refers to this gathering at the college, that is. But does 'Dutch' mean we are after a Dutch conspirator? Should we be looking to the Dutch for help? Does it even have anything to do with the evening? If not, what are we meant to accomplish by going? There are still so many questions."

"Well, you won't answer any of them by getting lost in your head. You'll end up chasing your thoughts round in circles and not making any progress at all. We can both

do without that.
Here, I challenge you to a game of chess."
Seeing that his friend's mood lighten slightly, Stephen reached for the board and pieces. It was a beautiful set of ivory and jade which would not have looked out of place in the King's own residence. He had diverted the attention of the man sitting opposite him, but Stephen felt there was something that had not been said. It clung to William like a shadow. Whatever it was that was he still held back must be something so awful he could not even bring himself to say it. It had been like this before. It was dangerous, had the potential to tear him apart. Stephen would have to keep an extra vigilant eye on his melancholy friend.

∞

William was restless. No matter what he tried, there was no way he could sleep. Something about the situation they found themselves in was not sitting right. Mind running wild with potentially disastrous scenarios, he attempted to figure out what it was that was plaguing him.
Time and time again his thoughts returned to Burns' notebook. Something drew him to it. Something about the remaining word that irritated like a barb caught in his skin. Dutch.
On first reading it with Stephen, it had been nothing more than a word. Another confusing word, but only a word. Even more than the others, it had been worrying away at him throughout the day, his gut telling him that it somehow spelt trouble. Now that the other words were seemingly related to the event the following

evening, he could only assume that this word did too.

Burns' words rang in his ears, 'neither of them are English…a woman would you believe…in Oxford.' Could that be it? A Dutch woman? It had been playing on his mind all evening.

Needing to clear his head, he made his way downstairs. Whispers echoing along the walls carried from the kitchen.

It was unusual for anyone to be awake at such an hour. Making his way slowly along the hall, he listened closely, attempting to catch what was being said. Surely anyone breaking into the house would not pause to talk in the kitchen? Not wanting to risk the same fate as Burns, he continued silently. Better to be overly cautious than caught sleeping.

Behind him, the creak of the second to last stair sent him into a state of calm that always fell on him before combat. There was someone else sneaking around the house.

Pressing his body into the darkest shadows, he waited for the night visitor to pass by. Were they making their way to join the other person in the kitchen, having found their target's bed empty?

A whispered hiss came from the top of the passageway. He relaxed.

"Will?" Stephen sidled up next to him. "What's going on? Is someone here?"

Signalling for his friend to be silent, William continued to move closer to the kitchen door. He found it slightly ajar, able to make out two figures. Feeling more than a little stupid, he identified them as Samuel and Hannah. His housekeeper stood by a large bowl into which she was pouring a variety of herbs, the rest of which were strewn across the table. Her husband sat by the table, picking at the bones leftover from the meals prepared earlier in the day. They spoke to each other in hushed tones.

Turning, William made his way back to the staircase.

"What's going on?" asked Stephen, confused by the late-night wanderings.

"I couldn't sleep and heard voices. It was just Samuel and Hannah."

"Are you alright? You don't look well."

"Just having trouble sleeping. I'll see you in the morning."

Stephen watched his friend make his way back up the stairs. He was about to follow when he caught a snippet of conversation from the kitchen. They were discussing Robert.

"I just think it's time he realised that he won't be able to follow William and Stephen around forever. They've been back less than a month and he seems to think he's one of them. I just don't want him to be disappointed. He'll end up doing my job, and that's a good life. He should be grateful for it."

Shaking his head, Stephen made his way upstairs. He had suspected Samuel had been purposefully keeping Robert from them. The young man had been noticeably absent since finding them in Oxford. Samuel might have a point, his son might never be wealthy like Stephen or William were, but that didn't mean the world was cut off to him. Stephen decided he would make a point of involving Robert in their work a little. The boy was intelligent enough and a willingness to work hard was far more useful than a lazy talent.

∞

Horses' hooves echoed a drumroll over the hills, huge clumps of mud thrown up behind them. The ground cracked. It had quickly dried out since the downfall weeks before, aided by the high winds the previous night. It provided little resistance to the heavy fall of the hooves as they galloped over it.

Stephen's perpetual concern for William had been amplified by the events of the evening before. His friend's strange actions by the fire and wandering in the night had confirmed that he had reason to be. Even for someone in their profession, sneaking around in the dead of night in their own home was not normal behaviour. With time to kill before the gathering at the college that evening, Stephen had suggested taking the horses out for a good ride might help clear their heads. William had been quick to agree. They had been at the house for some time now, but he was yet to properly inspect the grounds.

Stephen knew this was not the real reason his friend wanted to take the horses out. For as long as he could remember, riding had been one of William's favourite ways to escape the world around him. Out in the open air, he could almost see the cares cast away. Feeling the forces of nature around him, William was reminded that there were greater powers at work. All worldly problems diminished in the realisation that much of what took place was out of his control. And with the wind flowing through his hair, carried across the fields at breakneck speeds, the great freedom made him feel truly alive.

Nearing the brow of a hill they had been racing up,

the horses slowed, great chests heaving as they fought to regain their breath. Halting by a single weathered tree that stood defiant at the summit, they turned to look back at the land they had just covered. Even as the sun continued to rise above the hills, the land was bathed in its gently warming rays. Though both men had witnessed the sight many times over the years, it still took a few minutes to take in, and just appreciate.

"Beautiful isn't it?" Stephen said, leaning over his saddle to his friend.

"It really is," William agreed, "I think sometimes people get so caught up in themselves that they forget to appreciate things like this. There is so much that can be gained from just stopping and taking a look at what's around you. So much of it is taken for granted. I'm as guilty as the next man, but whenever I stop to really think about it, it never fails to have an impact.

All the work we do for the King, it makes no difference to this really. Wars may come and go but there will always be beauty when people stop to realise it. All we can do is try to keep others safe so that they might have the chance to grasp the delicate splendours that so often go unnoticed."

Stephen nodded in silence, taking in the full effect of the dappled lights that emerged over the fields. As the vibrant strokes of reds and purples faded into the bright blue of a morning sky, the two men sat back in the warm glow. Stephen thought the ride had achieved the desired effect on William, he certainly seemed more at peace with himself, returning to the pleasant mood he had shown since their return from London. Only time would tell if the current mood would last. There was no knowing what the evening would bring.

After a brief pause to enjoy the sight one last time, they kicked the horses on, reluctantly trotting down the other side of the hill before charging on to complete the loop that would bring them back toward the house.

∞

Since that wonderful night at the Conway's, things had moved fast for Valentine. As he had hoped, there had been many influential members of society in the room that night, some of whom evidently had the King's ear. His summons to court had arrived only days after Lady Conway had been healed.

He was more convinced than ever that this was his destiny; God-given. He had fully trusted in the new vision for his life unveiled by the Almighty, but doubt over his own ability had always followed. It was too often that he had to remind himself that he was just the vessel, it was the Lord's power that would give him all he needed to bring about revival.

God had stayed true to his word. Very soon Valentine's task would be complete. The nation would be set free, unshackled from the darkness that held the nation back from the vision of heaven on earth.

Feeling the increasing strain of the pressure of such a huge task weigh upon him, Valentine began his journey to London, his journey toward the King. Very soon it would all be over.

∞

Tall shadows cast by Bodley's Library reached out over the street. Normally she would have been careful to stay hidden in their dark embrace. Today, however, was different. All reports from London were extremely positive. Plans in the capital were progressing rapidly. The schedule for what was to come might even be moved forward.

In Oxford, she was allowing herself an evening to relax. The meddling thief Burns had been out of the scene for a while now and the two King's men were clearly at a loss. Her informants had told of how they spent time between the house outside Oxford and the city itself, asking questions but getting nowhere. They had spent the last week or so wandering aimlessly. As far as her people had been able to tell her, neither man was any closer to the truth.

It was with an air of satisfaction that she was allowing herself this evening of self-congratulation. Even she had expected more from her pursuers. Their complete lack of information was the reason she was able to take some time for herself. It had been a long time since she allowed herself the pleasure of mixing with high society; the risk of recognition was too great. Her time was dedicated to the workings of the Children of Aeternitas now.

Gatherings at masked balls, such as those in Venice, where her identity was hidden were the only social occasions she allowed herself. Those, and the meetings of the Children, which were equally anonymous. But not tonight. She had talked her way into an invitation weeks before in the hope that she might take the evening for herself, and as things stood the plan was proceeding far better than she could have imagined.

Dressed in the finest clothes she possessed, she made her way into the college. Wooden heels clicked against the large stone slabs that made up the walkway around the quadrangle. Her large silk skirts rustled with every step, the deep blue material bunching up around her waist if she walked too quickly. Not even the fashionable parting at the front of the dress, revealing an equally elaborate underskirt in a paler blue, provided much range of movement. But tonight was not about speed or practicality. It was the glamour of the occasion and she would enjoy it fully; finally allowing herself out in public now that plans were so far along that nobody could stop them.

Very soon the country would be free, able to look forward to a future with limitless possibility and potential. The restrictions of the tyrannical rule of man removed. There would regrettably be casualties, but progress could not be made without them. Phoenix had convinced her of that. Besides, in the end, time conquers all. The death of a few mattered little in the progress of humankind.

Inside the college buildings, the library had been transformed for the evening. The long room, still lined with books, was filled with lines of chairs facing a cleared space at one end. She presumed it must be where the musical entertainment would take place. Seeing that many of the seats were already taken, she moved forward to a seat nearer the front, left inexplicably empty.

As she moved forward she was able to scan a few faces, any that noticed her looked back without recognition. Good. There were a few in the city that might have known her, even now. She was sure that none would be there that evening, nevertheless, it was reassuring to receive confirmation. If anyone raised any suspicions, she had an easy story to slip into. It was with this false identity that she had been able to gain entrance to the evening's gathering.

At her seat, she deposited the thin cloak that had covered her lean shoulders and sat down.

13

After the long morning ride, William and Stephen had been champing at the bit to get into action and find out who, or what, it was Burns had meant for them to see. The excitement of the unknown left them both pacing around the house, unable to remain still for even a short moment. Before long, Hannah had grown weary of their uncommunicative restlessness and sent them away.

William and Stephen arrived at All Souls College even earlier than they had planned. The College staff didn't seem too concerned by the early appearance of guests and allowed them access. The two men made the most of the opportunity to scout out the layout of the college. The room they had been directed to offered little in the way of vantage points. The uniform layout of the chairs meant that the best chance of maintaining a good view of the whole room would be to sit right at the back. It would mean they would not be looking at faces, but better than not being able to see anyone at all. Being so far from the performance would be disappointing, but the desire to finally gain some insight into the plan against the King outweighed any personal regret.

As the two men milled about in the otherwise

empty rooms, wondering what to do with themselves now the plan was in place, their ears pricked at the subtle strains of music coming from an adjoining room. They looked at each other, a smile spreading across their faces at the realisation they shared the same thought. Agreeing that a preview of the evening's performance would allow both an enjoyable and informative visit, they stole through a small side door.

Their sudden entrance caused the previously sole occupant of the room to jump in surprise, almost dropping the beautifully carved violin held at the chin in the process. Had they known anything about instruments, they would have recognised it as the creation of Nicolò Amati, the master craftsman from Cremona, and therefore worth a small fortune. The small man juggled the instrument for a moment, eyes wide in fear of damaging the precious object, before finally securing a firm grip and drawing it back to the safety of his embrace.

"We're so very sorry," began Stephen, almost immediately, "we were very early and couldn't help but hear you playing. Naturally, we had to see who it was that plays so exceptionally well."

"You are too kind." The reply came in a thick French accent. The man was still breathing heavily from the shock of their entry, but recovered well; no longer appearing flustered by his unexpected visitors. "So you are here for this evening's little performance?"

"Absolutely." Stephen introduced William and himself. "I'm afraid that our host for this evening has been rather remiss with the details of the program for tonight. I don't suppose you'd mind awfully filling in the gaps for us?"

The young man, who introduced himself as Frederick Guchard, was helpless against the endless flattery from the large man, and happily indulged them. They passed the remainder of the afternoon enjoying each other's conversation. William felt completely out of his depth, he knew the music he liked and would always enjoy listening to good musicians, but the often pretentious sermons spouted by those who considered themselves well educated in music were far beyond him. He allowed Stephen and Frederick to discuss the complexities of modern music as it all washed over his head, chiming in his praise whenever the young violinist took up his bow to play.

As the hour of the young Frenchman's performance approached, the two old friends extricated themselves, allowing for any last-minute preparations. Walking back out into the library, they found most of the seats had been filled.

"We must have been in there longer than I thought." said William.

The door they had just passed through brought them out at the front of the room. Not wanting to be mistaken for the evening's performers, Stephen pulled William quickly past the front few seats before making their way to the back of the room. It was then they were thankful to have had the forethought to reserve their seats at the back with their cloaks, many of the rows of chairs now only held solitary seats.

∞

As the small door opened at the front of the room, she watched the two tall men enter the library. Jovially they made their way to the back of the room. Her heart sank into her stomach as they passed. Blind panic was only seconds away, the taste of bile rising in the back of her throat. What were they doing there? The rat Burns must have managed to contact them somehow before she had dealt with him. How had informers failed to notify her that they too would be at the college that night?

They moved past her chair, apparently not looking for anyone specific. But if they saw her, they would know. She couldn't afford to be there anymore. They might see her if she left, but staying in place would leave her trapped. Even if she was not recognised straight away, the night would be torture. The threat was too real. All thoughts of the relaxing evening she had planned back in the company of normal society disappeared. She had to leave. Now. Before the music began and social convention forced her to remain seated.

Heart beating out of her chest, she silently got to her feet. Sweeping her cloak back over her shoulders, she thought better of throwing up the hood. In an effort to remain inconspicuous as others still bustled for their seats, she walked slowly out of the room, taking care not to look toward the two men. It was only when she was sure she was out of view that she broke into a run, cursing her prohibitive skirts as she disappeared into the shadows that embraced the city.

∞

A flash of blonde hair and the rustle of skirts caught his attention as the woman darted out of the small side door to the college. He had been waiting all evening for signs of anything unusual, a fleeing woman certainly merited his attention. Shifting his weight in the shadows, he pushed off against the cold stone wall. Silent in pursuit.

∞

Stephen swore. William looked up at him with a combination of shock and amusement, curious as to what could have elicited such profanity in polite company. His friend was staring to his right. He followed his eye line to the woman moving away from her seat. With a gasp he clenched his hand, fingernails digging painfully into his leg.

They had both seen. Before she had a chance to pass them, they had both clearly seen her.

Stephen uttered a single word, sending a chill down William's spine, "Ana."

A Dutch woman, thought William, Ana.

14

William and Stephen were on their feet in a split second. Paying no attention to the disturbance, they crashed along the aisle of chairs, racing for the doors Ana had just passed through. Reaching the large college gates, they rushed out into the cobbled streets.

The Radcliffe Camera loomed tall over them, moonlight picking out the details of its curved roof. The street was empty. Anyone wishing to remain hidden would be quickly taken by the dark night. Skidding to a halt, their shoes providing little purchase on the stones worn smooth through use, they threw frantic looks along the length of the street. There was no one to be seen. William grasped the situation quickly. In the dim light, they held little to no chance of finding Ana again.

Stephen turned to his friend, about to suggest they alert the watchmen on the gates. Before he had opportunity to utter a single syllable, William took off towards High Street. It took the larger man a couple of seconds to register what had just happened before he began the chase.

William was fast, and he had a head start. It was times like these that Stephen was glad he forced himself to exercise regularly. It was unusual, and most people didn't understand why he made sure to stay fit, but in his line of work it paid to be able to hold your own – that and chasing distraught friends fuelled in their running by the sight of a painful memory.

Turning right on the High Street, towards St. Martin's tower, they then took a left, past the newly constructed Town Hall, considered by many in the city to be an abominable monstrosity. As they reached Christ Church College, Stephen managed to draw up alongside William, matching the steady rhythm of his footfall. Knowing that it would be a fool's errand to try and stop him, he simply kept pace. Soon after the college they passed through the South Gate to the city. Still William did not relent. A ferocious look adorned his face; jaw clenched, eyes fixed ahead as he glared through his eyebrows.

Stephen was beginning to struggle, breathing became ragged as the pace refused to drop. They just ran and ran. The crazed man next to him showed no sign of slowing. He was having to do everything he could just to stay close to William. He had even discarded his jacket in an attempt to allow the cool night air an opportunity to cool his sweat-drenched skin.

They ran through fields, along worn paths, past bends in the river, and dodged through small clumps of woodland before William finally suddenly stopped. Hands on his knees he fought for breath. All at once his exhaustion seemed to have hit him, his back shuddered in a combination of anguish and physical pain. Straightening up with a bestial cry that came from somewhere deep within, he was a wounded beast howling defiance at the moon.

As if noticing Stephen for the first time since All Souls, he rushed at him, seizing the larger man by the collar of his shirt.

"Dead, Stephen…Dead…I saw what the disease did to her…I saw it, she's dead…" A terrifying fire burned in the eyes that stared back at Stephen. It flickered, and then was gone. Releasing him, William crumpled to the floor muttering his repetitive assertion over and over again.

Unsure how to react, Stephen stood back, observing the pitiful shell of a man. More broken than he had ever dared to believe, the building good humour of the past weeks came crashing down to reveal the truth of his friend. With a deep breath, he helped William to his feet, supporting him with a weary shoulder.

"We'll find her, Will, she can't get far in one night. We'll get to the bottom of all this."

"But it's not her. It can't be." A level of clarity appeared to have returned to William, as if the animalistic display only a few moments ago had never taken place, "I don't know how they did it, but it can't be her. I saw her die, Stephen. They're baiting me."

"Baiting? But why? Burns' notes led us there, why would he send us to something that was only a distraction?"

"No, you were right before. His notes could have meant anything. So much was lost. They know us, Stephen, this isn't just about the King. They want us too. There must be something we missed. There must be something else."

"But Will, finding that woman must lead somewhere. She would know something, if only the people who told her to be there tonight. Burns did warn us that these people might be capable of more than we could understand."

"No. It was a distraction. They want us to follow. It would lead only to a woman, a maze to occupy us and take us away from the real investigation. We must be close to something, we need to carry on."

There was no arguing with him, not as he was. A manic paranoia had set in, coupled with a fixation that he was in some way being made to jump at ghosts. Stephen didn't know what to think. After all, he had seen the woman too. She had looked just like Ana, but William was right – she was dead, the doctor had confirmed it over a year ago.

What was it William thought they were meant to carry on with, thought Stephen, that evening was the only lead they had. Still, it would not do to tip Will any further over the edge, he wouldn't push the issue now. What they needed was to get back to the warmth of the house, or the city, whichever came first. Stephen realised, after all the running, that he had only a vague notion of where they were. Using the pale specks of the stars in an attempt to find a bearing, the large man adjusted the arm slung under his friend's weary frame, and set off in what he hoped was the direction of Oxford. The cool night drew in as they began the long walk home, leaving Stephen regretting discarding his jacket earlier in the chase.

∞

Ana was sure she hadn't been followed. There had been no sight of anyone, she had even cut back on herself several times to make sure. But she had definitely been seen, and there was no doubting they had known her.

Stephen's loud curse had confirmed it, but there was no sign of them.

How had they known to be there? Could Burns have managed to contact them before he had been killed? They had obviously not expected her there, their reaction was proof enough of that. Perhaps then, their information was not complete. With no way of knowing how much they knew, plans would have to be brought forward. A return to London would be required. Phoenix would need to know what had happened. There was no doubt in her mind that he would know how to proceed.

She had thought the plan foolproof; that if William and Stephen ever got too close they would be removed. But seeing them had been far more painful than she had expected, even after all she had been through. They could not be disposed of, but she couldn't let them get in the way. The Children could not be let down by her own weakness, for that is what it was. She would perform her role without fail. If they came for her, she would pull the trigger…wouldn't she? The vision of Aeternitas had to outweigh any individual circumstance.

The tumultuous predicament ruled her mind as she entered the tall house to the north of the city. It acted as her temporary home. So consuming were her own thoughts as she entered the house that she failed to notice the outline of the small figure watching from the street corner before it disappeared back toward the city.

15

It had been a long night for Stephen. William's manic energy in the flight from the city had disappeared as quickly as it had come upon him. A supporting shoulder had been required for the entirety of the long walk back toward the city. It was fortunate they were known to the gatekeeper, Lewis. Some would have left the two men standing in the cold until morning. Although he had not been happy at being woken late in the night, he had allowed them passage. Stephen quickly babbled his thanks. The gatekeeper clearly wanted to return to his bed. Being outside in the cold night air with the added weight he had been forced to bear was exhausting enough without having to navigate around the city walls and back to the house. Once more inside the city, they had sought out the Bear Inn. Good fortune was again on their side as the innkeeper allowed them in, showing Stephen to the final free room, not far from William's lodging.

Stephen had little time to enjoy the comforts of the room. Once sure that William was asleep in his own room, he had crashed onto his bed the moment the door closed behind him, falling into a deep sleep in moments. But rest was not to be his that night, the early hours of the morning brought a knocking at the door. It started as a scratching that he was only vaguely aware of in the depths of sleep. It was not until it developed into what, in the silence of the dead of night sounded like a violent barrage against the thin door, that he became fully aware. Finding himself more tired than he had been before his brief respite from the concerns of the conscious, he staggered over to the door. Opening it a crack to see who had disturbed him at such an unsociable hour, he was met by the sight of an equally weary-looking Robert.

"I'm sorry to wake you so late, or early, nevermind. It took an absolute age to find you. There was no sign of either of you back home, but I wasn't sure if you were still in the city. I thought the inns might be the best place to look for you, but there are so many, and people get suspicious of anyone running around so late. At first, I wasn't even sure you had left the college, but there was no sign of you there."

Putting his hands up to calm the young man down, Stephen nodded, reassuring him that everything was alright. Robert realised he was blabbering, stopped abruptly and waited for a response. In an attempt to prevent further information overload, Stephen asked one question.

"Did you see her?"

"Yes, I did just as you asked. I don't understand though. How can it be her? I only caught a glimpse of her face before she ran, but I'd recognise her anywhere – she was always good to me."

Ignoring the gushing reply, Stephen directed the conversation where he wanted.

"Did you follow her?"

"Yes, she cut back a few times but she didn't see me.

I've been running these streets since…"

"Good. Where did she go?"

"A house further north. Past St. Giles' Church. It's near where…"

"Robert, listen to me. You've done well but I need you to keep this between us. Not even William can know. In fact, he most of all cannot know. I can't tell you more yet. To be honest with you, I don't know much more myself.

Early tomorrow I'm going to try and keep William busy for a while whilst you show me where she went. Can you do that?"

"Yes, of course."

The young man was evidently mystified by the night's events. For now, it was best to keep it that way. Stephen hoped that the tone of the conversation would make the seriousness of what had taken place clear.

"Do you need somewhere to go now?"

"No, thank you. I can stay with a friend up by St. Michael's at the North Gate."

"Well, good night Robert. I will see you back at the house tomorrow morning. And remember, no one can know who it was you saw tonight."

With that, he dismissed the younger man, closed the door, and crawled back into bed in an attempt to rescue some sleep. So, she was still in Oxford. But how? There had been that nagging thought in the back of his mind since Burns' note. He had been able to put the pieces of information together – a Dutch woman, but he certainly hadn't reckoned on it meaning she was alive. He was not even sure how it could be true, William had seen her dying, the doctors had confirmed it. But tonight he had seen her, and so had Robert. Despite what William believed, it was her. His friend could never know though.

It took an age before his thoughts allowed him to fall back into the fitful sleep that had characterised the last weeks, and it was not long before streams of early morning sunlight began glaring through his window to wake him again.

∞

William slept surprisingly well. The shock of the previous night had sent him into a deep, comatose sleep. The moment his head touched the pillow he had been out. No dream of any kind had visited him in the night. Despite his undisturbed sleep, he woke in a haze; his mind not properly able to process anything. Void of clarity, his numbed senses prevented him settling into the clear, darting thoughts that so often aided him in his work. His mind drifted between blurred, dreamlike pictures; unable to focus properly on anything. It was almost as if he was floating along, even his footsteps on the streets as he walked home did not feel their normal, solid selves. In this state, he was incapable of any certainty of thought, only a vague sense that he should follow Stephen.

During the journey back to the house, Stephen attempted to start conversations that might get William talking again. He grew increasingly frustrated at the total disregard shown for his efforts. Knowing that he was more prone to quick, unreasonable bouts of anger in his fatigued state, Stephen eventually decided it best to walk in silence; William would talk if he wanted to.

For William it was almost as if Stephen's words were in a different language, so little did they register with him. All he could take from the situation was the look of concern mixed with a wave of increasing anger that played across his companion's face. So easily distracted, he would become fixated on singular words as they were spoken, missing their context and meaning entirely.

Robert met them back at the house, helping William into a chair by the fire. It barely made any impact on the state of the shocked man. He seemed completely unaware of the hushed tones in which Stephen and Robert conducted their conversation by the doorway as they flicked their gazes over to him.

William stared at the fire, watching the flicker of the flames. Reds and golds danced and writhed, taking the wood below in their embrace. Beautiful in its destructive power, he pictured a great bird rising amongst the flames. As they formed, the featherlike dancers combined to create unfolding wings that filled the fireplace. The eyes of the firebird stared out at him, a jet black that drew him in; more terrible than the scorching flames that created it. Throwing its head back, it let out a high, keening cry that pierced deep into his being. Then it was gone.

He snapped out of the trance-like state. Only the fire remained. Once more aware of his own thoughts, he called over to Stephen, shaken by what he had just imagined.

"Stephen, I think I'm going to have another look at that notebook."

Taken aback, Stephen did not immediately reply, instead gawping wordlessly. William repeated himself, allowing his friend time to process the idea.

"Are you sure you're up to doing anything? I thought last night had taken its toll on you. You haven't been well all morning. Maybe some rest would be better? You could take a look later?"

"No, I was just in shock. Thank you for your concern, but I'm more than capable of sitting and looking through the pages of a small book."

"Right, of course. I was going to suggest something similar myself later." The change in his friend was extraordinary. It was like the night before had never taken place. "I was thinking I would go back into the city; see if I can uncover anything new there."

"Good idea. I think we might have missed something in the booklet though. Perhaps the apparently random letters mean something after all."

"A code?"

"Oh, I wouldn't have thought so." William smiled at the flicker of hope on the larger man's face, "Why write the majority of the booklet in code only to leave a message in plain English? No, I mean maybe they are algebraic sums for something, or a system of measurements for a building."

"How will you know?" Stephen looked with renewed concern, surely this was a return the paranoia of the night before. William had lost rational thought – there was no way anything more could be gleaned from that booklet.

"I don't really know yet. It's worth a try though. We don't have much more to go on." William noticed Stephen was itching to get out of the door and back to the city. "Let me know if you find anything helpful. I can always come and join you if you need me."

"Of course I will, and vice versa." Taking his leave, Stephen began towards the door.

"Oh, and Stephen," the large man craned his head

back around the doorframe, "Thank you."

"Think nothing of it, old chap." Smiling weakly, he made his way out to the horses, where he was met by a waiting Robert.

∞

Stephen and Robert pushed the horses harder than either would normally have dared. Making sure that William was safe and occupied with something other than Ana had taken precious time, time they could not really afford to have lost. Arriving too late at the house Robert had tracked Ana to the night before could leave them with nothing. It could not be allowed to happen. Thoughts of all else vacated Stephen's mind as they thundered across Magdalen Bridge. His concern for his friend would need to be put aside for a while.

Reining his mount in slightly, Stephen was forced to slow as they veered around a plodding cartload of what looked like clayware, heading toward the city gates. Instead of following the road to the East Gate, they followed the outskirts of the city wall, past the semi-constructed Sheldonian, and towards the church of St. Giles.

On Robert's signal, they came to a halt. Stephen slid off his horse, his expression betraying a seriousness that the younger man had not seen in him before. He was about to follow, his feet already swinging out of the stirrups, before Stephen gruffly told him to stay. It was not open to discussion. The potential danger became clear as the large man reached into his saddlebag, pulling out a pair of vicious-looking pistols. Robert had not reckoned on his riding companion being so heavily armed. Happy to be involved, regardless of whatever intrigue was unfolding, he had asked no questions. He had not seen the weapons Stephen was carrying before. They did not look like the elaborate guns William had bought, now resplendent above the fire in the snug. Their barrels held no finery at all, though the flintlock firing mechanism had evidently been meticulously cleaned and maintained. Robert wondered where the pistols had materialised from. He had certainly not seen them amongst any of the luggage Stephen had brought from London. He hoped the appearance of the weapons was precautionary. Even so, the revelation of the pistols made it abundantly clear that he was out of his depth. Waiting with the horses would be alright with him.

Pointing to the house he had come to the night before, Robert watched as Stephen confidently strode toward the front door. He had tucked the two guns into poachers' pockets, cleverly concealed in a long leather riding coat. Gone was the majority of his customary finery, replaced by the hard-wearing garments more fitting to a soldier.

As he approached the door, Stephen noticed that it had not properly been shut. Was he too late? He pushed with a booted foot, allowing it to swing open, displaying a grand hallway dominated by a large staircase that split along the back wall so that the house had two clearly defined wings. It was more richly decorated than the outward appearance led to believe. Although significantly smaller than William's family home, it was dressed in the latest tastes and to the height of fashion.

Thinking it best to search downstairs first, Stephen made his way to the left of the large, sweeping staircase, spotting a small door tucked away in the shadow of the ornate stairs. It opened to reveal a small passageway just tall enough for him to walk through. Following it along for a few feet, he came across another doorway similar to the one he had just passed through. Listening carefully for any sign of life on the other side, he gently eased it open.

It revealed another lavish reception room. The passage he had come through was most likely a rat run for the servants to move about the house discreetly. The new room joined the front hall by a large door that had not been visible from the other side. Like the adjoining room, it was adorned with the latest fashions. The entire room was put together in shades of blue. The walls were draped with a deep blue silk that ran into paler decorations adorning the upper and lower sections. The ceiling was sculpted into a depiction of the sea. Various forms of sea-life projected from its edges toward a central mural of the world. Even the flooring had been stained a subtle pale blue before the varnish had sealed in the colour.

There was little in the way of furnishing that inhabited the room, but what there was had evidently been carefully selected. Dark mahogany chests of drawers were visible in each corner, their deep wood drawing the eye whilst looking completely in-keeping with the stylish surroundings.

The wall, adjacent to the door by which Stephen had entered, housed a towering grandfather clock. Its face was framed by two columns, each with the carving of a snake wrapped around them. Their heads met above the numeral twelve. Down the long front piece of the clock was carved the depiction of a scene from some ancient legend, the origin of which Stephen could not tell.

Light infiltrated the room from the other two walls, each held a floor to ceiling window, tall and narrow. Only one looked as if it could open. As he walked over, Stephen noted a set of stone steps leading out onto a small formal garden that had not been immediately visible from inside. The door built into the window showed no signs of regular use. A quick look through the glass panes was enough to assure him little could be gained from searching outside.

Using the large doorway, he made his way back into the entrance hall, marvelling at the way the door blended once more with the wall so that only those looking for it would have any hope of finding it.

Immediately opposite stood another door, one he had previously ignored in favour of the servant's passage. Through this door was a very different room. Completely fitted with large desks, its walls were lined with tall shelves reaching the full height of the room. It was evidently a library. However, it was a rather peculiar one; it housed no books. Other than the occasional stain of candle wax on the desks closest to the door, there was no indication that the room had ever been used at all.

Thinking it strange, Stephen took a closer look at the shelving in the hope that some clues to its purpose might become clear. Eventually ceding that the lack of any evidence, other than being strange, made it not worth further investigation, he returned to the hall and progressed upstairs.

The first floor followed a similar layout to the ground floor. He was left with the decision to go left or right. Favouring the left first, Stephen moved above the blue room. Within was a bedroom, sparsely decorated but evidently in use until fairly recently. The bed was made, with fashionable women's clothes laid out on top, as if ready to be worn that day. A large valise on the other side of the bed suggested that the clothes were in the process of being packed before someone had left the task unfinished.

Stephen was alert at once. He strode over to the bedside table, checking the wick of the candle for heat. Still warm. Ana was there, or she had departed only recently.

The bedroom contained another doorway. He drew the pistols as he entered. It revealed nothing more than a large dressing room. Not wanting to waste any more time, he made his way back across the staircase to the right-hand wing of the house.

It was set out in a very similar way to the bedroom on the left. Instead of a bed, it was fitted with a collection of more comfortable looking chairs. This must be a less formal living room.

A clattering of many horses' hooves on the street outside sent him racing to a small window looking out into the streets below. A large black carriage had pulled up into a side road, waiting for a woman running from the direction of the house. Ana must have concealed herself somewhere just outside the front door. He would have passed within a few feet of her and been none the wiser. There was no way he could catch her now.

Stepping up into the carriage, she looked up at the window as if she knew exactly where he stood. Her blonde hair fell from beneath a hood that attempted to conceal her features. With a smile, her flashing blue eyes made contact with his before being whisked away.

Lashing out in frustration, his foot made heavy contact with the wall. Cursing as his toes began to throb, he turned away from the window. The sound of a rider following a good distance behind the fleeing carriage brought his attention back to the window. A deep burgundy cloak betrayed the rider as Robert. It was the cloak Stephen had lent him for the ride into the city.

Good lad, he thought, then realising the danger the young man had just placed himself in he muttered, "Be careful, don't do anything stupid."

16

William stared down at the blotched pages of Burns' notebook, determined to somehow make sense of the seemingly random scrawlings. Despite his best efforts, nothing was becoming any clearer to him. He had moved from the comfortable spot by the fire downstairs, opting instead to work in the small, upstairs library that seconded as his private workspace. William found the warmth of the fire had made him drowsy. It muddled his thoughts. Moving to the library, though less cosy, would be more productive. The colder climate kept him sharp and on task.

The water damage that had distorted Burns' message also obscured much of the work in the rest of the booklet. For what seemed like hours he had been inspecting the ruined pages without the slightest success. It remained a baffling mixture of what looked like mathematical theory and apparently random markings. What mystified him further was that whole pages, containing nothing but random letters, were strewn throughout the compact leather booklet. They had no apparent order or purpose. Each page was different. One page held only a Q written once in the top left. Others contained multiple figures scattered over the page, but only ever a single alphabetical letter repeated. There was no pattern to it. Nothing in the spacing or the order that pointed toward any code he had ever seen before. Frustration was taking over.

Lack of success in his task left his mind free to wander. Though nothing had been said of his breakdown the previous night, he knew Stephen had gone in pursuit of the woman. Who it could be, he did not know, but it could not be Ana. William knew that much. He had seen the plague take hold of her; watched every rasping breath as she struggled to fight off the disease that had inflicted itself on so many households across the country.

They had been in London when she had first complained of feeling unwell. Whilst he worked, they split their time between their home in Oxford and a small set of apartments close to Westminster. The illness had come on suddenly. No one had expected it, at least not in the magnitude in which it struck the city. People got ill, that had always been true, often it led to death. But nothing as devastatingly ruthless had taken place in living memory.

Ana had been caught in the first wave of indiscriminate killing. No demographic of the population had been spared: young, old, male, female, rich, poor, all were taken. It was at its worst in the cities. Doctors blamed anything they could think of. Only the rich could afford to flee the miasma that many claimed had corrupted London. Fanatics preached the wrath of God, choosing whatever sin served their purpose; divine retribution for turning from the Catholic faith, or for the murder of their King. Not a day after her death, William had fled. Fled London, fled the plague, fled work and everything that had made up his previous life. Not even permitted to take Ana's body for burial for fear that it would spread the disease further, he had not known how to mourn her. Disconsolate, he ran from everything and everyone. She couldn't be back. It was impossible. Some evil trick designed to derail him once more. Not this time, he would not let it. Instead, he refocused his study of Burns' book. A new determination not to fail set in. He would not be beaten down any further.

William continued to work in the cooler study, opening a window to encourage the flow of air around the room. He found the presence of a breeze more conducive to clear thinking. The heat from the fire downstairs would only have encouraged a lethargy that bred daydreams, daydreams he could do without.

Sitting behind a large wooden desk he had inherited along with the house, he searched the room for inspiration. The desk itself was practically empty, only the palm-sized leather-bound book and a small selection of unused candles clustered close to his sitting position. The rest of the room was not well kept; the one room Hannah could not control. The study was primarily the family library and archive. Everything that had ever been collected by past generations could be found stacked on the shelves and overflowing into piles on the floor. Often topping these stacks of books and papers were items collected by William and Ana during various overseas missions they had been sent on by His Lordship: hats worn only by a specific band of condottieri in Italy who had aided William whilst he worked in Milan; small carved figures presented to Ana by a village in the Alps after she had stayed with them whilst her husband was further confusing the political situation in Prussia;

assorted bottles of glass, clay and porcelain; masks; and the odd elaborate knife or small sword.

None of this provided William with any sort of revelation. No earth-shattering moment of clarity that would solve all their problems. Thinking that perhaps it would help to occupy himself some other way for a short time, he set about dusting off some of the piles of books on the floor. As he uncovered more and more of the family volumes, he sought out a system to order them all onto the shelves. Eventually, after deciding to divide them roughly by subject matter and then by alphabetical order of the author, he began to make progress. Tales of the ancients and natural histories made up the vast majority of the collection. They had always been William's favourites; legends of how the world had been, and the brilliant delicacy of each majestic design. There were a few theological works and political discourse, but he found them dry, lacking in any spark. Much more could be seen of God in the beauty of creation than in wordy arguments. The perfect complexity of a bird in flight, apparently so effortless, filled him with far more wonder than a lashing tirade from the pages of another broken and fault-filled writer.

After a good couple of hours, he was seeing the fruits of his labour. At first he had just been exchanging one pile of books for another, but gradually a semblance of order was starting to show. With the order came a reduction in the numbers of piles residing on the floor, although, he had to admit he might need further shelving to house them all.

As he was sorting through the final few stacks, a piece of paper fell from a copy of a well-worn copy of Homer's Odyssey. Reaching down to retrieve it, he found himself struggling to read what was printed. The letters all appeared to flow into one another, making no discernible language he had ever seen before. Was this a return to the fogged thoughts of the morning?

Feeling the paper between his fingers, William realised it was folded in half. Unravelling it brought it to life. The print that had moments before looked unreadable was clear as day. Folding it back over, William noticed that the paper was thin enough that, when folded, both sets of text merged into one. An idea flashed into his head.

"Surely not." He mumbled.

Grabbing the notebook, he held two of the pages together. Nothing. He tried holding them up to the light. Still no difference, the paper was too thick. What would happen if he were to write all the letters out on a single page though, as if they had all been written on the same piece of paper?

With nothing to lose, he began painstakingly copying them all out. It was not long before his persistence was rewarded as a pattern began to emerge.

∞

Stephen moved away from the window. There would be no catching Ana's carriage now. She could have gone anywhere. But Robert was in pursuit. He would have to await notice from the younger man once they reached a final destination. He only hoped the boy was up to it. Following the road without being noticed was a skill not many could boast of. Even if he managed to track them, it could be weeks before Robert managed to get news back to Oxford. By then Ana could have moved on. An endless game of cat and mouse would ensue.

There was nothing Stephen could do to help now. His time would be best spent scouring the house for any sign of what Ana was involved in. How she was still alive, he did not know, but it was something he could not waste time dwelling on. She was alive and somehow involved in a plot to undermine the security of the country, which was all that mattered now. Except it wasn't. Not really. William could never know, it would destroy him. This was one piece of information that would have to remain hidden.

Stephen began his search of the rooms upstairs. His initial assessment still held true, it was a room for use rather than display. Where the formal rooms were decorated to impress with their cold grandeur, this room held a warmth only everyday life could bring. From the slightly worn edges of the elaborate Persian rug, to the scuffing of the chair legs and creases in the cushions where they had been crumpled for comfort, every detail whispered life.

Collections of papers rested on a small table next to the most used chair. Stephen rustled through them, looking for anything that might be deemed important. None were of any use. Only copies of the Oxford Gazette and a few older papers from London. The room also held a few books; most were tales of ancient heroes, a passion Ana shared with William, but nothing out of the ordinary.

A small door facing the rear of the house drew his attention. It took him a moment to realise why - it should not have been there. There was no room downstairs to match the layout. Ducking through the frame he found himself in a spacious room full of collected oddities. The only light came through the door by which he had just entered, it fell upon various statues in the Greco-Roman style, catching the tips of wings, outstretched arms and picking out the hollows of a marble face. Amongst the statues were glass cases full of an apparently random collection of objects, ranging from stuffed animals to musical instruments of unknown origins. Across several of the cases were draped skins and furs of indistinguishable beasts. The space had an eerie stuffiness to it, completely out of character with the rest of the house. It held no obvious purpose. A collection of items hidden from the world.

Stephen had seen similar collections before. He, William, and Ana had been shown the vast assembly of the Holy Roman Emperor, Leopold I, when they had been sent to offer assistance. A series of deaths in the royal household had taken place, members of the staff suspiciously close to the Emperor. William had solved the mystery after noticing the fragile nature of the casing that held a spear taken from a tribe in South America. The spear had been falling and scratching those looking around the collection, but the victims had not died until a poison – found on the tip of the blade – had taken effect nearly half an hour later. No one had been able to link such small cuts with such painful deaths.

But this room held a different mystery - Stephen could not understand how the room was even there.

Rushing downstairs once more, Stephen double-checked the empty library. There was no door leading to a room below the odd cabinet of curiosities. The bookshelves were solid. So where was the door? Thinking again of the passageway he had found on first entering the house, he searched every inch again. Lamplight danced off the stone walls of the narrow walkway. Twice he traversed its length. He was sure he had missed nothing. Moving out into the gardens, he tried to make sense of the missing room. It was clear from the outside that there was a room there, but no way of entering.

Again he traversed the servants' passage, exploring fully the hidden warren that allowed the running of the house to remain separate from the grander rooms. There was a small kitchen and level of empty servants' rooms below ground level. Nothing was unusual about them. They connected to all other rooms in the house. A small hidden staircase provided access to the upper floor. But there was no entry to the hidden room. He had pushed walls, inspected floors for trap doors, felt for levers that might open a hidden entrance - all without success.

Back in the library, he stood facing the shelving, wondering if he could break through the wall somehow. He had seen secret doors before, but none of the bookcases gave any impression of being false. Deciding that perhaps a more delicate approach would prove more fruitful, he methodically began to scrutinise each section of the shelving. In keeping with the rest of the house, it was well put together, the result of work from a master craftsman. The outer edges of the panels were covered in an intricate ivy design reaching across the entire wall of book casing. Running his hands along some of the outer shelves, he found a thick layer of dust gathering on his fingers. It was clear books had been absent for some time.

Nothing was coming from his search. Stephen had been in the house for hours. All he had managed was to upset much of the dust, reducing him to several sneezing fits. And yet, there had to be a way into that room.

If so much trouble had been taken to prevent entry,

it must have something of importance contained within. He had thought about bringing William to the house - he might have been able to think of something or at least speed up the search. But in such a fragile state Stephen could not rely on the aid of his friend, plus there would be too many questions. So he carried on alone.

On reaching the final section of casing he was on the verge of giving up. It was then that his fingers brushed over smooth wood. It was not until he had reached the other end of the shelf before it registered as strange. There had been no dust there. A glimmer of hope sparkled in the back of his mind as he retraced his steps. Between the layers of dust there was a very definite groove of smooth wood. He pushed down. Nothing happened. Disappointed, he looked around for inspiration. It had to be the way in. An idea sprang to him. Running back up the stairs, he grabbed a pile of books he had seen in the living room, selecting those of similar width to the gap in the dust.

The first two were placed on the shelf without incident. Was there more to it than just the placement of the book? They had both been the correct size. The third book was a title Stephen had not noticed before. It was a tale of Egyptian legend, the Bennu, a great firebird. Lifting the book, he noticed its considerable weight. It must have held lead in the binding. This had to be it. he placed it on the shelf, releasing his breath only at the satisfying sound of a mechanical click from within the wall.

∞

The weather had drastically altered the quality of

the roads. Heavy rainfall earlier in the season caused deep ruts as carriages passed over. This downpour had given way to days of endless sunshine, drying the dirt roads under the Sun's blistering rays, and creating treacherous tracks jutting out from the road surface.

As the black carriage had sped away from the north of Oxford, Robert had immediately known Stephen wouldn't be able to reach the road quick enough to mount a pursuit. In a split second he had made the decision to go by himself. It was essential they knew which direction the fleeing woman had gone once out of the city. With that information gathered, it would be easier to hang back, asking after his quarry from passing travellers, and at station houses to make sure he was still on the correct trail.

Following too closely would only alert them to his intentions. He knew enough of tracking prey to know when to fall back. It was not so different to stalking a deer really. The slightest indication of his presence would result in panicked flight. From there it would be very difficult to find them, let alone get close again. It was best that they remain completely unaware of him.

From the north of the city Ana's carraige had taken a roundabout route, skirting the edges of the outlying villages before connecting back with the main route to London. Robert had been in two minds as to what to do next. The most likely route would be to the capital, but if that was the case then he needed to know where in the city they were based. He couldn't go back to Stephen with just a vague sense that they were heading towards London. A specific location would be needed. Which was an issue for Robert, although the streets of Oxford were well known to him, London was a different beast. The only trips to the big city had been to accompany his father on business. He wouldn't be able to pick up the whereabouts of the carriage if it reached the city without him.

Robert knew the journey would take the best part of two days, but if the carriage horses were really pushed, he supposed it could be done in one. Fresh horses could be hired from the station houses, increasing the chances of his quarry pulling away from him. As it was, his trusty horse would be slower than the four pulling the carriage, even with the extra weight they pulled.

His decision had been a gamble, putting faith in the hope that a private carriage would not want to lose their horses by swapping them at a coach house. It would lengthen the journey for them, but there would be no hurry if they were unaware of his pursuit. If, on the second day, he could push his mount a little harder than he should, he might reach a city gate and wait for them there; ensuring he could follow them to their destination within the walls.

The plan was risky. Not only did it rely on the journey taking two days, but he would also have to overtake without being identified and then hope that he went to the correct city gate. But Robert didn't have much choice in the matter. With so many variables weighted against him, he had to make do and pray that everything came together.

As his horse brought him to the summit of a steep hill, Robert was able to look out over the valley below. The road wound for miles. Tucking into the trees to remain hidden, he looked out from his vantage point. Not so far ahead he could make out the steady progress of his quarry. For now, at least, he remained on the right trail.

∞

That they were words was undeniable. But they were of no language William had ever seen before. For a long while, he had simply stared at them, as if over time they might suddenly decide to reveal their true meaning. He played with the letters, thinking perhaps that it was an anagram, without luck. There were just not enough vowels to come close to a language of Latin origin. Wondering if he had vastly underestimated Burns' education, he searched through his small library for any books that might shed light on this unrecognisable script. Could it be a variation of a Cyrillic language, translated into Latin lettering? Was this message even for him? If not, any further attempt to decipher it would be a colossal waste of time. Surely the fact that it was so well hidden signified that it was something of importance, even if it was not meant for William and Stephen to see it. With that in mind, he carried on searching the collection of books for inspiration.

A knock on the doorframe dragged his attention away from the volumes he rummaged through.

"Ah Hannah, to what do I owe this pleasure?" he asked, flashing the housekeeper a smile.

"You haven't eaten today William, not even a bite." She looked at him with concern. "I worked for this family long before you were born and I will not hear it said that anyone starved whilst under my care, no matter how charming they could be."

The housekeeper finished her light-hearted scolding by setting down a tray on one of the stacks of books that William had repositioned around the room.

On it was a simple lunch, fresh bread baked downstairs that morning, a selection of cheeses picked up from the market, as well as a thick stew made from vegetables, bought from the St. Ebbe's market gardens, and home-grown beef.

"I will be back to collect the tray later. I expect that all to have disappeared." With a final flourish of motherly severity, she looked despairingly at the new mess William had created, tutting before leaving the room. William followed her gaze, realising the steady progress he made earlier in the day had been completely undone in his rush to find answers.

The thought of food had been far from his mind. So absorbed had he been in his task that he was completely unaware of the passing hours. A waft from the meal quickly made him realise just how hungry he actually was. A loud rumbling emanated from his stomach, announcing its displeasure at being neglected.

Submitting to the wishes of his housekeeper, he settled down on the floor, leaving the tray on the stack of books to act as his table. Hannah would never act in such a way in front of guests, but he was glad that despite his age she felt the need to look after him. In truth, she was the only mother figure he had ever known. His own mother had died in childbirth, leaving only his father and the house staff to raise him. He couldn't fault the job they had done, his had been a happy childhood filled with laughter. It was not until later in life, away from the shelter of family, that his moods had darkened. Still, he had found light in people too, friends and a wife that outshone any shadow. It was when he had married Ana that the house had become his, a present from his father, who had moved to a much larger estate out towards

Gloucester where he could live away from the politics of the cities.

William made short work of the meal left for him. He moved the tray, almost polished clean, onto the desk so that he could reach the books below. Thoughts drifted back to the note as his eyes settled on the book that topped the pile; Suetonius, Lives of the Caesars. Rushing back to his desk, he placed the note in front of him, grabbing a scrap of paper to assist his work. Perhaps he had not been so far off with the idea of an anagram. He recalled reading about the secret missives Julius Caesar had sent to his generals. A code had been used to prevent others from reading his instructions. However, if the code was known it was easily read. All that it required was the alphabet copied out twice, with the second copy shifted along so that the letters no longer matched up. Caesar had used D as the starting point in his code, so that was where William began.

Words that had previously held no meaning were soon translated into clear English:

QEB MELBKFU FP YLOQ COLJ FPQ LTK XPEBP

ILLH ELO QEBFO JXOH QEBV XOB KLQ
VL ZBII DFAABA XP TB CFOPQ QELRDEQ

TXQZE QEB ZXMFQXI FG TFII YROK TFQELRQ VLR

THE PHOENIX IS BORN FROM ITS OWN ASHES

LOOK FOR THEIR MARK THEY ARE NOT
SO WELL HIDDEN AS WE FIRST THOUGHT

WATCH THE CAPITAL IT WILL BURN WITHOUT YOU

William stared at the writing. It was certainly directed at him, but why had Burns gone to such extreme lengths to hide a message that was in riddles anyway? All that William could assume was that Burns had been concerned that, in the wrong hands, the message could alert their adversaries to their investigation.

The small leather book had led from one frustration to another. The only clear message was to 'WATCH THE CAPITAL.' Well, thought William, that's nothing new. The capital is always being watched – it's the capital. But what did all the imagery about mythical birds and fire mean? He knew Burns had said the phoenix was the symbol for the secretive group they were up against. Its mythology contained a message of continuous rebirth – the dead phoenix reborn in its own ashes. Burns must have been indicating that the capital would be the centre of death for one regime and the birth of another, hence the city burning.

He sat back in his chair, running his hands through his hair in frustration. Although it was now clear that they must turn their attention back to London, this was something he and Stephen could probably have guessed. But it was a big city, there were plenty of places and opportunities for plots to emerge. It was simply not enough information. And what did the middle line mean? 'LOOK FOR THEIR MARK', a phoenix? There must be plenty of statues, coats of arms or heraldic phoenixes around the city, leftover from past centuries.

"At least they're hidden in plain sight though," he

muttered irritably, "it's good to know that everything is so blindingly obvious...so much so that we only heard of them a week ago."

The flutter of tiny wings at the window caught his attention. A tree sparrow had found its way in through the window but was having trouble relocating the point of entry. As he moved towards it, the small bird increased its panicked attempts to break through the panelled window. It was too fast for him to cup his hands around. Giving up, he placed his hand just below the terrified bird, palm up, thinking it might be a less aggressive way to approach the tiny creature. To his surprise, no sooner had he opened his hand when it perched itself on the middle of his index finger. Slowly he moved the hand toward the open section of the window. Cocking its head, the sparrow looked over its wing at him, as if questioning whether it was really free to go. When no further threat came from William, it turned back to the window, opened its wings and launched back out into the clear skies.

Realising that he was going to achieve nothing by bemoaning the lack of revelation he had thought the pages of the book might hold, he set about looking for all mentions of the mythical birds. If nothing else, they could now be sure that London should be their destination. Oxford could, for now, be ignored as a red herring. Hopefully, Stephen's day was proving more productive.

FROM THE DIARY OF SAMUEL PEPYS.

August 8th 1666 – Met my fellow Gresham College member Robert Hooke in the street today. We talked of his most recent work; a study into sound vibrations. He told me of how he was working with the concept that different vibrations create differing tones. He has been able to use this to tell how many times a house fly beats its wings by the note that they respond to whilst flying.

Though I can see how he arrived at such a conclusion, I must admit some scepticism. The conversation was however, highly engaging.

17

"Here goes nothing." Stephen said aloud to the empty room, he began to push against the book casing. After the click from the secret mechanism, nothing more had appeared to happen. The shelf was now visibly higher than those next to it, a small gap of about an inch could be seen between the flooring and the case, but nothing resembling a door had materialised.

Still puzzled, Stephen had resorted to brute force to complete the job. As it turned out, he needn't have pushed so hard. The whole section of shelving shifted almost a foot backwards, before swinging open so that it crashed against the wall. Stephen was sent stumbling forward by the sudden movement. He could just about see, between two sections of shelving that created the hinge, a system of weights and balances that had allowed the door to open. Although it appeared complex, he could see that it was quite a rudimentary piece of apparatus. The real genius had come from the master carpenters, allowing the entrance to remain almost undetectable from the library side. Stephen assumed the craftsmen were the same creators of the hidden doorway from the hall into the large blue room he had first entered; they must have held considerable skill. Perhaps this had been a room built to hide Catholic Mass. It was more tolerated than in the past century, but outward displays of Catholicism could still cause trouble.

Peering further into the dark room, not much more could be seen. Like the room above, no natural light made its way directly in, the only source of illumination was the daylight from the library coming through the open shelves. The majority of the room remained cast in deep shadow. A lamp would be required to explore the space fully.

Ducking back out of the room, Stephen made his way to the main section of the house in search of a light. Finding a small oil lamp in one of the rooms, he returned to the library. The small flame, though vastly better than nothing, did little to illuminate the space. What became apparent immediately was a long table running down the centre of the room. Bathed in the orange light of the lamp, it sent a series of odd, distorted shadows projected against a back wall that had been left empty of adornment.

What else was in the room, Stephen could not have said. His attention was entirely focused on what lay on the long table. At its centre was the layout of a city, one he instantly recognised, even looking at it with a bird's eye view. Miniature buildings set out along the table, responsible for the long shadows dancing against the wall, were positioned in a near perfect imitation of the capital. He could pick out all the landmarks; St. Paul's, the Palace of Westminster, even the masses of newly constructed shantytowns were present. It was unnerving for reasons Stephen was not entirely sure of. Such precision must have taken months. But why? Was a normal map not sufficient? It was eerie, but rather in keeping with the similarly strange collection in the room above.

A lone piece of paper on the corner of the table wrestled his attention away from the model. It had been placed under one of the buildings, as if left there for safekeeping. The message was crumpled, it must have travelled a long way in the pockets of its possessor, but remained legible. As he unfurled it, a second, smaller note dropped to the floor. Before reaching down to pick it up, he quickly scanned the first. Though he had not seen it before, it was clearly the fake letter His Lordship had sent them after. Despite all the odds being stacked against them, they had somehow managed to muddle their way to the correct place. Begrudgingly Stephen admitted to himself that much of their good fortune had been down to the efforts of Burns. But he was there and that was what mattered.

Holding the notes up to the lamp, Stephen's sense of unease, originally a result of the strange room, grew. The original message was just a jumble of numbers, but below each line lay the decoded message. It was indeed a letter detailing the King's wish to continue with John Dee's exploration of conversing with angels, nothing suspicious there. But Stephen could see that it was a very simple code. All that His Lordship had done was attribute each letter of the alphabet to a number. It wouldn't have taken prodigious intellect to figure it out. And by all accounts, the people they were dealing with were no village idiots. The smaller scrap of paper, looking like it had been torn from a larger page, felt very wrong. It held a short message, nothing more than,

Our man has made his way to London.

So, their destination was once again London - as if the model hadn't confirmed that. But what struck Stephen was not the message, which was fairly mundane. It was something else. Something that, if he was right, meant they were in far more danger than either he or William had first thought. Taking both letters back to the clear light of the library, he placed them on a desk by the window. There was no denying it. The handwriting was identical.

∞

Valentine remained patient. It felt like months had passed since King Charles had made it known that he wished to view the miracles for himself. In truth, it had been no more than a few weeks. Many notable members of society were beginning to write of him. Surely the King could not ignore him for much longer. He had even been mentioned in a copy of The Philosophical Transactions of the Royal Society. Robert Boyle himself had taken a huge interest in him, keen to prove that the miraculous was not dead. Valentine, knowing Boyle was highly regarded by Charles, hoped his interest might provide a prompt to the King. Yet still he waited.

In the meantime, he would have to continue his ministries. Setting up in areas of London with the highest concentration of those afflicted by serious illness, he remained on task. Striding through the crowds that gathered, he struck an impressive figure. The tall, well-dressed gentleman in stark contrast to the varying degrees of poverty the masses were reduced to.

On the periphery of the crowds stood members of polite society. Intrigued by his reputation but unwilling to intermingle with the dirty and potentially contagious. Some even remained in private carriages, content to watch from what they had deemed a safe, respectable distance. Valentine, though appearing not to care, made sure to always remain in their line of sight. He waded through the throngs of people, his reputation doing the work for him as he placed hands on them.

His nickname 'The Stroker' had gained even more momentum since his arrival in London. Now, many only knew him by that title. His real name was no longer sufficient for his celebrity role.

As those watching from the edge of the crowds began to disperse, Valentine slowed his ministrations, happy that they would relay news of his good work to many more. Careful to remain a while longer than the last member of his audience, he then made his way back to the lodgings he had taken.

∞

William was having more trouble locating Phoenixes in heraldry than he had initially anticipated. 'NOT SO WELL HIDDEN AS WE FIRST THOUGHT' was proving to remain fairly well hidden. His instinct had been to look at the heraldic device of Queen's College in Oxford. It was a device he had often seen; three large birds, wings displayed, and depicted in red. However, despite the colour choice, in the lists of heraldry he managed to find, they were labelled as eagles.

Throughout the long, tedious search, the only

record in English heraldry he could find was the Seymour family. Jane, Henry VIII's third wife, had owned a device that included a crowned phoenix rising above a castle, between red and white Tudor roses. However, Francis Seymour, the current Duke of Somerset, was only eight years old. It was highly unlikely that a child was mixed up in a plot to overthrow the country, especially one that was rumoured to have roots in a civil war long before he had been born. By all accounts he was a difficult child, but not that difficult.

Rifling through the mass of texts contained in his personal library had made for an enjoyable, if more than a little frustrating, day. 'How time flies.' He thought, noting the sun creeping down behind the trees that lined the edge of the estate. Lost completely to his task, he had failed to notice the passing of the day. Hannah's brief interlude with lunch had provided some respite but since then he had not rested.

Watching the sunset, he surveyed the land around him, realising how tired the day had made him. He wondered where Stephen had got to. There had been no communication from him all day. That could either mean he had found nothing and was still searching, or he had found something worth pursuing. There was no telling what he might have uncovered.

William only hoped his friend had stayed true to task, not a return to that barmaid. As soon as the thought crossed his mind he regretted it. Whilst Stephen had a reputation that even he could not deny, the large man was also very good at his job. He would not stray. He had never let any of his nocturnal excursions impact on their work. A few times William had seen him return worse for wear the morning after a heavy session at the local inns, but he always recovered miraculously. If anything important had been found, William was sure his friend would return as swiftly as he was able. Still, if he was following a lead it could be days before he returned. He had Robert with him though, he could always send news back.

As the sun finally dropped below the horizon, taking with it the deep reds that had adorned the sky, William gave into the fatigue of the last week. Still in his chair, he allowed himself to fall into a deep slumber. Through the window, the final shades of peach clung to the darkening sky. Hannah, returning once more to check on him, tutted at seeing him asleep at the desk. She had already returned halfway through the afternoon to retrieve the lunch tray. William had been completely oblivious to her presence, lost in the papers strewn across his desk as he mumbled to himself.

She had not seen him like this before. William and Stephen had always worked hard, she was not sure what on, but the state they had been in over the last week was different somehow. Whatever it was they were doing, she hoped it would end soon. They were pushing themselves too hard, the pace was unmanageable. Soon one of them would crash, and William couldn't take that. She worried endlessly that another hit would leave him in pieces too small to reassemble, he was barely whole as it was. Whispering a quick prayer of protection, she pulled a thin blanket over him and closed the window. The weather was warm, but the heat of the day quickly gave way to cold nights.

∞

Stephen panicked. Unsure what to do with the

mess of information now whirling around his head, he decided to settle his nerves with a quick drink before returning to the house. He reasoned that a drink would provide time to think through everything he had just seen, and what it would mean for the rest of their investigation.

Returning by the North Gate to the city, he had passed the tavern in which they had met Burns. Imagining that the atmosphere in that particular establishment might be a little tense after the death of their patron, he ignored the welcoming glow of its front door. Instead, he opted for an old favourite from his time as a student in the city. Making his way a short distance along the High Street, he ducked into The Mitre and found a shadowy corner in which to muse over his situation.

Despite the large tankard placed in front of him, the drink did little to reduce the fear that had taken hold. Every so often he would find his hands had drifted to his pockets, ensuring the presence of the two scraps of paper that might change everything they thought they knew about their investigation. Thinking that a second drink would go well with a plate of food, he placed enough money on the bar and returned to his seat. It was often the way with work, things moved so quickly that eating was regularly overlooked. Stephen always made sure to compensate with as many large meals as he could lay his hands on. To not be eating was a wasted opportunity, and everything was more manageable with a full stomach.

A large slab of meat, doused in a thick sauce, and accompanied by a selection of greens was brought over by a barmaid. Setting the meal down, she winked in recognition at the large man. Remembering her from the visit they had paid in the first few days in Oxford, he flushed, recalling how he had been publicly reprimanded by William's boot. But he's not here now, he thought, and really, it can't hurt to have a couple more drinks – they'll help me think.

Wolfing down the meal, he moved over to the tall stools by the bar, making sure to sit as close to the girl serving as possible. The barmaid proved to be a more than willing drinking partner. Stephen considered himself an able drinker, but by no means drank as heavily as some. Still, he was surprised to find his tally matched drink for drink by the petite girl, without any apparent effect on her sobriety.

As the drinks continued to flow, she maintained a vigilant control over her territory – supplying further beverages to the clientele as the need arose. Her flirtatious nature, a professional courtesy, ensured that the area around the bar was packed to capacity. Stephen wondered if every man living in the vicinity was now crammed into the confines of The Mitre's bar. Despite maintaining a constant stream of conversation the whole way along the bar, she made sure to reward Stephen with eye contact every few minutes.

He was enjoying himself. The attention of a pretty girl, an abundance of alcohol, and the cheerful bustle around the bar had entirely taken his mind off everything else. He hadn't even checked his pockets for the papers for hours. The soothing embrace of the beer dulled the feeling of panic that had set in earlier in the day. Something in the back of his mind must still have been at work as his ears pricked at a conversation a short way down from him.

"...King's summoned him to court...big Irish fella... miracles in London and all over..."

Immediately on guard and struggling to revive his beer-soaked mind, Stephen instinctively clutched at the papers in his coat. Could this man in London be the one in the note? Had the fake letter really been part of the true plot? It had said the King was looking for new miracles and magic, and now he had summoned someone to court for exactly that.

Gingerly stumbling along the bar, he sought out the speaker.

"What did you just say?" he demanded, more aggressively than he had intended.

"Woah there big fella, what's that you say?"

"The King...who has he summoned about miracles?" Stephen slurred his words, breathing deeply in an attempt to control the effects of the alcohol.

"You haven't heard? It's a good story. They've been calling him the Stroker. Giant from Ireland, taller than you I dare say. Goes around performing miracle healings just by touching folk. He's been turning heads in London recently and now the King himself wants proof."

Stephen's face went sheet-white as panic threatened to settle back in. Mistaking his appearance for overindulgence in the beer, he was quickly guided outside by unseen hands. He went without a struggle, too lost in thought to notice what was happening. Surely it couldn't be a coincidence, William would have to know.

"Come on." A female voice said as he felt a tug on his shirt sleeve.

"What?" Realising he was back out in the street, he turned to identify the voice. "Oh, hello."

Evidently the barmaid had been the one to escort him outside. Pulling again at his sleeve, she beckoned for him to follow. Conflicting thoughts flashed through his mind, the alcohol making his previous urgency to get back to William dissipate as soon as they had come on – William would be asleep anyway. And it was a long walk back. Struck dumb by the swirling thoughts, he allowed himself to be led down the High Street.

As they approached the large front of Queen's College, the barmaid stopped. From a side road came a voice followed by the emergence of two burly looking men.

"Well done Modesty, that's him."

The men weren't any he had noticed in the Inn, he had no recollection of ever seeing them before, but apparently they knew him.

"Modesty," Stephen said, "well that's a misplaced name if ever I heard one. This isn't going quite the way I imagined."

Not wanting to engage in whatever the two men had planned, he took a step back, only to find himself shoved forward.

"Not just two then, well done Stephen, you've outdone yourself this time." He said to himself, "Sorry Gentlemen, I think you must have me mistaken for someone else. We have never met." Not wishing to aggravate the situation any further, he attempted a polite, swift reconciliation.

"No, we haven't," came the reply, "but you did meet Burns. And then he died. Hit over the back of the head by a giant of a man. One of the street boys saw it." The man advanced as he spoke, drawing a knotted wooden club.

"Hold on." Stephen said firmly, hands held out in front in an attempt to calm them, "Why would I kill him? He was helping with a few questions my friend and I had, that's all."

"I don't much care why, but there aren't many giants around these parts. You'll just have to do." He swung at Stephen, throwing his full force behind the thick chunk of wood.

The threat of violence had done wonders for sobering Stephen up. As they had been talking, he had assessed the physicality of the two men before him, guessing by the shuffling of feet at three more behind. Both men facing him were thick-set, obviously used to some form of physical labour, and their confidence suggested this was not their first fight either. But chances were they had never faced a man who knew how to fight back, wrongly assuming Stephen to be a cowardly dandy only capable of killing from behind.

Stephen instinctively darted to his right, away from the majority of his opponents, and helped guide the club onto the head of a man standing behind him. He had guessed right, three men behind – now two. The stuck man lay still on the floor, blood pouring from a large gash across his cheek and nose.

The attempted attack had left his assailant off guard. Stephen sent a swift kick to his ribs, sending the man barrelling into two of his companions. He was now one on one with the second man to confront him. His adversary did not react quick enough, met with a rapid punch to the throat he collapsed into a gurgling pile on the floor.

The original attacker recovered fastest, connecting a well-placed kick to Stephen's knee that forced the large man down. The following swing of the club should have taken Stephen's head off, but he ducked just in time, then sprang back up onto both feet. A blow from behind connected with his shoulder, preventing his elbow from smashing into the man's temple. Moving with the club that met his shoulder, Stephen lessened the effect of the impact, seizing the weapon and throwing the man over his head. There was a crack as a skull met the slabs of stone in front of the college, but Stephen had little time to assess the damage as the other two men recovered.

Now wary of the fighting capability of the larger man, they circled him, not wanting to go within reach of his long arms. Together they moved forward, swinging their clubs in sync. Sacrificing his ribs to one attack, Stephen gasped in agony as he felt the impact on his left side. The sacrifice had left him able to draw the man in. Grabbing him by the collar, he swung him into the second man. The club met the unprotected back of the assailant's companion. By pure luck, Stephen's swing cracked the two heads together; leaving all his ambushers in an unceremonious pile of bodies in varying states of consciousness.

Breathing sharply to avoid the pain that wracked his body with every deep breath, Stephen straightened up. By his reckoning, he had at least two cracked ribs and the blows to his shoulder and knee would probably leave him feeling their effects for a good few days.

"So, Modesty, where were we?"

The barmaid, frozen throughout the conflict, turned and ran. Watching her disappear into the night, he let out a soft chuckle – immediately regretting it as a wave of nauseating pain swept over him.

Not wanting to hang around for the five semi-conscious men to come around, Stephen began a slow shuffle back to William's house.

18

The journey back to London had been stressful for Ana. She had decided that to rush would have only drawn unwanted attention. It was unusual enough for her to be travelling such a distance alone, people noticed such things, and she could not afford to be so conspicuous. The driver had been instructed to remain at a steady pace once out of Oxford. Every glimpse of other travellers had sent her heart racing in trepidation. The jovial smiles and subservient nods of the head from those they passed only left her questioning who they were and what they knew of her.

The overnight stop in Wycombe had been near torture for her. Even locked in her room at one of the less popular inns, she had flinched at the slightest sound from the corridor outside. The restless sleep she had managed to fall into, between bouts of paranoid wakefulness, had left her exhausted and irritable. It was not until the carriage approached London, late in the afternoon on the second day of travelling, that she was able to relax enough to drift into a much needed slumber.

Instead of entering the city, she had directed the carriage driver to take her south of the river to

Southwark. This location provided an opportunity to be close enough to London without spending so much time there that she might become recognisable. Even in such a large, cosmopolitan city, anonymity was always useful.

She ordered the driver to drop her off some way from the house. No one knew the exact location of her residence. She was careful to keep it that way. There was a good reason that, among the Children, the identity of their compatriots was guarded so closely. Such a revelation could lead to a power struggle, undermining everything they had spent years working towards. As the carriage disappeared from view, she wound through the busy streets, habitually ensuring she was not being followed. The winding roads provided further cover before she emerged at a small lane, containing a handful of cottage homes. The other inhabitants knew her, or rather, they knew a version of her, and had no suspicions as to who she really was. To them, she was a kind young widow, too distraught at the death of her husband to face socialising with the outside world. They gave her little trouble, only the occasional attempt to draw her back into society. None of them would ever come to the house, they would wait to catch her as she left. But in her absence, someone had been there. As she walked toward the front door she could feel it. Something wasn't quite right.

There was no sign of forced entry. The front door remained locked and windows undamaged, no scratching around the lock suggested any attempt at picking it. Though unassuming, the locks on her house were of the highest quality. She had left nothing to chance when she moved in. As the door swung open she noted that even the thin layers of dust behind the door remained undisturbed. And yet, someone had been there, she was sure of it. Whoever it was had been highly skilled, but no one could go anywhere without leaving some trace. The house smelled wrong. The candles used by the intruder had not been made by the same chandler she used. Different oils in the wick, or a slightly different environment in which the wax was moulded had left a scent that lingered, betraying their carrier.

Following her nose, she moved cautiously into the small room that was her dining room. The state of the long rug on the floor confirmed the presence of an intruder. Any doubt was banished. Where the rug had been scuffed at one corner, it now lay perfectly straight. Such a basic mistake. People couldn't help fixing the way it lay. Something in the human psychology assumed that they must have caused it to scuff up.

Approaching the dining room table, Ana noticed the message that had been left for her. Sitting on the edge of the table, a small piece of paper with a familiar image embossed at its centre. It looked like a red figure of eight laid on it's side, the symbol for infinity. She knew what it meant, but flipped over the note to see if any extra information had been provided. Nothing was there. The image was enough. No words had been necessary. The Phoenix had summoned her.

∞

All Robert's risks seemed to have paid off as he asked one last effort from the tired horse beneath him. Judging by the slow speed of the carriage, his haste was not really necessary, but he had not wanted to be seen staring. The quick glance he sneaked as he passed had not revealed much. He had been glad to note the relaxed nature of the driver and horses, they were not pushing hard to be anywhere. He hoped this meant his presence had gone unnoticed.

But it had now been hours since Robert had overtaken the carriage on the road to London. The creeping confidence that had been growing throughout the journey was beginning to wane. Even at a slow pace it shouldn't have taken them that long to reappear on the roads. Had they not been destined for London after all? Should he remain in place, or would he be better off abandoning his post and searching the outlying towns to the south of the capital? In reality there wasn't much choice, he didn't know the area; wouldn't know where to start looking; and who was to say they wouldn't still come through where he was? Searching alone would be like trying to find a needle in a haystack. He didn't have that much time. The cloak Stephen had lent him held a few coins, but even with his frugal attempt at saving money by sleeping under the stars, the coins would quickly run out. He would have to remain put. No sign of the carriage by the end of the day would mean he would return to Oxford unsuccessful.

He really didn't want to return empty handed, Stephen had shown great faith in him. Robert had taken the opportunity to prove his worth and could not fail. He was still not sure what was happening, but the reappearance of William's dead wife was more than enough for Robert to want to find out.

Stephen had been insistent that William could not know about their visit to the house. But Ana had always treated him well. If it really was her, he wanted to find out what she was up to. How was she even alive? She had been at the house only a couple of weeks before her death.

After two weeks in London, William had rushed home with Stephen in tow. For days they remained silent before Stephen had sat down with the household to explain how Ana had been taken by the deadly sickness that was sweeping through the city.

Robert remembered the frail wreck William had become in the weeks that followed, before disappearing altogether for almost a year. Was this why Stephen was keeping everything so close to his chest? He knew both older men had worked for the King in some capacity. Were they mixed up in something now? Questions, given time as he waited, continued to evolve in his mind. Theory after theory developed and was shot down by their increasing ridiculousness.

Around him, the busy traffic on it's way to London bustled by. It never showed any signs of slowing, and the regular steady stream of people made their way in and out of the city. Occasional waves of increased footfall came every hour or so as groups that had set off and travelled the roads together reached their destination. Robert was beginning to recognise some faces, people he had passed on the road. Perching on a fallen ash tree by the roadside, he grew more downbeat with every passing familiar face. Where had the carriage gone?

"Hey...Mate?!" a cry from the road cut through his daydreaming. "Hey, up on the tree." Looking over at the road he picked out the man calling to him. "Any chance you could give us a hand? The wheel's come off the cart."

The broad-shouldered man was pointing over to a cart that had fallen foul of the rock-hard roads. By the cart stood an enormous bull; slow, but strong enough to pull a heavily loaded cart that would normally rely on at least two beasts.

"Of course." Robert replied, jumping down from his perch. There was already a small crowd gathering around the offending cart. It would take as many hands as possible to lift, piled high as it was with sacks of flour. This man was evidently supplying from a local mill, with the growing numbers in the capital it would be good business if he could keep up with the demand.

Joining the crowd, he hooked both hands under the cart frame, planting his feet in a solid position and bracing ready for the lift.

"Three, two, one...lift." called the driver. At first, nothing happened. The cart appeared to have defeated them. But, just at the point of giving up, it began to inch up. Sinew-strained and sweat beginning to pour, the group managed to raise the structure just high enough to get the wheel slotted back on. With a final groan, it was lowered back to the ground, once more sitting level. Breathing heavily from the exertion, Robert placed his hands on his head, looking up to increase the flow of air into this chest.

"My thanks lad." The heavy hand of the miller clapped his shoulder. Turning to accept the praise, his eyes caught a movement behind the wide man that sent him sprinting over to his horse. An ungainly scramble onto his mount followed before he took off in the direction of the city. Bewildered, the miller shrugged at the strange youth before clambering back aboard his cart.

A flash of blonde hair had caught Robert's gaze. Immediately he had known it was her. He wasn't sure how, or why, she no longer rode in her carriage. Instead, astride a large bay, she trotted past the fallen cart and into the city. Praising the Lord for the fortunate twist of fate, he set off after her – not wanting to lose her once more in the busy city streets.

∞

It had not taken Ana long to find a horse. The stables of a wealthy merchant were located not far from her safe house. They had been unwilling to part with any of their stock, but the offer she had made was one they would have been foolish to turn down. The Children never wanted for money. Ana was not sure if certain of their members were incredibly wealthy, or whether an inexhaustible fund had built up over time. It was most likely a combination of the two.

The ride into the city had been slow. A hold up at the gate, caused by some inept trader, had clogged the roads for a while before she had been able to pass. Eventually, tired of waiting, she had forced her horse around the hold-up, ignoring the resentful mutterings as she trotted past. Once in the city, her pace had slowed significantly. The sheer numbers of people massing on the streets took movement out of her control; able only to follow the flow of the crowds through the winding roads of the capital.

She had never been summoned before. All initiates to the Children were taught what it meant, but if any others had ever received one it had not been mentioned. Though, she supposed, it was not the most likely topic of conversation in an organisation where secrecy was so highly regarded.

A carriage would be waiting by St. Paul's Cathedral. From there it would take her wherever it was that Phoenix had decided they would meet. She knew no more than that. She was not even sure when the summons had been left for her, the carriage could have been waiting for days. But that was not her concern. She had followed the instructions to the letter, any more than that was up to the Phoenix.

The area around St. Paul's was teeming with people. It had been popular with traders for centuries, particularly higher value professions such as printers and portrait painters. Amidst the smell of ink and paints, Ana could also detect the more pungent odours suggesting at least one apothecary had opened up in the area. Acrid notes of burning materials mixed with strong floral scents that would have given her quite a headache had she stayed in their fog too long.

Above all the traders, peacocking for business, rose the old cathedral. It vastly overshadowed the buildings around it, making them appear nothing more than a shanty town thrown together at a whim. The large building had seen better days. Though it had stood for the better part of a century, the last few decades had not been kind. The spire had been destroyed in a lightning strike over a century before. A sure sign of God's displeasure at the war waged between Catholics and Protestants. The forces of parliament had not treated it well during their occupation in the civil war. Many of the buildings in the churchyards now lay defaced or razed – their remains recommissioned to act as trader's workshops.

Spotting a carriage waiting in the agreed position, Ana directed her horse toward the West entrance to the cathedral. As she approached, the drivers made eye contact with her, watching as she moved over to them. Drawing closer, she reigned in the horse, standing level with the drivers' seats. The man closest to her, clean-shaven and very plain looking, spoke first,

"How may we help you, my lady?"

"I seek a fire." She gave the phrase that would identify her as the one they waited for.

"It will burn, my lady." Came the required reply.

"But it will also refine."

With the exchange complete, both parties were content that they had met with the correct contacts. The second man on the carriage dismounted and made toward her. She was helped down from her ride and into the carriage. The man assured her that the horse would be returned to her in due course, before he closed the door.

Predictably, the windows to the carriage were well covered with heavily woven drapes, thereby preventing any chance of retracing her steps to the rendezvous point. As they forced their way through the crowded roads she sat back, resigning herself to the conclusion that all would soon be made clear.

On three occasions they stopped as the driver exchanged greetings with passers-by. Ana could not have said how long the journey took, all perception of time skewed by lack of landmarks to use as a reference. At the fourth stop, she was instructed to adorn a blindfold, which she found resting on the cushion of the seat opposite her. Once this was done she was bundled out of the carriage and into a building. Her echoing steps let her know she was in a narrow corridor before she was directed through two sets of doors. There, Ana was helped into a chair and the blindfold removed.

The room she found herself in was small, barely large enough to fit two chairs and a small writing desk. These were the only items of furniture. The rest of the room was bare, only a fireplace took up any space along one of the walls. It was impossible to guess where she might be. No light came into the room, the crackling fire provided the only source of illumination. Ana noted that there were two doors to the room; probably a room between rooms, kept for precisely this kind of inconspicuous meeting.

Opposite her sat a familiar figure, the man who had first brought her into the Children. As she recognised him, it took all her willpower not to react – this man was meant to be dead. It could only mean one thing; he must have faked his death in order to become Phoenix. For the first time, Ana realised she was not wearing the mask that would normally be required of a meeting of the Children. It mattered little, this man was fully aware of who she was.

As these thoughts flickered across her face, the man smiled a greeting.

"I suppose you have questions," he pre-empted, "How am I here?... Why are you here?...so on and so forth. I'm afraid they will have to wait. You were not my only set of eyes in Oxford. You waited too long - you were seen by La Penne and Berry. What do they know?"

"That evening was, I believe, coincidence. With Burns out of the equation, they have no leads. They know nothing. As I left the city Stephen saw me but could not follow. There is nothing they can learn at the house." Ana worked hard to keep the nerves from her voice, though she was not convinced of her success. She was confident that the hidden room would yield no information, even if broken into. The friendly tone of the man opposite her had quickly gained an edge of venom as he glared accusingly across at her.

Phoenix sat for a moment in thoughtful silence before continuing.

"I cannot believe anything here is a coincidence, especially with those two, but it does appear that they will be more distracted by your sudden reappearance than anything else. I had planned for you to keep them away from London. It was a case of leading them in a dance, I had even thought you might plant the letter with Burns, that could have been entertaining. But you were never meant to reveal yourself. You were only to join me here once we were sure they could not possibly know anything. Plans in London are all set, we will have to remain vigilant in our patience."

Ana knew all this already.

"When will it begin?"

"This may actually play into our hands." He ignored her question, continuing to think aloud. "All reports show William to be in a very fragile mental state, almost a complete recluse over the past year. Seeing you may have pushed him over the edge."

"You said he wouldn't be harmed." She whispered, hating that she still cared.

"And he won't." Phoenix snarled back. "Not by my hand. Do not forget your role here. This task is bigger than either of us."

He fixed her with a piercing stare, searching out any weakness. Refusing to give anything away, Ana nodded her consent, maintaining eye contact the whole time. Seemingly content, he dismissed her with a wave of his hand,

"Go. Further instruction will follow in the usual manner."

Hands behind her returned the blindfold to her eyes. She heard the opening of doors as footsteps exited the room. The meeting was over. She was firmly escorted her back to the waiting carriage. Sitting back in the blackness Ana breathed deep, warding away the panicked sob that sat like a lump in her throat. That man had increasingly terrified her before she thought him dead, his mood so changeable at the smallest prompt, and now she knew he had been controlling her all along.

With a lurch, the horses pulled them away, back to the meeting point at St. Paul's. The slightest flicker of wind swept through the carriage window, for a split second drawing the veil away from the it's edge. Through the crack, Ana managed to make out the unmistakable façade of the buildings around Westminster Palace.

19

When William finally woke, he was lying in his bed. He didn't remember making the move back into his bedroom, but guessed by the soreness in his back that he had spent a good few hours asleep in his chair before moving. His first thought upon waking had been to exchange information with Stephen, there was a lot to be discussed. But, as the morning wore on, there was still no sign of his friend emerging from his room. Hannah and Samuel had been unable to answer his questions about what time his friend had returned. They had heard nothing from him all night and were only sure he was back after noticing the door to his room had been closed. Hannah had been reluctant to wake the man for breakfast, having heard deep snoring when she went to enquire whether he wanted food.

William's renewed sense of purpose at the deciphering of Burns' note had put him in good humour, but patience was wearing thin as the morning turned to midday. He had expected to act upon the information he had gained immediately. It was not much, but he now knew they were in the wrong city. Getting to London as soon as possible would surely give them a better chance of uncovering whatever was being planned.

Deciding that just waiting was a waste of time, William revisited the books in his library. There might still be some information that had been overlooked, some clue that would link the note's metaphors to an actual event. Burns had said Aeternitas was a Roman deity, perhaps some legend involving her would help point the way forward.

William was still rifling through texts when Stephen eventually made an appearance. William was shocked at the sight of him. Dishevelled features only stood out more against the fresh clothes he was wearing. He was walking with a severe limp and one shoulder was definitely hanging lower than normal, held in what was clearly a painful position.

"What happened to you?" asked William, jumping to his feet and rushing over. He was immediately hit by the lingering stench of stale beer. "You were drinking?"

Taking a step back in disbelief, he thought of the time that had been wasted during the long morning. It quickly turned his concern to frustration at the betrayal. With so much resting on both of them performing at their best, had Stephen really thought it appropriate to be out drinking so heavily?

"Let me explain." Came the groggy reply.

"So...yes."

"Will, I'm sorry." The larger man managed before launching into the speech he had rehearsed on the walk home. "I uncovered something, something big, and panicked. I didn't know what to do, how to deal with it. I thought...well, I didn't think...I just did. But then I got carried away, and there was that girl, and then some men decided we were the men that killed Burns. It was a...I am a mess and I'm sorry."

"Wait, slow down." William could see there was more to this than he had thought at first glance. The surge of anger began to wane as curiosity took hold.

"What exactly did you find?"

Two pieces of paper were placed on the table in front of him. William quickly scanned both, neither particularly long or complex, however, their significance was instantly apparent.

"But this means…"

"I know," Stephen cut in, "so I panicked."

"Where did you find them?"

"Robert tracked the lady that they sent to Oxford. He's following her again now. I found them at her house, hidden in a secret wall."

"We need to go. Now. There can be no denying it, both these letters are by the same hand. And I'd know that writing anywhere. We need to get to London. He must have sent us here to keep us away from his plan."

"There was a complete miniature of the city in the house. I think you should see it before we go. You might gain something from it that I missed."

"Very well, you can tell me the rest of your escapades on the way there. I have something to tell you about Burns' book as well."

∞

Stephen was asleep again. The carriage rattled through Oxford, toward the capital. The house to the north of the city had sent a shiver down William's spine. The sheer emptiness of it had made its grandeur very cold, the ghost of a house.

His friend's further accounts of the night before had thawed the tension between them. He could, to some extent, understand Stephen's blind panic. It was a different coping mechanism to his – but they were very different people. He couldn't feel anger anymore, the information gained from the evening had been invaluable. William had to admit that, had Stephen not gone off on his drunken adventure, they would not have heard anything of the suspicious Irishman.

News of the 'Stroker' in London fitted perfectly with the letter His Lordship had told them was fake. How many missions had they been sent on only to fulfil the goals of His Lordship? It didn't bear thinking about. All they could do now was focus on stopping him.

The model city Stephen had shown William had been odd. It had to be important, no one would go to so much trouble otherwise, but neither of them could work out its relevance. They were heading back to London, it was clear that they needed to be there, but what would a miniature of the city be for? Why not use a map? - over the last decade, their quality had increased dramatically.

Their best lead remained the news of the 'Stroker' and the letters. His Lordship would have to be confronted, but the immediate threat to the King was the more pressing issue. More information would be required about this Greatrakes causing such a stir in the capital. Finding him was the priority. His Lordship would face them in due course.

Every new piece of information gained only led to further questions. It was the nature of their line of work that they had to make decisions based on very limited knowledge, that was just part of the job. Even so, William couldn't remember a time when they had so little to work with – and all of it so confusing. That they had both been sent to Oxford made some sense; His Lordship wanted them out of the way, but why involve William at all? He could have been left in Oxford and continued none the wiser to anything that was taking place. Unless, they were being set up in some way, and would find themselves scapegoated for the death of their King. All manner of possibilities began to work their way into his head, even the most ridiculous managing to appear logical.

The overriding question William was having trouble coming to terms with was, why now? His Lordship had been in a position of power for years, he was a close confidant of the King and sat in the centre of a web of influence across the whole of Europe. With all that in place for years, what had been the trigger for him to turn on his country now? Or had it all been building to this from the start?

William suspected that such questions would never receive a satisfactory answer. Cornered men rarely divulged such information, when next they met it would be swift and brutal. He would be offered no mercy and knew none would be expected. Their reappearance in London in the next few days could well be enough of a signal to His Lordship that they were on to him. Once there, they would have to watch their backs. Every shadow would hold a threat. For now though, no one knew they were coming. The element of surprise was in their favour and they would have to maximise this to stand any chance of success.

William looked down at the hand gripping the window edge of the carriage. His knuckles were white, the blood pushed from his hand as he clenched. Realising his fixation on the mission was fraying his already tattered nerves, he sought to take his mind away from all the unknown. In an attempt to relax he watched the country pass by from the window. Finding that this did nothing to distract him from his own thoughts, he stuck a rough elbow into the ribs of his sleeping friend.

"Wh...ow! What was that?!"

"Must have been a hole in the road, the whole carriage jumped." William lied, feeling awful that he had forgotten the state of his friend's ribs. After a moment of silence to regain his composure, Stephen began his usual stream of nonsense.

"Oh, I was having the most wonderful dream. There was a table set out with all the greatest foods you can imagine: a boar, venison stew, one of those elaborate centrepieces made up of who-knows-what. And every time I ate something it reappeared, each time it tasted even better than before. And I never got any closer to feeling full. Bliss."

"Sounds marvellous." William chuckled his reply, heavy with sarcasm. "Though I don't recall a time when you ever complained of being too full to pack more food in."

"Well sorry for not living like a saint." At the remark William raised his eyebrows, giving his friend a look that made the large man's cheeks redden. "Yes, alright. Point taken." Stephen lowered his eyes.

"Seeing as how you're awake now, you might as well tell me about the girl."

"Really?" Not waiting for a response, Stephen snapped up the opportunity, launching into a rather exaggerated version of the tale he had already told.

Content just to let his friend ramble on, expunging

all thought of what would happen once they arrived at their destination, William sat back and let the journey pass by.

∞

In a small set of rooms in the central-eastern side of the capital, Valentine sat at his window and stared out at the cloudless sky. The midday sun provided no respite for the city workers. The warm, dry weather that had marked the summer months had only persisted. Now, as the year wore on, there was no indication that it would abate. The occasional storm did little to lessen the effects of the drought. Food supplies grew thin as they spoiled in the extreme heat. Flies swarmed around the city, an endless droning that was unavoidable even to the wealthier inhabitants.

At present, none of this was a pressing concern for Valentine. He stared, not at the city, but instead thinking on the letter that he held in his hands. It had finally arrived. No more vague assertions that the King wished to receive him. No more playing to the crowds gathering around his ministry. The letter had come. The date was set. He would stand before the King in just a week's time. And there he would achieve his goal.

He must have read the letter a dozen times already. The words played round his head as he read them again and again.

Charles R

Charles the Second, by the Grace of God, King of England, Scotland and France and Ireland, defender of the faith &c. Greetings - You are a person of known abilities above the understanding of many witnesses in whom I show great trust. Your presence is respectfully requested that we may better enjoy the gifts that might so well serve to remove the strife of our great country.

You shall be seen one weeks hence at our Court at Whitehall.

By His Majesty's Command,
E RAWSON

This was it. He had almost done it. Now, all that remained was to meet with the King.

∞

It was a little over a week before Ana heard from Phoenix. Again, she found a note on her table. This time it contained more than just an image. It was a detailed, yet concise, plan for the upcoming event. Their man was due to be in place at the allocated time, a date had finally been set. The countdown to the new England could now begin. And it would not just be a new England. The impact of their actions would reverberate across the globe. Like the fall of Carthage, the sack of Rome, the destruction of Byzantium; it would be an event that would resonate through time as the beginning of a new world.

If all went to plan, there was little left for her to do. Though, as she was now in London, she would play her part. The event itself would be quick. She knew no glory would follow. Only a select handful of people would know the reality of what had taken place. Once the fuse had been lit in the capital, it would not be long before the rest of the country began to burn. From there it would be a matter of time before the rest of the world would follow suit.

Since the flight from Oxford, there had been no sign of William or Stephen. She was sure that, had she been followed, they would have presented themselves by now. She was the only lead they had. They must have got stuck in Oxford, bogged down with trying to find more information. Or perhaps Phoenix had been right, maybe seeing her really had broken William.

Whilst she wished no harm to either man, it was not worth dwelling on their involvement for too long. She had loved William, perhaps she still did, but he and everything she had left behind were part of the problem she would help solve. As Phoenix had said, this was bigger than any feelings she might still have. Besides, William had lost any claim to her when she had been abandoned at the very time she had needed him most.

Ana's mind drifted back to the hazy memories of her illness. It had hit her fast. There were no warning signs, no tell-tale swellings. Her skin had remained free from the rash-like black and red spots. The first anyone had known of it was the white hot fever that struck, at once confining her to bed. She had called out deliriously at shadows. Phantoms crowded her, driving her into further madness as no one else responded to their presence. The apparitions had set upon her, delivering daily beatings that raised her skin into deep black bruising. She had tried to tell them; cried out that the demons were to blame for her Promethean torment. Not one of them had listened to her, allowing her to slip further and further away.

Then there had been only darkness. It was not something Ana let her thoughts turn to often. Even the idea chilled her. When, at last, she had been plucked from that abyss, she was met by a face she had not known, in a place that she did not recognise. There had been no sign of her husband. Not even their regular doctor remained. She had no inclination of how long the darkness had enveloped her.

The man, who had introduced himself as John Fenneck, assured her that he was there to bring her back. As she recovered they talked. He told her of how she had been abandoned by everyone she knew, left for dead. He explained how it was the same for so many across the country, the men in power leaving them to die as soon as they were deemed useless. She had been chosen, reborn out of death to live a new life; a life of service, resetting the balance of power. Working in the shadows as a purveyor of a new world. All that she had been would be left behind, she too would leave her past life to die.

Those weeks had opened her eyes, seeing the unjust manipulation of the few in power over the rest of the world. John had told her she could help right the wrongs of centuries. She was in the perfect situation to undermine the established power base.

Soon after she was back on her feet initiation into the Children had followed. The reality of their struggle was made even more real by the death of her mentor shortly afterwards. In a foul blow almost half a dozen of their number had been taken by a man under the King's orders. She now knew this had been staged, her mentor taking the role of Phoenix. But, at the time, it had only thrown fuel on the fire for those remaining.

Very soon they would be vindicated. As she walked

the streets of London a smile crept over her face. The stallholder standing opposite her took it as approval of the breads laid out before her. Unwittingly, she was drawn into conversation about the array of freshly baked wheels. Feigning interest, she allowed herself to be talked through the different processes that went into producing the finest breads. Processes which, of course, no one else in London was capable of reproducing.

Eventually the vendor's persistence paid off as she left with more bread than she could possibly consume before it went stale. As she set off there was a small commotion behind her, the busy streets not allowing anyone to push against the flow. An elderly stallholder had stopped a young man, a tattered hat in her hands.

"Is this your hat, my duck?" she asked.

"Yes, thank you. It must have knocked off in my rush." The young man replied. There were maybe four or five people between Ana and the young man, obscuring her view – but there was something familiar in that voice. Even during peak trading times it was unusual to hear that particular twang. It was unmistakably an Oxfordshire accent. But, more importantly, she was sure it was familiar.

She pushed her way back through the crowd, receiving angry mutterings as the bread in her arms was discarded without a thought. Surely hearing that accent was a coincidence, but it was not something she was prepared to leave to chance.

Ahead she saw the hat bobbing away from her, carried along by the tide of people crushed into the street. Gaining ground, a burgundy cloak became visible beneath the ragged hat. Doubling her efforts, she cut the gap between them, leaving furious cries behind her.

Reaching out, she lunged at the cloak, catching an edge in her left hand. Around spun the man.

"Hey! What are you playing at?" Before her stood a man she had never seen before. Squat, hunched shoulders framed a thick neck. His greasy, silvering hair hung limp around a weathered face, deeply lined with age. Puffy features overpowered a set of squinting black eyes. This was not her man.

"My apologies, sir. I thought you were someone I knew." Quickly searching around her, she sought out any sign of the young man without success. Not wanting to hang around the old man any longer than she already had, she ducked back into the crowd. Any chance of finding the origin of the familiar voice was long gone.

Gaining some comfort from the idea that she had been aware enough to pick out the accent of the young man, she continued home. She would have to be more observant from now on, daydreaming was a luxury she could not afford. Her task was not over yet.

∞

Tucked back against the drapings of a leather merchant, Robert gave a deep sigh of relief. Though he knew there was no way Ana would be looking out for him, one sighting of his face would give him up. Ducking into the stall to discard his cloak had been his first thought as he saw her rush at him. He had watched the scene unfold from there, knowing he had let her get too close.

He had been following Ana for weeks now without detection. He knew that William and Stephen had arrived in London a few days ago but had received instruction to remain on task. Stephen had somehow managed to track him down. With all regular forms of reaching each other unavailable to them, Stephen had managed to use his network of less desirable contacts to find him; the network of street children and traders were able to track him down quickly enough. Correspondence by letters, left at a discreet inn, was their only means of communication for the time being. Robert was yet to meet him to properly discuss all that had occurred.

Stephen had provided extra funds and told him to keep his head down. The letters he received were short and succinct. Robert was increasingly sure that something of great importance was being kept from him. The lack of meeting clearly indicated William and Stephen were attempting to keep their presence in the city known to as few as possible. Robert was not even sure if William knew he was there.

The information Robert had been able to provide had apparently been received well. Stephen's letters gave the impression that he was very impressed. Still, following one person, however mysterious, was wearing thin. On several occasions his concentration had lapsed. That day's blunder was one of a series of mistakes, though it was by far the most serious. He hoped something would happen soon. He had shown his worth, now he longed for action. Stephen's continued call for patience only magnified Robert's desire to be at the heart of the goings-on.

Peeling himself away from the wall, he took a deep breath. There was still a job to be done, however tedious it was becoming. Setting off at a steady pace he made sure not to let Ana get too far ahead.

20

They had been in London for well over a week before William and Stephen were able to catch even a glimpse of Valentine "The Stroker" Greatrakes. Though many claimed to have seen him at work, the man himself had proved to be frustratingly elusive. All the stories they ha heard spoke of his persistent ministries to the poor, but this was not the reality they had been faced with. They hadn't been able to find him anywhere.

It seemed that, since receiving a set date for his audience with the King, the Irishman had almost disappeared. This suspicious behaviour only increased William and Stephen's desire to confront him. To cease serving was not the attitude of one working for the glory of God. This man had an agenda. With a date set, he no longer needed to be out on the streets. Clearly, all that mattered was the meeting with the King. They needed to find him before he got too close to Charles, and time was fast running out.

Greatrakes' withdrawal from his public life had not been the only struggle William and Stephen faced on arrival in the capital. Somehow they needed to remain undetected by His Lordship's agents. They were both known by many in the city, and with everyone's loyalties in question, attempting to find a man, whilst remaining hidden, was no easy task. In the end, it had been Stephen's growing frustration at the lack of progress that had given them the first sighting of their quarry.

Late one day, the two men were staking out Greatrakes' suspected lodgings for a third time. The rundown old building had been pointed out to them by a washerwoman who claimed to have seen the rangy Irishman enter the building on more than one occasion. There since the early morning, William and Stephen were yet to see any sign of the healer. Plenty of the building's other inhabitants had been and gone throughout the day, but not one held any resemblance to the increasingly famous miracle healer. At the end of his tether, Stephen had given up.

"Come on Will, this is useless. We've been here all day, and this is the third time we've tried – he isn't here. I can't do this anymore. Sitting in this sweltering heat, staring at the same building for hours on end is not a good use of time. Let's go for a drink."

"A drink? How is that a better use of our time? I know keeping a low profile doesn't come naturally to you, but drinking is not the answer to all life's problems. We need to find Greatrakes before he gets to the King." William snapped irritably. The incessant heat was not helping either man deal well with the stalled investigation.

"It might not solve anything, but at least it would make you bearable." Stephen muttered.

"Excuse me?"

"I said...taking a step back can't hurt. We're not making any progress just sitting here. Greatrakes obviously hasn't been here for days. We can clear our heads and come back with a clear perspective. They might even have some information on Greatrakes, something we've missed." Noticing a softening of William's expression, he added, "I know some very discreet places we could go."

"Are you really suggesting we go to one of those horrendous God-forsaken dives you inexplicably make a habit of frequenting?"

"Dives?" Stephen spluttered in mock affront, "I'll have you know they are some of the finest establishments I have ever had the pleasure of setting foot in."

"Yes, well I think that probably says more about you than their quality. Besides, won't they recognise you?"

Stephen could tell his friend was coming round to the idea.

"I make sure never to visit the same place enough times for them to know me; habit of our trade. Even the ones that might recognise me wouldn't know who I actually am."

"You really have taken drunken debauchery to a whole new level!"

"Why thank you," the large man replied with a flamboyant bow, "Come on then. I know the perfect place close by."

"Fine. Just one drink though."

"Of course, my good sir. When have I ever overstepped the mark." He winked at William, ignoring the reproachful look he received in return.

They made their way to a dingy area of the city, not far from where Greatrakes had conducted the majority of his ministries whilst in the capital. On either side of the street, the original structures were hidden, covered completely by sprawling new wooden lean-tos sticking out into the street. These homemade extensions were typical of new builds. The cheap materials and ease of construction made them much more economically viable for the many that came to the city for work.

Further along, they stepped into a side street so dank and dark that William wouldn't even have noticed it if Stephen hadn't tugged his coat to direct him. Here, the bustle common on the main streets abated into a silence so at odds with the rest of the capital that it sent a shiver up William's spine.

Following his friend, William ducked under a low hanging balcony, coming face to face with a small door. Stephen knocked twice, waited a few seconds, before knocking once more. A hatch to the side of the door opened, a pair of heavily made-up female eyes looked back at them expectantly.

"Rupert, plus friend, for a drink." Stephen said confidently.

"Just a drink?" The eyes twinkled back at them.

"Well...I mean...We could probably..." A cough from William saved him, "Just a drink today please."

The hatch slid closed, a girlish laugh audible as the door swung open to reveal their host. She must have been in her late forties thought William. The elaborate dress and makeup she wore did nothing to hide her age. The finery of the costume she wore was, at a closer look, of poor quality. The materials were cheap and ill-fitting.

"Anyone else here?" asked Stephen, making his way further into the building. The girl shut the door behind and followed them in.

"One other, he's busy at the moment."

It suddenly dawned on William just what kind of

establishment he had been brought to. It should have been obvious – what a fool. Grabbing Stephen's shoulder, he pulled him aside.

"What are we doing here? In this…place."

"Where did you think we were going? I said discrete didn't I?" Stephen's face was a mixture of confusion and amusement. "I'd have thought the conversation at the door made it pretty clear."

"Discreet yes, but not this."

"It's just a drink Will, calm down."

"You actually come here often?"

"Not often. But yes, occasionally I do." The large man was struck by the self-righteousness of his friend, he had nothing to be ashamed of, visiting places like this was very common – even expected of men his age. "It's alright for you, you had Ana. Sometimes…"

"Alright for me?" he interrupted angrily, "How dare you compare my dead wife to some common whore."

"I'm sorry Will, that's not what I meant. And of course her death hit me hard too. But at least the woman you loved felt the same way for you."

Stephen's misty eyes shocked William to silence. He had always thought the large man had not wanted that life. His friend's comments on the matter had always been clear; he would not settle when there were others he could chase. William could only stare as Stephen continued,

"I also found young love. But for her it was only a fleeting infatuation. She left for some marquis up in the northern cities. It was a long time ago now, but I've found a lack of emotion, and places like this, work better for me."

"Stephen, I didn't know. But you can't really think that it's best that way can you? It might not be harming anyone else, but think of what it does to you. Why have you never said anything before?"

"I gave up Will. So I drink, and I visit places like this. Nothing to leave behind, no one to worry when you're gone - apparently that's the perfect attitude for someone in our line of work."

"But..." William tried to cut in, still shocked at Stephen's outburst of emotion.

"Well, not entirely true. There's you of course. And day to day I suppose I get by."

"Look at the both of us." William grabbed his companion by the shoulders. "Both given up on the world. And we haven't even had that drink yet." William laughed, pulling the larger man into his arms.

Stephen's sombre face cracked into a beaming smile. The two men filled the room with frantic laughter. Unsure how safe the pair of them were, the woman, who had just reappeared after realising she had not been followed, backed toward the nearest door.

"Uh, sorry sirs but if you're looking for that kind of entertainment you'll need to look elsewhere."

"Oh, no. We're not...apologies. It's been a very stressful few weeks." Stephen tried to ignore William, who was now laughing even harder. "How about that drink?"

She beckoned them on, still keeping her distance.

"Who's the other chap then? Anyone I know?" asked Stephen.

"Strange one. New to London. Been here all week though." She replied, happy to see the two men had returned to normal.

"All week?" William cut in. "That's strange. Isn't it?"

He looked over at Stephen.

"What's he like?" The tall man asked.

"Oh, well, tall. Probably your height." She pointed at Stephen. "He says he's magic."

"And Irish?" Both men said at once.

"Yes, a friend of yours?" She looked at them. "I can let him know you were here."

"No, that won't be necessary. Thank you." William responded quickly. It wouldn't do for Greatrakes to know he was being followed. "We'd love that drink though."

As they sat down, doors opening in the hallway drew their attention. Looking back into the hallway they had passed through, they caught a glimpse of a tall, thin man with broad shoulders being playfully dragged between two of the rooms. They only saw him for a second before the doors closed, but it was enough.

"So, that's him?" asked Stephen. "Doesn't seem like much of a vessel of God's will to me."

"No, more like an assassin who knows he won't live long after his mission is complete. We need to warn the King. If we put a stop to him now, His Lordship will know. We just have to make sure he fails, then we can dispose of him."

In grim silence the two men gathered their coats, dropped a few coins on the table, and let themselves out of the building.

21

John Fenneck leant over his desk. He was reading through a report that had recently been delivered from an agent sent out to Bologna three months before. He was finding it hard to concentrate on being His Lordship; his building anticipation for the event he had spent so long planning left him utterly distracted. But there was more to it than just the restlessness of expectancy. He hadn't heard a whisper from either William or Stephen since they left London. Ana had supplemented the reports from contacts in Oxford, but even her news was weeks old now. There should have been more communication from them. Protocol required them to report back every few weeks, even if they hadn't found anything useful. He knew they would be reluctant to report back with nothing, but their silence made him uneasy. Had they managed to find something? Had Ana made a mistake? If they were in London, none of his people had reported seeing them. But the lack of news from Oxford made him increasingly sure this was the case.

He had sent the two men on a fool's errand, chasing ghosts in the wrong city. It hadn't been planned, but the sighting of Ana should have been enough to sufficiently derail William. Stephen would have been left with enough on his plate to distract his focus. Despite this, doubt continued to gnaw at Fenneck. How much had the meddlesome Burns managed to pass on to them? He was not even sure how much Burns had known. It had taken an age to locate him. It had been luck their man was on hand to find Burns alone that evening. In the time it took to remove him some information must have slipped through. Fenneck only hoped it had not travelled far. The only consolation was that, with the centre burnt out of it, Burns' web of control was already beginning to collapse. Infighting had set in within days, a struggle for power that left the Children's operations in London free to proceed with only minimal interference.

Fenneck remembered when Ana had first woken from the coma-like state she had been put in. It had not taken much to bribe the doctor into pronouncing her dead. The carefully created concoction of low dose poisons had had the desired effect. To the untrained eye there had been no doubting she was another victim of the plague's destructive force. Getting the poison to her had been the hardest task, William la Penne never seemed to leave her side. But Fenneck had chosen her, and even William's home was not impenetrable.

The choice of Ana wasn't actually essential, the work of generations of the Children could not possibly rest on one person, but the thought of William eventually discovering the role she would play gave him a great deal of satisfaction.

In the time it had taken for Fenneck to perfect the charade of nursing Ana back to health, he had begun feeding her his doctrines. Her thought processes distorted by the foul drugs; it had not been hard to convince her she had been abandoned – the life she had known nothing more than a façade hiding the reality of a world shaped by corruption. He had told her of the injustice of government, how actual policy and intelligence came second to wealth and prestige. It was the story of Fenneck's life. He held personal experience of how his politics had been brushed aside by the la Penne family name; William's father forcing him away from government for a long time. It had been the experiences of his younger life that had driven him to join the Children of Aeternitas. All this bitterness and anger he passed to Ana.

  John realised he must have been sitting at his desk for hours without making it past the first correspondence lying before him. His letter had been read through several dozen times but he was unable to recount anything beyond the first couple of lines. Reaching over to a jug left for him on the table, he poured a large glass of wine. The rich notes of plum and blackcurrant did little to calm him. Taking a long swig of the deep red liquid, he gave up on the pile of paperwork in front of him. Even the fine vintage, selected personally from a vineyard in the Loire Valley in France, could not be fully appreciated – his mind was busy elsewhere. Finishing the glass of wine, he poured another before deciding a walk in the city might do a better job of clearing his head. The hustle and bustle would provide ample distraction. The events of the next few days would certainly be more productive. He rose, made his way toward the door, before thinking better of leaving a full glass of wine on the desk – it would only spoil in the heat. Throwing his head back, he drank its entirety. Already feeling more positive, he strolled out into the city.

∞

"If there is such a threat, why did His Lordship not come personally?" King Charles II toyed with the lace cuff of his shirt, he was reluctant to believe anything the two men were telling him. Both were known to him. The big one he had seen once, he remembered his clothes, but they had never spoken and had certainly not sought a private audience. Their claim of a threat to his life was one he heard regularly, yet something in the demeanour of the two men in front of him had made him hear them out. They seemed earnest enough, but why was this information not coming from the head of his intelligence? That was, after all, His Lordship's entire purpose.

"Your Majesty, we had not had time to tell His Lordship of our discovery and this is not really a matter for a spy, rather a physician. Your life is far too pressing a matter to delay by reporting to him first." Stephen's reply held the perfect mixture of flattery and logic for Charles. "All we ask is that we are permitted to view Greatrakes from the moment he enters the building, and respectfully suggest that you do not allow him near you."

"Not allow him near me? If your information is correct, and I could catch whatever unpleasantness lingers on him, surely I should not see him at all?"

"Your Majesty, are you still not curious to see his healing power for yourself? All we suggest is that contagion is prevented by removing yourself from any miasma that may pass from his breath. The contact with the poor of London should not be passed to you."

"Very well. I shall take these…precautions. I have

no desire for Greatrakes to be required to heal me after all." The King laughed at his remark, echoed by the two men standing before him. With a wave of his hand, they were dismissed.

Out in the corridor, William turned to Stephen.

"I still think we should have told him everything. We just lied straight to the King's face."

"Come on now Will. If we told him of the real threat panic would have set in. The best way of dealing with the King is by skirting around the real issue. That way he remains blissfully ignorant, but safe. Plus, His Lordship would immediately know of our interference. This way we can keep Charles alive, and pursue the old man afterwards. There's no way Greatrakes will get near him with a pistol or knife, it must be poison. I think warning him of risk of illness was a masterstroke personally. You never know, it might even be true."

With a chuckle, both men left the royal residence. There was a lot of planning needed before their plan to save the King and flush out His Lordship could go into full effect. Besides, Stephen had information on Ana's whereabouts, passed on to him from Robert, to think over. He would have to confront her without William's knowledge. If not, the whole operation could get very ugly.

∞

The long-awaited day had finally arrived. Valentine had barely slept. His anticipation had woken him before sunrise, leaving him unable to receive the benefits of deep sleep. Not content to wait, he had set out into the city – walking the streets as the Sun rose over them. From the bank of the Thames, he watched as the first rays of yellow gold stretched over the rooftops before finding rest on the twinkling water.

The streets of London were never quiet, but with the rising of the Sun they became fully awake, gradually reaching their full volume. Early morning traders touted their wares before the heat of the day had an opportunity to spoil their produce, and prices. To supply the capital required vast quantities of food. Some arrived in carts, and by river; merchants hoping to cash in on the premium prices of a city in constant demand.

Valentine had let it all wash over him, taking in the scents and sounds. He had gained a reputation, but soon every single one of the great city's inhabitants would know his name. After this day was done, none would doubt his power.

He was met at court by two men, both tall and dressed finely – though with very different styles. The taller, barrel-chested, man was more flamboyant in his attire than any Valentine had ever seen. They had shown him through to a room in which he was told to wait. The King was not yet ready to receive Valentine. Though they had never met before, the Irishman was surprised the two men seemed to know exactly who he was. They were very inquisitive about what it was he planned to do, though mainly questioning where his effects were – did he not require any tools? This had made him laugh. He assured them all that was required was his presence. This was met with apparent confusion from the two men. Both men left the room soon afterwards, leaving Valentine to wait until Charles was ready to see him. Content to wait, he sat in one of the many comfortable looking chairs that lined the small room. None of them provided the comfort they advertised, but he didn't mind, this was the last time the King would keep him waiting for anything.

It was not long before one of the men reappeared to usher Valentine out of the door. Following through elaborately decorated corridors, he marvelled at the magnificent adornments lining the walls. Everywhere he turned was another masterpiece: wall to ceiling tapestries of past battles, portraits of previous monarchs, collections of armoury, sculptures of ancient heroes, great stuffed beasts snarling from alcoves – a level of grandeur he had never thought possible.

In comparison, the hall into which he was finally led had been sparsely decorated. What it lacked in quantity, it made up for in quality. Fine wood panelling ran the entire length and breadth of each wall, upon which hung a collection of exquisite tapestries. The ceiling displayed a central hunting fresco. Gilding picked out the teeth and claws of the savage beasts. Around the outer edges of the ceiling stood carved woodland animals so lifelike they appeared to be chasing each other around the perimeter of the room.

Gathered around the room stood those lucky enough to be selected by the King to view the prestigious event. Bodies jostled for position, wanting a clear view without encroaching on the empty space in the centre provided for Greatrakes. Opposite the entrance sat the Monarch, surrounded by the closest members of his retinue. Charles II had dressed for the occasion in a coat of rich blue, bordered by the frills of a shirt so white Valentine had never seen the like. On each hand, no less than three rings of unwieldy size made up his most elaborate pieces of decoration. He was finely dressed, and flamboyant, but not to the standard of some outfits the

Irishman had heard graced the courts. Perhaps this was the King in his practical attire? Valentine smirked at the thought as he advanced to the centre of the room.

"That's far enough sir." The voice of his guide put a halt to his stride. "The King does not need you standing on his toes in order to see you."

Valentine made a mental note to be rid of that man as soon as he was able.

"Very well." He conceded. As he was announced to the room, he presented himself with a sweeping bow, hands almost scraping the floor. He remained there until acknowledged by the King.

"Get up man, that's plenty long enough." The King's voice was not as Valentine had expected. It was not the commanding tone of a man born to power, rather a nasal whining like that of a spoilt child. He did his best not to show his shock, slowly bringing his eyes up to the monarch as he straightened up.

Charles wasted little time with small talk,

"So, you are the famous 'Stroker'. I very much look forward to viewing one of your miracles for myself. Much talk has preceded your visit today. I have been told you put on quite the show."

Show, Valentine had almost gasped at the word. I'll give you a show that won't be forgotten in a hurry, he mused.

"Indeed, Your Majesty." It took all the self-control he possessed not to speak his mind.

"Well done, well done. Let's get on with it then, shall we? No time like the present and all that." Turning to the weasel-like man standing next to him, Charles could just be heard to say, "Isn't this such fun. He even looks biblical – some sort of wild prophet, a veritable

Elijah!"

The noise of a side door opening had all eyes turn to view the procession of an unfortunate man chosen as the subject for Valentine's display of healing. The room filled with a buzzing of muttered conversations; the man paraded in front of them like a savage animal captured from an exotic land. The subject of the crowd's attention looked thoroughly miserable, not least due to the obviously painful skin condition that afflicted him. Visible on both hands and reaching up his neck onto the left side of his face, it left the skin cracked open to reveal raw flesh. Each laceration in the scabbed skin wept a clear fluid, causing the man to appear scaled.

Once the room had their fill of barely suppressed disgust, they grew silent once more. The man was brought to stand next to Valentine, his eyes cast down at the floor after feeling the humiliation of his entrance.

Amongst the crowd, William had re-joined Stephen, content that the Irishman was not armed, and distant enough from the King's person not to cause any immediate threat.

"This is disgusting." He hissed. "No one should be required to suffer such indignity for the amusement of the King and his playmates."

"He's far from perfect." Agreed the big man. "The alternatives don't bear thinking about though. That's why we're here. Try and ignore it. We have a job to do."

William grunted his acknowledgement. They could not be distracted at a time like this. Any further conversation was prevented by the interruption of a disgruntled, suave looking young man in military attire. He was the sort of dashing officer that would cause swooning at all social occasions with talk of his career, despite never having dirtied his boots in conflict.

"Will you two kindly desist from your chatter. The Stroker is beginning his routine."

Sure enough, in the centre of the room, Valentine had begun to lay hands on the sick man. Very quickly, all eyes were fully focussed on him.

Valentine wasted no time once the diseased man was next to him. He had not travelled all that way to be upstaged by the man he was meant to heal. Not wanting to engage in conversation, he had only asked if the man was ready before he began.

With hands on either side of the man's face, Valentine began slowly moving his palms over the afflicted areas.

"I command you to be healed." He announced.

Nothing was happening.

Beneath his hands he could still feel the weeping of the cracked skin. There was no heat...no healing power passing between them. In the silence of the room, he was aware of the King's whispers.

"Is it done? Did he do it?"

Still nothing happened.

The whispers were growing more regular and gaining in volume. The buzzing was returning to the room as more and more voices repeated the King's questions to their neighbours. As time continued to pass, the room's disappointment grew in volume before being silenced by Charles.

"Stroker, the Lord appears to have deemed this man unworthy of a miracle on this day. How very disappointing. I held such hope for you."

"As did I Your Majesty." Valentine reluctantly lowered his hands, his head bowed in defeat. The King had already turned his back, he was talking to those around him again. Valentine's moment had passed. He was escorted out of the room by the two men that had met him at the door.

The tall Irishman passed through the elaborate corridors in a daze. What had gone wrong? He had been chosen. He had demonstrated his power time and time again. Why had it deserted him now, when everything rested on his success?

Behind him, William and Stephen exchanged questioning looks. They were equally confused by the situation.

"Greatrakes." The man turned to look at William, eyes glazed over as if in a dream. "You failed today, but we cannot permit you to leave yet – even though no attempt was made on the King. Tell us all you know of the group Aeternitas."

"Who?... I don't understand. Attempt on the King? What do you mean? I was here to help the King, make him great again through divine power. I was to be the vessel of supernatural power that would secure the nation. At his side, I would rid him of the deceit and lies around him."

Stephen looked confused, but William could not help believing the Irishman. Greatrakes looked utterly dejected. They had made a mistake. This man had offered no threat, made no attempt to approach the King. He appeared to be just a man gone astray in his perception of his own power, humbled by God in the most public way.

William thought to soften the blow to the man's pride.

"What will you do now? The King did not judge you a fraud, just unfortunate."

"I don't know…" Valentine hadn't thought that far

ahead, "I...I had thought..."

"Perhaps you will continue your ministry to the poor? Continue the Lord's work?" William prompted.

"The... the Lord's work..."Greatrakes repeated. Like removing a blindfold, the situation became clear. That was it. The Lord, the Almighty, God. He had forgotten Him, the one who had made it all possible. He had believed the hype of London. Influence had become the goal, turning his back on his previous convictions he had begun claiming the power as his own – somehow placing himself above all others. A meeting with the King had become more important than following the will of God. He had been humbled for his hubris.

Valentine thought back to how he had spent his time in the capital, guilt building as he realised how far he had strayed. That was it, enough. He would atone for his betrayal. Ministry to the poor would be resumed with fervour. No longer for his own fame or power, but to spread the glory of the Almighty.

With a new light shining behind his eyes, he turned to the two men escorting him out of the building.

"Yes, I will continue my ministry. Thank you. The Lord has pointed the way and I must follow."

The two friends held the door open for Valentine as he re-joined the busy streets. Disappointment at his own failure had been quickly replaced by the renewed fire to serve. Pride would no longer control him. Vice was no longer his to bear. He was a vessel of God once more.

In the doorway, William turned to Stephen,

"We need to move fast. Greatrakes was a dead end. Clearly he was never the threat."

"Just another person tempted to stray from their path." Noting his friend's serious expression, Stephen added, "So the threat is still out there. We need to find His Lordship."

22

Ana's nerves had reached breaking point. She had become increasingly convinced someone was following her. She may have confronted the wrong man in the street days before, but every instinct told her she had been right to think someone was close by. It got to the point she was so sure of this that for a couple of days she hadn't left the house.

Ana was certain that in every crowd there had been prying eyes watching her. They followed her every step, down every street. Any attempt to double back on her route only compounded her insecurity. Swishing cloaks became the tell-tale sign of her pursuer's quick get-away, conversation nothing more than a cover for people to get close to her. There were probably multiple sets of eyes watching her. Each shadowy side street the post for another lookout intent on tracking her movements.

Eventually, after days of feeling trapped in her house, Ana had worked up the confidence to walk through London. The regular sights and smells on show at the wood-framed trade stalls reassured her, steeling fragile nerves. The familiarity of the hustle and bustle settled her; locals calling greetings to each other from windows or across the street, merchants attempting to attract buyers, the mundane conversations that made up the continuous background noise of a busy city. All this encouraged her that nothing was out of the ordinary.

A week on from her self-imposed confinement, Ana was back to her regular daily routine. She still had to be ready for what was to come. Her paranoia would occasionally manifest as a sudden panic. It had been triggered more than once. A trader, selling fine leather goods, had picked her out of the crowd, calling for her to inspect the new wares he had brought to the capital. Why was she being picked out from the crowd? Surely her pursuers would not fail to see her now. She had turned tail and run, jostling through the swarms of people to get away from the man who continued to call after her.

That had been two days ago. She had hidden in an inn for a while, sure that her house would be watched, before finally returning home. The promise that everything would soon change was now strong enough to help her fight the panic she felt - panic at the thought of what might happen if she were confronted by William or Stephen.

Now, the feeling of being followed was little more than a nagging doubt in the back of her mind. Yet the feeling remained. There was no actual evidence of even one person trailing her, she told herself this time and time again. If the plan was to go ahead without a hitch, she could not afford to be trapped in her own home.

Back amidst the swelling crowds, she felt reassured by the sheer mass of people. No one could possibly follow her here anyway. She followed her regular route. The route she would take on the fateful day, a day rapidly approaching. Phoenix had made clear the importance of familiarity with her surroundings, visualising the events that would take place to ensure nothing could stand in their way.

Passing through the main road on her route, she walked along the edge of the River Thames. Its banks stretched as far as the eye could see, enlarged by the low tidal waters that had receded to leave an empty-looking trough. Along the waterline lay the signs of discarded city living, flotsam and jetsam thrown, unwanted, into the thick brown waters.

Ana stopped by the river, watching as scavengers trawled the shore looking for any items of value or interest that may have been washed up. As she came to a halt, she became aware of a heavy set of footsteps that stopped not far from where she stood. No, she thought, it's just your mind playing tricks on you – just continue on your way as normal.

She proceeded along her route for a few feet, listening for the heavy footfall to resume. Sure enough, there it was. Only yards behind her. Quickening her pace, she made for the nearest side street, hoping from there that she would be able to lose whoever it was. As she sped up, so did the heavy steps. There was no doubt in her mind now, she was definitely being followed.

Her pursuer was getting close, gaining ground. Her change of speed had evidently alerted them to her awareness of their presence. Dashing out in front of a fast travelling carriage, she risked injury for the extra time she would gain, her follower prevented from resuming their chase until the traffic had passed.

Ducking into the street she had been aiming for, she pressed herself up against a doorway. The overhanging houses provided a dark cover even in the midday sun. It was typical of many of the capital's smaller streets, an easy place to hide, the warren of houses all looking the same. Fumbling inside the bodice of her dress, Ana pulled out a long thin blade, an Italian stiletto. Where most women would use bone to structure their dresses, she kept the knife. She didn't need anything to help enhance her figure, and it paid to be careful.

No one else had entered the alley. Waiting another minute just to be sure, she stepped out from the shadow. Had it been her imagination after all? If someone had been following her they would surely have entered by now. Still, no one was there.

The clatter of a pebble against wood sent Ana spinning to confront whoever had displaced it. Too late she realised her mistake. The stone had been thrown further down the path in order to capture her attention. In the split second of distraction, her adversary had entered the street behind her. The cold of a steel blade could be felt against the naked skin of her neck, its sharp edge resting just below the lobe of her left ear.

"Good day, m'lady."

The gruff voice came from over her shoulder. She recognised the voice immediately, though it was not one she had thought to hear again so soon.

"What are you doing here, you fool?" She whirled around to face the man, flicking the knife away with a fingertip. "You're not meant to be here. None of us are to be seen together."

A bear of a man faced her, so tall he almost entirely blocked the Sun from the already shaded street. This man had been responsible for the death of Burns and the retrieval of the letter that felt like years ago. He had not been with her in Oxford for long, only there to dispose of the troublesome criminal at her behest. His time had been required elsewhere, there were other aspects of the Children's plan that required his attention.

"Others have been worrying about you - sent me just to keep an eye out. You know they're very conscientious like that." The large man sneered, rolling his shoulders and making them crack menacingly. Ana felt a shiver run down her spine at the noise. This man, Thomas Russell, had always disgusted her. He was not truly one of the Children, she was not even sure if he knew they existed, merely a rogue agent who had proved a valuable asset in removing unwanted obstacles. His talents were well paid for, but she didn't trust his loyalty to anything other than his purse.

"Well, you can assure them that everything is still going to plan. Though I would appreciate not having to watch my back for people that they send after me. As I'm sure he will appreciate, my time could be much better spent ensuring the success of the plan." She managed to keep her voice in control, preventing the anger at Phoenix's mistrust from erupting from her. "Now, if you will please leave me alone, I shall resume my day."

Russell whistled a long, discordant note, mocking her tart reply.

"Calm down, m'lady. As you wish. I'd pay a little more attention if I were you though, you're getting sloppy." With a final scornful bow, he turned on his heels and lumbered back out of the alley.

Alone once more, Ana leant back against a nearby building. In an attempt to steady her nerves, she took long, deep breaths; feeling her rapid heartbeats slow in response.

So, Phoenix did not trust her as completely as she

had thought. That was hardly surprising, he could not afford anything getting in the way of the plan so late in the process. Her failure to entirely release the feelings she had for William must have sent alarm bells ringing in Phoenix's head. Try as she might, her emotions still had a strong hold over her.

The rest of the plan must be progressing smoothly, she mused, the appearance of Russell was a testament to that. Phoenix would not have spared him if there was any doubt of the Children's success.

After taking a moment to compose herself, Ana made to move back out onto the main road following the riverbank. Catching herself just in time, she realised the dagger she had pulled from her dress was still clutched tightly in her hand. Disappointed with herself at the near blunder, she shook her head and tucked it back into its hiding place. It was not the most conspicuous weapon once drawn, but would definitely have turned a few heads – not many well dressed women brandished blades in broad daylight. Content that she was once more presentable, she stepped out of the side street and continued along her route.

∞

Robert was growing increasingly weary of the task given to him. His daily routine for weeks had been to follow Ana through London, always the same route through the same streets. Each day she travelled from her house to the city, once there proceeding to walk without any obvious purpose. He barely had to think about directions anymore; his feet carried him across the worn paths as if he was born to them.

Not so long ago he had arrived as a stranger in the city, unfamiliar with everything. He was now able to recognise faces, joke with friendly merchants at their stalls, and could disappear into the crowds in seconds. Traversing the same route everyday had made his task easy. He had thought people might question why he always passed the same way, at the same time, day in day out. It didn't take long to realise there was nothing unusual about his routine. People are creatures of routine. Crowds passed the same way each day, held the same conversations, bought the same produce from the same market stalls. There was nothing to mark him out as unusual.

His regimen had the added benefit of providing familiarity. Robert knew which side streets would be empty if he needed to hastily disappear. He knew which stalls at the side of the road provided the best cover from which to watch Ana's progress. The merchants were friendly with him now, and would happily launch into conversation when he needed to appear as if he had been bartering all morning. All this he was able to do without thinking.

The ability to blend in and remain hidden had quickly become second nature. Yet it bored him. He questioned what it was that Stephen expected him to look for, what was it that he was so intent on finding? Following her had revealed no answers to the many questions the young man now had. Why were William and Stephen not confronting Ana themselves? There was a supposedly dead woman roaming the streets of London, surely that was worthy of their attention.

He had traced her steps all the way from Oxford. The other two men joined him in the city and yet stayed away. They still hadn't even met up with him, still relying on letters to pass any news. He had not seen either of them since leaving home. Without further information, he had no aim. Left just to follow and report unusual activity. The only thing unusual about Ana's activity was that it never changed. There had been a couple of days when she hadn't left the house, but whenever she did it was always the same. If she really was involved in something untoward, surely there would be more to her everyday life than just wandering. He was beginning to think that Ana might just want to be alone. Perhaps she had kept away from William for a reason unknown to Stephen. But he had known Ana before, there was no way she would have chosen to stay away from William; they had been so happy. So the tedious game of cat and mouse continued.

Robert looked up from the stall at which he had been inspecting the fresh selection of shellfish, collected earlier that morning.

"You alright matey? Those crabs seem to have put you in rather a quandary." The stocky fishmonger brought Robert's attention back from the daydreams. "I can assure you, they're the highest quality."

"I don't doubt it, Simon, they always are." He replied. Simon was one of the regular stops on his tour of the city.

"Ah, Robert. Didn't recognise you with that pensive look on you. What can I do for you today?"

Robert looked over to where Ana had last been standing. There was no sign of her. Quickly scanning the area he realised he had lost her for the first time. How long had his thoughts diverted him?

"Sorry Simon, just realised I need to get away. Lost

track of time."

The fishmonger thought nothing of it, watching as the young man rushed off. That boy was always distracted by something. Instead, he redirected his sales pitch at another potential customer inspecting the day's catch.

Where could she have gone? He couldn't have been distracted that long. Continuing to scan faces for any sign of her blonde hair, she should have been easy to spot, he jumped up onto a mounting block outside a large inn. The increased height gave him a much better view of the street, but still no sign of Ana.

Thinking perhaps she had spent longer at a stall than usual, he swept his gaze over the wooden benches lining the sides of the road. She was not there. This was crazy, where could she be?

Cursing his luck that this had to be the one day he was not on his guard, he stepped down from his elevated spot. All he could do was carry along the route and hope she was further along.

Resigned to the fact that he may not find her again, something caught his eye. There, further up the road, was the unmistakable bright gold of Ana's hair, bleached further in the strong rays of the summer Sun. She must have been obscured by the awnings at one of the stalls. Sighing with relief, Robert re-joined the melee of the street. Worming his way through, he closed the gap on his quarry.

∞

William had been watching the entrance to His

Lordship's building all afternoon. He had only seen him come to the door once. The old man had talked briefly with someone William had not recognised before returning inside. Next to William, the space Stephen had been occupying that morning lay empty. The two of them had decided to work in shifts. Though William had remained with his friend all morning, Stephen had taken William's watch as the opportunity to follow up another lead. When asked about it the large man had muttered something about Robert following the woman from Oxford, but had left in a hurry before he could be pressed for more information. Not wishing to sour his mood by dwelling on it for too long, William had left his friend to it. He knew it was a reasonable line of enquiry.

They had stationed themselves outside the building three days before, waiting for a chance to confront their employer away from the centre of his influence and power. For three days now they had been disappointed. There had been signs of activity, His Lordship had even left the building a few times, but on no occasion had he wandered more than a few hundred yards. Both men had begun to question whether he even owned a separate residence.

There was no questioning His Lordship's involvement in whatever was being planned, the letters left no doubt in William's mind. But they could not simply kill him. Without confronting the man, they remained ignorant of any plans that may already have been set in motion. If they were to kill him without interrogation it was back to square one, unless Stephen's vague need to talk to Robert yielded any results.

William could understand his friend's reluctance to give him any more information about the woman and, truth be told, he hadn't wanted to talk about it either. Their last encounter had shaken him badly. However, if it really was a potential lead, the information needed to be shared. His emotions would just have to be put aside. In his head he made a note to remind Stephen of this when he returned.

Rehearsing the upcoming conversation in his head, William almost failed to acknowledge His Lordship's exit from his building. The old man had turned down onto the main street toward the river before William could be up on his feet and in pursuit.

It was not difficult to keep pace. The older man was travelling surprisingly slowly, even for a man whose hair had long ago turned from granite to snowy white. William made sure to trail at a good distance, aware that His Lordship probably had his own men watching for security.

At no point did the Head of Intelligence look round for a pursuer. He did not attempt to double back or change direction quickly to avoid being followed. He did none of the things William expected of him; adding to his assumption that there must be others looking out for him. In turn, William was sure to keep an eye on those around him, making certain he was not providing an easy target for one of the old man's cronies.

From Westminster they followed the curve of the river, remaining on the more heavily populated north bank. Even late as dusk approached, the river traffic continued in full force. Small fishing vessels were heading out to ensure they were ready to catch the morning tide, they jostled for priority over the transport ferries taking people between the two sides of the capital, amongst them large trading craft displayed their superior size – tearing through the busy waters with little regard as the smaller boats scattered before them.

Along the banks, washerwomen were still finishing up the day's work. The open air by the river provided better conditions to dry out the many sheets and items of clothing in their charge. The unseasonably warm September weather worked to their advantage, quicker drying allowed them to cash in on any extra work they might be able to get their hands on. Even so late in the day, a few could be seen hanging newly washed items out on long lines they'd strung from any available fixed point.

His Lordship was maintaining the slow, steady plod of a man unconcerned by the length of his journey. William still kept his distance, content to indulge passers-by in small talk in the knowledge he would not lose sight of him any time soon. Countless cries of "Good day sir" had been followed by offers of hot pudding pies, sausages, drinking glasses, spices and herbs. Some even carried small collections of metalwork fresh from the nearby forges.

After a good few hours of walking, His Lordship increased his pace, making his way onto a street running parallel to the river. There he ducked through the doorway of a public house. The sign above the door read 'The Olde Wine Shades'. It stood just off the river, in close proximity to London Bridge; one of the jewels of the capital, a landmark on the lips of all that visited the city.

Along the bridge's many arches stood three-story buildings, some even reaching four, so tall the rooms towered over the largest of the river vessels. It was under the bridge that traitors would be taken to the Tower of London, passing the grisly heads of past criminals displayed on spikes to remind potential insurgents of their fate.

William did not immediately follow after His Lordship, thinking it best to find out a little about the establishment first. He waited for the first person to leave the pub, calling over to them,

"Pardon me, good sir." The man looked up, startled at being called to so soon after exiting the drinking hole. "I'm not from around here. And I happened to wander across this place, could you tell me a little about it? How is their wine?"

"You looking to sell or drink? Most of what they sell is cheap, basically water." Looking over the nearby crowds, he added with a wink. "Ask for the special vintage and you get the good stuff."

The man had evidently taken William for a trader, he decided to play along.

"Ah, so they already have a special arrangement with someone?"

"Ha! You know the kind!" The man laughed, hefting what looked like a good sized bag full of books onto his shoulder.

"My thanks." William nodded appreciatively.

"Pleasure." The man set off, making his way north, presumably toward St. Paul's.

So, mused William, this pub was a front for smugglers. And His Lordship was inside. He could really do with Stephen's help with this one. Still, no point wishing for things that weren't about to happen, he would have to cope alone.

Adopting the casual swagger of a well-off merchant, he walked over to the pub's entrance. Taking a second to ready himself, he pushed open the door and

E. J. MYATT

stepped inside.

23

After waiting for days outside His Lordship's building in Westminster with no results, Stephen had left William to watch for their employer alone. He'd promised not to be long and finally gone in search of Robert. He was feeling more than a little guilty for leaving the young man to follow Ana day after day, whilst he had remained caught up with Greatrakes. The subsequent realisation that they would get nowhere without confronting the head of the King's intelligence had left no room for any thought of Robert's task. But, now that he and William had once again hit an impasse, thoughts of Ana's role in everything returned to him.

It was time Ana was confronted. She was somehow involved in the whole affair. It was in her house that he had found the two tell-tale letters from His Lordship after all. And there was the ever-present question of how she was even alive.

Despite his reasons for wanting to talk to Robert, the large man knew his departure from William's side was far from ideal. Desperate though he was not to let his friend slip into another state of melancholy, Stephen had still needed to provide adequate reason for leaving their post. In the end, he had settled for a vague, mumbled version of the truth. He had sped through his explanation, watching his friend's unmoving expression. Perhaps what he had said had not fully registered, but it did not appear to have concerned William in the slightest. Not waiting to find out, he had left before further details were asked for. William was more than capable of watching the building by himself. Besides, Stephen had stood his watch all morning – it was William's turn now. But what if His Lordship did finally appear? The devil on his shoulder whispered, "you've left him all alone when he needs you – just like you did when Ana died, left him, only able to stand the misery of the man by contacting him through letters." Stephen shook the thoughts from his head; ridiculous. Not true at all. Were they?

No, of course not. He had done what was best – allowed necessary space and time to heal. Anyhow, it was not the time for a crisis of conscience. William was good at this kind of work. He had faced more dangerous men than the old man and come out alive. Stephen would probably be back by then anyway.

Stephen had so far only managed to communicate with Robert through a series of letters. The use of his trusted network of street urchins was slow, but far more secure than any other means. By Robert's accounts, Ana had not done much since arriving in London. One trip to Westminster had been followed by weeks of traipsing the same route around the streets of the capital. There was nothing particularly worrying about her actions, though the visit to Westminster compounded Stephen's belief that she was closely linked to His Lordship. As far as he was concerned, it was a sure-fire sign of her guilt.

"Stephen, good to see you...Are you alright?"

Robert's enthusiasm drained as he saw the tall man's grave expression. The tempest of thoughts must have shown on Stephen's face as he reached their agreed meeting place.

"Hmmm?... Oh, yes. Sorry, thoughts were elsewhere. Everything is as well as could be hoped for."

"And William is..."

"Oh gosh yes, he's fine." He quickly replied, causing Robert to let out a sigh of relief. Stephen realised his expression must have been truly awful for the younger man to have assumed William was the issue. "He has eyes on another target at the moment."

"I'm glad to hear it. So, what's the plan? Are we going to confront her?" Robert had followed Ana for weeks and was not about to let his opportunity for action slip away.

Stephen looked at him with concern etched across his tired features.

"We aren't going to do anything. I need to do this alone. You have performed admirably up to this point Robert, but now it gets serious."

"So, I'm just meant to go home? After following her for weeks without knowing why? You just expect me to leave?"

"Look, Robert," Stephen put a hand on the young man's shoulder, "All will be revealed in due course, but so much is uncertain at the moment that I can't let you wander in blind. Too much is at stake."

The flash of anger turned to disappointed acceptance. Shoulders slumped, Robert stared down at his feet, kicking loose pebbles with flicks of his toes. Stephen continued,

"Look, you obviously have a talent for this. I'm very

confident that there will be plenty of opportunity for you in the future. But right now, in these circumstances... You're still young and whatever is going on here requires more experience. Understand?"

Robert nodded, not wanting to make eye contact. Stephen knew this would be a great disappointment for the younger man. He did not want to discourage him entirely. The boy had done well, it was only fair that he told him as much. But confronting Ana and His Lordship would be dangerous, there would be no pleading youthful ignorance, and he could not bear the thought of the return trip to Oxford without Samuel and Hannah's son. They would be beyond devastated.

The devil returned to whisper in Stephen's ears, barraging his conscience with guilt – another friend let down by his actions, and all within hours of each other.

No, he reassured himself, I did the right thing. Who knows how Ana will react to their discovery she was still alive. She had run from Oxford, but when cornered it would be a different story.

"What will you do? Stop her in the street?" Robert asked. Stephen shook his head.

"I think it best to keep this out of the public eye. And fewer people to get injured if it kicks off."

"You really think she could be dangerous?"

"Yes. Well, she could be. For her to be mixed up in everything that's happening suggests she has the potential to be very dangerous, or at least be with dangerous people."

"What do I do now then? Go home?"

"Here." Stephen passed him a piece of paper. "This is the address of my house out towards Westminster. Go to the house and tell them you are waiting for William and me. If you reach the marshes at Five Fields, you've gone too far. There shouldn't be any trouble. We will join you in the next couple of days. If there is no sign after four days, alert the rest of the house to where I have been. Of course, it shouldn't come to that."

"Good luck. I will see you soon." Robert took the paper handed to him.

"Yes, you will." Stephen smiled at him, turned his back, and began the short journey to the house Robert had identified as Ana's.

The young man watched as he walked away. Slipping the note he had just been handed into a jacket pocket, he stepped behind the cover of a slow-moving cart that was making its way in the same direction as Stephen.

He'd spent too long following not to be there when something actually happened, he had made his decision even as the older man explained the dangers he might face. Besides, if it really was going to be that dangerous, Stephen could need someone to back him up.

Robert continued to follow the cart along the street. The skills he had acquired over weeks of following Ana might finally result in some excitement. And to remain hidden whilst trailing Stephen would require everything he had learnt.

∞

Stephen reckoned he was almost at the house before he had any idea he was being followed. That boy was better than he thought, he smiled to himself, glad that it was no one more sinister. He was actually quite relieved at the knowledge someone was with him. As long as Robert remained hidden he couldn't get himself into too much trouble. Hopefully, their previous talk would be enough to prevent any foolhardy intervention from the young man. It was the knowledge of a friendly presence nearby that was reassuring, even if it proved to be little help if things started to get messy.

Pushing all thoughts of his pursuer from his mind, Stephen approached the house Robert had identified as Ana's. Sidling along the wall of the houses on the same small street, he grasped the handle of a small pistol he had tucked into his coat. It would not be ideal to go in all guns blazing, but equally foolish not to be prepared. Better safe than sorry. The small firearm had got him out of a few sticky situations in the past.

The layout of the street meant there would be no cover as Stephen approached the house. Although he could make the majority of the distance concealed by various buttresses and walls, there would be at least fifty or sixty yards that held no cover at all. As long as no one was watching for him, it shouldn't cause too much of an issue, he was pretty quick on his feet for a tall man; but it was still a big risk. Out in the open, he would make an easy target for even a half-decent shot.

Though still expensive, firearms were increasingly common – the war had ensured that many now had ample opportunity to get their hands on old weapons. Stephen was sure Ana would have some form of protection. Even a rusty old musket would be the end of him, and he was well aware that even poorer households were investing in more reliable munitions. If Ana was working with His Lordship, she would surely have access to the best weapons available.

All it would take was a glance out of the window

at the wrong moment and Ana would get a clear view of him running towards the house. Unfortunately, there didn't appear to be a better option. He would just have to be lucky.

Watching from the shadows of the next building, Stephen identified a window that had caught on the latch as his best chance of an entrance. There would be no way the door would be open. He had not caught sight of Ana since his arrival, but her movement was clear by the candlelight illuminating the few windows that looked out from the front of the property. The window that was his target entrance lay in an area of the house that had remained in darkness for well over twenty minutes. He hoped that meant it was unoccupied.

Stephen reached inside his coat, once more feeling the settling presence of the hidden pistol. Taking a few moments to load, he took a deep breath and readied himself to charge the building. He took the first step, thought better of it, and returned to the shadow. A sudden rush of movement could actually draw more attention than just walking nonchalantly over, not to mention the noise he might make running. Steeling himself against the growing tension in the pit of his stomach, he set off on the long walk to the house.

Every fibre of Stephen's being was telling him to run. He was too exposed. Surely she would spot him, and then it would be a clear shot from a window to end him. He had to assume she was dangerous, it could be his downfall if he allowed her past to cloud his judgement. Ignoring the surge of his heartbeat, he took each stride as if he were on nothing more than a pleasant evening stroll. With every step he was a little closer to his goal, the window still lay ajar. The light from Ana's candle remained on the far side of the house. And still no shot came.

With a sudden scurry, Stephen completed what felt like the longest walk of his life. Now, hidden by the shadows, he stood with his back against the cool stone wall. Able to breathe freely, he took stock of the situation.

It had not taken long to identify the window as the best means of undetected access. What had escaped him was how he would actually reach the window. Though slightly open, it was on the first floor; out of reach, even with his height. Looking around for something that might act as a ladder, or even a step, Stephen could only see a large trough that would act as a water butt. With the heat they had been experiencing, he was almost certain it would be empty. Even so, it looked heavy. He could hardly start dragging cumbersome objects around the street without someone noticing. No, there had to be another way up.

He raised a hand above his head in an attempt to estimate how much extra height he would require to reach the window ledge. It was not a tall building, even so, he was a good five or six feet short. With barely contained frustration he stared up at the window. There had to be a way, there was no way this was going to defeat him.

The click of a booted heel on the paved street beside him almost caught him off guard. With a deft flick of the wrist, a knife came shooting from a hidden sheath in his sleeve. The point of the blade came neatly to rest at the throat of the person creeping up next to him.

"You can stand on my shoulders," whispered Robert, apparently nonplussed by the weapon a breath away from slicing open his throat.

"Jesus wept boy," growled Stephen, "What in all that is holy do you think you are doing? You're lucky I need to stay quiet or it would've been the pistol."

"Well you can't get up there alone can you?"

"I sent you back to my house for a reason. Go. Now."

"I'm here now. I might as well help."

"Oh God. I should have sent you back when I saw you a few streets back." Stephen slipped the blade back into the hidden section of his sleeve.

"You saw?" Robert's face dropped in disappointment. He recovered quickly. "But you didn't send me back, so you must know you need my help. I won't go inside, but you can't reach that window without me. Let me help."

Stephen was scanning the front of the building for something that might act as a frame to climb up. A few vine-like creeping plants could be seen, nothing that would take his weight. He was not even sure if Robert would manage. Despite his best efforts to find an alternative, Stephen had to admit the young man was right, there was no other way.

"Alright." He muttered. "But on no account are you to enter this building. No matter what you hear. Do you understand?"

"Of course." Robert stood with his back to the wall, knees bent to act as a step.

"This is not a good idea." Stephen placed his foot on the braced knee.

"But you don't have a better one." The young man smiled, his evident enjoyment clear.

Stephen kicked up onto the young man's knees, scrabbling for a handhold on the wall. With a tentative step, he moved up onto Robert's shoulders. Reaching up above his head, he grasped at the window sill. Still too short.

"I can't reach." He hissed. He was flailing uselessly at the space inches below the edge of the window. A jolt came from below, the tall man was sure he was about to fall. His weight was too much for the young man, Robert wouldn't be able to hold him much longer.

Stephen tried to step down, not wanting to fall and have any noise from the crash alert Ana to their presence. He found himself unable to move his feet. Robert had gripped both ankles, securing him in place on his shoulders. In an attempt to stabilise, Stephen reached up once more for a handhold. To his surprise, he found he could now feel the edge of the sill. Robert's strength had not failed at all. He was actually pushing Stephen up, straightening his legs to increase the reach of the man on his shoulders. All that back-breaking work helping his father in the fields had made him deceptively strong.

Stephen could now comfortably loop his forearms over the edge of the window. He pushed the window open further to ensure he would fit through, noticing that the latch had worn smooth so that it did not shut properly. He reached through into the room and placed the pistol on the floor to allow better use of his hands, before drawing himself up into the open space. From below, Robert was able to guide the large man's flailing legs before he disappeared into the house.

Both men paused, unsure whether their noise had alerted anyone. Nothing. Stephen stuck his head back out of the window to show he was uninjured. He shooed the younger man off with a wave of his hands, watching as he disappeared into the shadow of the house. *I'll thank him later*, he mused, *but right now I have more pressing* concerns.

Stephen made a hasty assessment of the room he found himself in. Unlit, the dark made it hard to tell the room's purpose. It appeared to be a storage room of sorts, full of nothing of importance; items strewn and stacked in messy piles. It was not the sort of room that was regularly visited. The window's broken latch must have worked open in the wind without Ana realising. Counting himself lucky not to have upset any of the precarious towers, Stephen moved for the door.

Checking the pistol was still primed, he made his way to where he guessed the light had been coming from. Treading as delicately as possible, he kept to the edges of the floorboards in the hope that they might creak less. Slowly, he crept down the stairs.

Downstairs the floor was flagstones, much less likely to give his location away. He trod lightly nonetheless. The lower floor of the house was something of a warren. No order to any of the rooms and all of random sizing. The first two he entered were empty. Bathed in darkness, they still held the heat of recent occupation.

A third doorway opened into a thin passage. Two further doors were visible in the gloom. Straight ahead the door frame showed the telltale glow of escaping candlelight. With a steely breath, Stephen moved toward it.

The latch on the door jumped up, opened from the inside. A female figure silhouetted in the doorway. Stephen held the pistol pointing directly at her head.

"Good evening Ana."

24

The Olde Wine Shades was crammed full of people. It was even more crowded than the heaving streets of the capital at their peak. Almost all of the thick wooden tables scattered around the room were laden with empty tankards, discarded by the many patrons packed inside. Most people had given up on finding seats, opting instead to jostle for position in a corner or around any surface that might act as a tabletop. The public house's staff were evidently struggling with the vast numbers of people. The high concentration of bodies around tables made it close to impossible to collect empty vessels.

William noted one barmaid expertly dodging her way around the room, unperturbed by the raucous behaviour around her. A young boy attempting to follow her was not having so much luck. The teetering tower of empties piled high in his arms swayed precariously every time he moved. It was not long before they finally came crashing to the floor when he misjudged his sidestep around one of the more inebriated inhabitants of the room. William could not hold back a bark of laughter, adding to the loud roar of amusement following the unfortunate boy's gaffe. Some of the men around the incident took pity, good-naturedly helping collect up the spilt tankards before they could roll further across the stone floor. With a face flushed the colour of beetroot, the boy greedily accepted the help before scampering back to the safety of the bar.

William had been scanning the room for any sign of His Lordship. The older man had entered only minutes before him, he couldn't have gone far. However, William had not counted on the large numbers within the pub acting so effectively as cover.

As the barmaid began another lap of the room, William managed to catch her eye, beckoning her over.

"I don't suppose you could help me? I was meant to be meeting someone here."

"Sorry Sir, we can't spare any tables at the moment. As you can see, we're rather busy." Her tone was respectful yet efficient. Message delivered, she began to turn away.

"I don't require a table." William pulled her back into conversation. "I just need to know if you've seen him."

"There are a lot of people here, I don't know all of them. Who is he though? A regular?"

"He came in just before me I think, but I can't see him anywhere."

"Does he have a name? As I said, we're rather busy – I haven't been able to watch the door."

William's vague requests were obviously making her increasingly irritable, wasting time, he was the last thing she needed on such a busy evening.

"Uh…he's an older man, average sort of height, bright blue eyes. He doesn't move like an old man though…"

"Are you sure you know this person without a name?" Suspicion showed on her face. William had no option but to go for it and hope that His Lordship was known to these people.

"Obviously he has a name – I just...don't know which one he uses here." He gave the girl a knowing look.

"Ah, I see. Say no more. He's in the back room, I'll show you the way." She winked at him in acknowledgement.

"Thank you."

Inside William's nerves were fluttering with anticipation. There was no way on earth that should have worked, he had half expected to be thrown out onto the street. The staff must all have been privy to the workings of the smugglers. He just hoped His Lordship didn't have company.

Weaving between the sea of people, he followed the barmaid. He had yet to see her put a foot wrong, keeping up proved to be a difficult task. As they approached the bar he spotted a door to the left which did not link to the communal area. His guide nodded him in that direction.

"There. Go through, follow the passage, you want the second door on the right."

He thanked her, turning away from the mass of people by the bar. Before he had got far she called to him, "Oh, and for future reference, he generally goes by the name John Fenneck here." She smiled warmly at him before diving back into the throng of the busy room.

"Fenneck," muttered William, "Fenneck... Fenneck's ... Phoenix...How apt." So he had been 'hiding in plain sight' after all, just as Burns' note had said. He inhaled deeply through his nose before exhaling sharply, puffing air into his cheeks. "Here goes nothing." He whispered, pushing through the door leading into the passageway.

There were three doors on either side of what turned out to be a long corridor. It was not clear where each lead, the building had not looked so large from the outside. Making his way to the second door, William patted down the pockets of his coat for the small pistol Stephen had left him. He was not a big fan of guns, there was nothing skilful or elegant about them, but at that moment he found it reassuring to know he was well-armed. Who knew what was on the other side of the door. A sword might be more graceful, but that wouldn't be much comfort if he was already dead.

Placing the barrel of the small gun against the door, he braced his left arm so that it was ready to swing the door inwards in one movement. Once inside, the pistol would be ready if required.

Knowing the longer he waited, the more reasons he would come up with to postpone entering, William made his move. Shoving the door open, he burst into the small space with his pistol searching for potential targets.

He was not prepared for what faced him. The room was empty besides a small oak desk sitting slightly off centre. Behind it sat His Lordship, head down reading a small selection of letters sitting in front of him. No one else was present. The old man did not even deign to look up at the sudden imposition.

"Good evening William, please do take a seat. My man said you'd followed the whole way from Westminster – that's a long walk."

Unsure how to respond, William remained standing, mute. How did the old man even know it was him? The many implications of this revelation flashed into his mind. Was this a trap? The man opposite him seemed alarmingly unconcerned by the pistol pointing directly at him. He had not even bothered to look up in acknowledgement of William's presence.

"I'll remain standing if that's all the same to you." He finally replied.

"Still here?" The old man mocked, "Suit yourself." Still he continued to read the letters at his desk. Why was he not talking? The shock of His Lordship's calm was increasingly turning to anger – how dare he just sit there in silence as if nothing was happening.

"The game is up your Lordship, or John, or whatever your real name might be. I know." Tired of waiting, William allowed his anger and frustration to boil over, something needed to happen.

"You know?" His Lordship said gently, finally looking up from the letters at his desk. "What do you know William? I must say, I've been disappointed not to have heard from you, it's been many weeks now. And though it's been rather amusing hearing about your escapades with that Irishman at court, you should have reported.

So what do you think you know? You heard a name I use from time to time, but what does that mean? As I'm sure you're aware, in our line of business it pays to be careful. It amounts to nothing. You know nothing. I'll wager you don't even know where that giant friend of yours is."

"Stephen is watching the door. He's just outside." William attempted an unconvincing lie.

"Call him in then." The old man smiled. "He's not outside William. Where is he? Come on…you don't know do you?"

William studied the older man's face. His bluff had been seen through instantly, but why was his adversary focussed on Stephen? Was this just stalling for time? Then it dawned on him, His Lordship didn't know where Stephen was either. He was worried because he didn't know. The old man looked calm, but Stephen could be anywhere, disrupting the plan without His Lordship able to stop him.

"He's gone to find the woman you sent to Oxford. I told you it was over."

"The woman?" A brief look of unmasked fear flashed across the old man's face before a grim smile took its place, "Oh but it wasn't just any woman, was it William? Come now, I would expect you of all people to recognise your own wife."

William froze, the barrel of the gun dipping for a split second. It was all His Lordship required. With a strength that surpassed his years, the older man flipped the table up at the man standing before him. It caught William's hand as he rushed to bring the pistol back into position. On impact the gun went off, wasting the only shot he had, as he fell back under the weight of the thick wooden desk.

"The city will burn," the old man shouted as he swept out of the room, "and it will set the world free."

William was quickly back on his feet. The table had cut into his forearms as he instinctively raised them to protect himself, but it was nothing serious. As he ran back out of the small room and into the corridor, he felt a warm trickle of liquid falling behind his left ear. Reaching up to inspect his head he found his hands slick with blood. The fall under the heavy desk must have opened up a wound as his head struck the floor. He had no recollection of hitting the ground that hard. There was nothing he could do about it without assistance, and there was no time to seek help.

Following the fading sound of fleeing footsteps, William made his way along the corridor. Further up, a door slammed. His Lordship must have gone that way. He approached cautiously. The old man had already proven to be faster and stronger than he looked.

His Lordship was not inside. The room was stacked to the rafters with beer barrels. Presumably it operated as an overflow room for the cellar. One barrel lay on its side on the floor, clearly it had been recently disturbed; still rolling slightly from side to side.

Approaching it, William noted the ring of dust on the floor where the barrel must have been standing before it had been moved. Below the dust, the wooden floorboards had been cut into an odd shape. They were also pointing in the wrong direction, the planks running against the pattern of the rest of the floor. A trapdoor. His Lordship must have put the hatch back on the wrong way in his haste to flee the building.

Wasting no more time, William scrabbled around the edges of the trapdoor for a finger hold. Without much difficulty, he succeeded in wrenching the door away. To his surprise, there was no ladder, only a barrel chute.

"No turning back now." He said, pulling a small knife from a leather sheath on his belt. Not wanting to lose control of his descent, he sat down on the edge of the opening in the floor and shuffled down the ramp. Bracing his arms against the walls, he was able to prevent his slide from gaining too much momentum.

The chute was long, about ten feet, but it didn't take him much time to navigate his way down. At the bottom, he found himself on a small platform sticking out into the Thames. It was well hidden. William didn't think the smuggler's route would be visible from the water, or the bank, due to the coverage of the bridge above. Even if the pontoon were noticed, it appeared no different from the many that lined the riverbank. Nobody would suspect the smuggler's entrance to the busy public house above.

As he landed on the jetty, William searched frantically for his quarry. No boats lay moored nearby. All around, the banks of the river were empty. He didn't think the old man would have been able to sail alone anyway, and highly doubted whether anyone would be able to climb the steep incline. His Lordship had to be somewhere along the jetty. Tightening his grip on the thin knife, William made his way slowly along the floating platform.

∞

John Fenneck was quickly running out of ideas. He had been well aware William had followed him for much of the afternoon, but the revelation that Stephen had pursued Ana had been a shock. He had no inkling that she might also be under their scrutiny. Still, William's reaction to hearing her name had been just as he expected. The two friends may have followed her, but they clearly still had no idea what was being planned. And he wasn't about to reveal anything that could jeopardise the plan.

Even if both he and Ana were stopped, the Children would strike back. There was some consolation in the knowledge. Even so, he would do everything in his power not to die today. The plan would suffer if Ana was prevented from playing her part. He supposed she should be warned, but that would have to wait. The current issue was the stalking figure of William La Penne moving down the pontoon towards him.

John was sure the younger man would catch him in a straight footrace. Simply running had always been out of the question. The climb up the bank was too steep, and there were no boats nearby. He had been relying on there being at least a small vessel to escape in, but the chase had been closer than he expected. He doubted he would have had time to untie and cast off anyway. Which left him with only one option.

William had to die. He had given Ana his word that William would be kept from harm, but there wasn't another way out of his current situation. Besides, he wanted to do it. William had always been good at his job, but John disliked him immensely. Rich, intelligent, successful, and always so humble about it. But really John knew that William must think he was better than everyone else and, of course, he was his father's son. He hated him. Yes, William's death would do nicely. He watched silently as the younger man progressed along the pontoon, closer to the hidden threat.

∞

A surge of water hit the pontoon as the old man threw himself at William, knife flashing across the back of his legs. He had lain in wait in the water; hidden, as his prey walked by, before he struck.

William was incredibly lucky. Hampered by the increased weight of his wet clothes, His Lordship had misjudged the attack. Unable to connect properly, the knife had caused nothing more than a thin red line behind William's knees. Any deeper and it would have crippled him.

Even so, the blow sent him staggering forward. Shock more than impact forcing him onto his knees. Behind him, the old man fought to regain a position on the jetty. Before William had a chance to move, a weight hit him square in the back as His Lordship bundled into him. He felt thin fingers on the back of his head, forcing his neck over the edge of the jetty. With all his strength he fought to keep his face out of the water, scrabbling behind him in an attempt to gain a hold of his assailant. As the strength in his neck failed, he felt the cold rush as his nostrils flooded with dirty river water. With the breath already knocked from him, he had little time before his lungs would give out. His vision was already beginning to dance with black specks.

A silent scream left William's lips as the last of his air ran out, his body going limp. Above him he felt the old man relax his hold, thinking the tussle was over. He had run out of air, but banked on one last attempt at freedom. With one last effort, William threw his body upwards. As His Lordship's weight shifted above him, he knew he held the upper hand. Raising his face from the water, he sucked deep breaths into his lungs, lashing out with his legs in a vicious attack that sent the older man reeling across the pontoon.

Both men recovered slowly, hearts beating out of their chests. Pain dulled by the thrill of the fight, the older man struck fast. If he was to win the conflict it would need to be done quickly, before William could regain his composure. There was no way he could sustain his strength in a long struggle, the younger man would surely overpower him eventually.

William felt a blade slice across his ribs as he spun to the left, unable to avoid the direct strike. In reply he lashed out at the offending limb, scoring a deep gash to his assailant's forearm. Keen to press home the advantage of being inside William's defence, His Lordship switched his grip on the dagger, bringing the blade stabbing up under the young man's rib cage.

William grunted in pain as the thin blade punctured up under his midriff. The old man had him, there was nothing he could do about it now. But His Lordship had also sacrificed his own safety to gain the hit. His defence was entirely open.

Ignoring the knife still protruding from his stomach, William mounted his attack. Reaching for the old man's head, he gripped the back of his neck by the greying hair. With his right hand, he struck. Forcing the panicking man onto the blade in his hand, he thrust the small knife into the soft flesh beneath the chin.

His Lordship's eyes sprung open in surprise as the tip of the knife burst through the thin layers of skin at his throat. His hands flailed uselessly at William's face, but the younger man's grip was relentless. As his strength dissipated His Lordship's body fell to the floor, blood pumping deep red over the wooden planks. As the body dropped to the floor, William stumbled onto his hands and knees. He still held the knife in his hands. Next to him the old man's throat foamed and gurgled, his figure thrashing as the blood continued to escape.

William reached down to the wound at his side, feeling the damp pool spread across his clothes. The knife remained in place, holding in much of the blood, but it was already too late. With a tremble, his legs collapsed beneath him, leaving him lying facing the darkening skies above. Sharp pain wracked his body every time he breathed. His vision blurred, swimming above him before the darkness of unconsciousness descended.

25

How are you alive?

Tell me what has been planned.

Why are you doing this?

The walk to Ana's house had provided Stephen with ample opportunity to rehearse his confrontation with William's wife. In reality, the planned speech gave way to a rambling sequence of confused questions; anger, fear, and uncertainty all vying for control of his actions.

Ana stood in silence, the gun still pointed directly at her, as she waited for Stephen to finish. Seemingly devoid of the conflicting melee of emotion within the man before her, she eventually spoke in a calm voice.

"Stephen. What are you doing here?"

Managing to gather a semblance of control, Stephen attempted to regain a hold on the situation.

"What am I doing here? Ana, what's going on? What are you mixed up in?"

"Where is William?"

"Answer my questions, Ana." Stephen gritted his teeth.

"What are you going to do? Shoot me?" She laughed, "Why are you here Stephen?"

"You're working with His Lordship, and some sort of secret group called Aeternitas to overthrow the King. That's all the reason I need to shoot you. What I don't understand is how you're even here at all. The doctor announced you dead. And why didn't you come back?"

"His Lordship? Who's that?" Her voice was too casual, giving away the slightest flicker of doubt creeping into her expression.

"Don't play games with me, Ana. The man you've been meeting in London, and writing to in Oxford. He's the head of the King's intelligence network. Are you really trying to tell me you don't know who you've been working for?"

The look on her face answered his question. Where before there had been calm confidence, there was now a steely grimace.

"That man saved my life." Her voice began to crack, "When you and William left me for dead and ran away, he showed me how you are both typical of the despotic regime that quashes the potential of humanity – nothing is of any worth to you unless it benefits yourselves."

"Left you...what? Ana, we saw you die. The doctor told us it was the plague. It broke William, he hasn't been the same since." She stared at him, silently taking in all he said. "Come with me. If we go now this can all be stopped. I can take you to William. Whatever you were planning, it's madness."

"A necessary war is a just war and where there is hope only in arms, those arms are holy." An unnaturalness had taken over Ana's features, giving a feral glint to her eyes.

"What does that mean?"

"It's Machiavelli. Our cause is just, our war is holy. I

may not know the whole truth, but I know enough."

"My God. What are you talking about? Didn't you hear me, we can stop this now."

At that moment there was a crashing noise from upstairs, the same direction from which Stephen had entered the house.

"Robert." He muttered. How had he even managed to reach the window frame?

A brief lapse of his attention allowed the woman to lunge at him. As she charged to catch him off guard, Ana was able to duck under the potential threat of the pistol.

Stephen acted instinctively. Using his large frame to absorb her momentum, he spun out of the grapple, throwing her to the floor. As she fell, her arms flailed at him; her reflexes looking to gain purchase to prevent the fall. Her left hand made contact with the butt of the gun, dragging it forward in Stephen's hand. His finger was still on the trigger. The grip she had found meant he no longer had control as the hammer flew down.

A searing flash of gunpowder sent the pistol kicking back in his hand as the shot buried itself high in Ana's chest. The ball of metal entered just above the left collar bone with a spray of deep red.

"You're too late. This city will be just the beginning." She croaked, blood rushing from her body, pooling on the floor around her.

There was nothing Stephen could do for her. He stared, transfixed by shock, as the final tremors passed over her body. It was the fastest he had ever seen anyone die. Death was common in defence of the country, but he had never seen anyone lose so much blood that quickly. The shot must have caught one of the large blood vessels leading from the heart as it passed into the neck.

Thundering footsteps coming down the stairs returned Stephen's wits to him. Robert came crashing into the room, freezing in the doorway as if hitting an invisible wall.

"Stephen, is everything..." he was cut off by the sight of the dead body slumped on the floor beneath his feet. Stephen still held the gun, the smell of gunpowder hanging in the air.

"Robert, listen to me," Stephen forced the young man to hold eye contact, "This was an accident. She rushed at me and set the gun off."

"But I heard talking. Did she not know it was you? How is she even here?"

"She knew me. I thought to reason with her, but this was not the same Ana that we used to know. I don't fully understand why she was here, but I can assure you she cared nothing for who she used to be. Someone got inside her head, Robert. We need to go now. William could be in more danger than I realised."

Stephen attempted to rationalise what had just taken place even as he calmed the younger man. It had all happened so fast, but he could not afford to let it overwhelm him now. If His Lordship had been the one to turn Ana against them, against the country, he must have been planning for years. And William was watching him alone. They had to go.

Robert took in little of what Stephen had said, but the urgency in his voice struck a chord. William was in trouble and needed their help, that much was clear. He looked again at the body lying on the floor. There was nothing horrifying about it once the initial shock had worn off. Even framed in blood it held a mysterious tranquillity to it. As he looked, he was amazed at how quickly after life had left the body that it became just another object in the room. Even so soon after her death, it was clear that Ana was no longer there; it was her body, but it was not her any more.

Stephen tore the younger man from his reflections. Grabbing Robert's arm, he directed him out of the room and toward the front door. There was no point attempting to remain undetected. The gunshot would have put an end to any hope of that.

With Robert in tow, Stephen cautiously stuck his head out of the door. He was sure someone would detect the body soon, but there was nothing that could be done about it without losing too much time. They would have to go back for it later. There would be lengthy explanations necessary, but time could not be wasted with the capital under threat of some still unknown terror.

Stephen's wary return to the street outside did not go as he had anticipated. Letting the door swing wide open, he stepped slowly into the dark night. Except it was not the night they had left behind them on entering the house. An unnatural glow lit up the city. Even from the secluded street they were on, the capital's skyline could be seen; opaque blackness picked out in reds and golds.

They were not alone outside. What could easily have been the entire population of the street had poured out of their houses to watch the skies. The gunshot from the house of their unsociable neighbour had not even registered. Every single pair of eyes was fixed, unwavering on what was unfolding before them.

∞

Flickering lights set William's eyelids dancing orange. He felt weak. A coldness had crept over him despite the warm September night. A faint scent of smoke filled his nostrils, causing him to cough. Pain crashed through his body. His eyes snapped open as he remembered all that had transpired that evening. Looking over to his left he saw the outline of another figure slumped face-up on the wooden pontoon.

Fighting the flood of pain threatening to knock him back into the darkness of unconsciousness, he forced himself to sit up. He was still alive, so chances were that he could survive the knife wound. But he would need to get the blade out. Leaving it in place up to that point may have kept him alive so far, but it would start to do more harm than good if left in too long.

With a huge effort, he began ripping his shirt sleeves into long strips, before binding his waist, allowing the knife to remain between the makeshift bandages. Once he had reached the stage where he could feel the strips compressing the wound, he reached for the handle.

"Here we go." He gritted his teeth. Holding his breath, he drew the thin blade from his side.

There was no time to let the pain take control. Dropping the dagger, he wound more strips of his torn shirt around his waist. Breathing was immensely painful, but he no longer thought he was at risk of bleeding to death.

Increasingly he was becoming more aware of his surroundings. William looked up at the dancing lights that had woken him. The acrid stench of smoke was still hanging in the air. It took a moment to fully understand what was happening.

The streets resounded with the panicked screams of thousands as all around them the crackling roar of fire took hold of the capital.

"Watch the capital, it will burn without you." he recited the final section of Burns' coded message. "But he had meant a metaphorical fire, surely."

And yet, sure enough, all around him London was ablaze. Across the still waters of the Thames, the reflection of flames swirled; majestically untroubled by the fate of the city built around it.

A wave of excruciating pain rippled across William's weakened body. It was more than he could take in his fragile state. His head dropped to the floor as he fell once again into unconsciousness.

FROM THE DIARY OF SAMUEL PEPYS.

September 2nd 1666 – I was woken just after three this morning. Some of the maids, still up to ensure that everything was in place for today's feast day, had seen a fire lighting up the city. It was quite some distance away so did not concern me. I returned to my bed.

When I woke again, this time at a more regular hour, the fire could still be seen burning. News reached us that over three hundred houses had already been destroyed overnight. It was now very close to London Bridge. In order to fully assess the potential threat, I removed myself from the house; watching from the highest place nearby.

The better vantage point revealed the full terror of the ferocious blaze spreading over both sides of the bridge. Its wrath showed no sign of abating, the dry months we have had previous further fuelling its rapid advance.

The Lieutenant of the Tower of London reliably informed me that the fire started in Pudding Lane. The King's own baker is thought to have owned the premises.

Throughout the day utter pandemonium has broken out over the city. All are doing anything and everything in their power to save their worldly goods. Entire contents of houses are being hauled onto riverboats in the hope of escape. Where there are no vessels, goods are cast into the water in the hope that they might be salvaged later.

A high wind continues to drive the fire further into the city. Little encouragement was needed for it to spread before, now it means an unbreakable tide consuming all in its merciless path.

At the earliest opportunity, I made my way to warn the King of the increasing danger. He remained spectacularly calm, giving the order to destroy a layer of houses to act as a break against the further spread of the flames. If there is nothing to burn then it cannot spread. Though evidently troubled by such a catastrophe, his control of the situation was admirable.

The mayor of the city came to ask for further instruction. He is lost for what to do; the fire burns faster than they are able to work. So far no barrier against the spread has been able to appear. All that could be suggested was that more bodies be recruited to help.

On the way home the sounds of the fire were deafening. Houses cracked and creaked as their timbers twisted in the furnace. The roar of the flames was like a great wind rushing through the city, its black smoke clouds engulfing all and blistering the skin.

I invited Tom Hater to stay with us after we crossed each other in the street. His house was already gone.

This evening we were forced to pack up our goods too. All money was placed in the cellar, where hopefully it will be safe.

September 3rd 1666 – Not content to leave the

money in the cellar, I had it removed to a safer location.

Leaving the house, the streets were filled by the fleeing population. Many tried to carry items from their houses but were forced to leave them as the fire continued to spread. The roads are now littered with debris.

September 5th 1666 – New cries of fire in the city. Those that were able to remain are now packing up and leaving too. In the evening I took a boat along the river to Woolwich. The city glowed in the dying flames, lit further by the cold moonlight.

September 7th 1666 – Slowly the damage of the past few days is coming to light. It is really quite remarkable that more damage was not caused. A great casualty was the cathedral of St. Paul. Its entire roof was sent crashing in. All that remains now is a ruined shell.

September 15th 1666 – We are once again in our own home. There are no signs of damage to any of our property but the city remains on edge. I have not slept well for weeks. My dreams are filled with the dancing flames, rushing in to destroy all they come into contact with.

26

In the days following the final devastating flurries of fire across the city, the extent of the destruction became brutally clear. Entire streets had vanished, the roads left lined with blackened shells of previous structures and carpeted with ash. Many of the capital's inhabitants had been left homeless, with only what they had been able to carry remaining of their worldly goods. Those with nowhere to go had been forced to return to where their properties once stood, setting up temporary slum-like tented homes until a solution could be found.

The purpose of the model in Ana's Oxford house had finally become clear to Stephen. An exact replica of the city had been needed to work out where best to start the fire, building size had to be taken into account to achieve the most damage possible. It was supposed that further fires had been planned, Stephen believed Ana herself was leaving the house just as he had confronted her in order to fulfil her role as arsonist. If multiple attacks had been successfully made across the city and its surroundings, little would have survived.

Stephen and Richard had not waited south of the river to see what damage the fire would do. Fighting against the fleeing crowds, they had joined the effort to combat the flames. It had felt like each time they quenched an outbreak, the fire spread even faster to take control elsewhere. They didn't sleep for days. And then they had been told about William.

The owners of The Olde Wine Shades had fled to the river and found William there, half-dead, choking on the thick smoke, and seriously wounded. Only a rough set of makeshift bandages had kept him alive long enough to find a physician. But they had shown compassion and taken him to safety. Wanting to identify him to make sure they received payment, word had been spread and eventually reached Stephen. He had been treated as best the doctor could manage, but he had not regained consciousness for many days.

On both occasions Stephen had visited William, the injured man had been lost in a feverish sleep. His skin burned to the touch, sheets soaked in perspiration. Once Stephen had managed to track him down, he ensured that his friend was receiving the best possible attention. No expense had been spared in the attempt to save him. Despite William's perilously fragile appearance, the doctors did not seem too concerned by his slow recovery. It did little to assure Stephen that even as the fever burned, they were convinced their patient would fully recover.

Stephen had briefly been called before the King to explain all he could of the past couple of weeks. Charles had personally asked for the large man's aid in the matter of clearing up the capital and the mess within the intelligence system. The efforts Stephen and William had gone to in protecting the King from Greatrakes had not gone unnoticed. The unexpected responsibility had been handed to him after His Lordship had failed to make himself available for service. His whereabouts were officially classed as unknown.

On hearing the news of His Lordship's treachery, those in the know had decided it would be best to keep any knowledge of the plot contained to a select few. It was still not clear who had actually started the fire, Stephen had been authorised to pursue any leads he could find. The King had acted quickly to move against further attacks on the capital, and his own person. Security heightened as the arsonist responsible was searched for.

It was early one morning when Stephen was woken by his house staff knocking on his bedroom door.

"Sorry to wake you so early sir, but something has been left on the doorstep."

"Something?"

"There's a note with it, for you."

Perhaps some new information on Aeternitas had been made available. Racing downstairs, he found a lumpy looking canvas sack by his front door. It looked as if it had been dragged a long way through the streets, there were patches of dirt clinging to damp sections of material. A note had been left carefully balanced so that it was immediately visible. It clearly instructed that Stephen alone was to open the unusual package. It ended:

Courtesy of the Burns Group

Intrigued, Stephen loosened the piece of thick cord that held it together and peeked through the hole he had created. Immediately recoiling in disgust, he took a moment to collect himself before returning to the grizzly sight. Within the bag lay the freshly hacked remains of a man. Limbs severed from the body, they had been piled on top of each other.

Looking down again at the note left to him, Stephen turned it over to find the rest of the message.

> This is your man, and ours. We found him by the docks in a drunken stupor. We've had a little talk and before too much persuasion he was singing of his talents as an arsonist and a murderer. Went by the name of Thomas Russell, you may know the name already. We believe he may have caused a few issues for you before. Our deepest regrets for any confusion that may have arisen in Oxford, you will appreciate that his description matched yours fairly well.

Stephen did know the name. The man now lying in a sack at his feet had caused plenty of trouble before further north. But reports had recorded Russell as dead in a raid over a year ago. He supposed it made a certain amount of sense, His Lordship must have identified his talents and recruited him; covering up any further investigations with a falsified death. That appeared to be a favourite ploy of his.

Turning away from the gory offering left at his front door, Stephen instructed some of his staff to help him load it onto a cart.

"If left much longer this will start to stink. All the dogs of London will be on us."

With the understanding that they were on no account to open it, he left them with the task of delivering the large sack to a discreet doctor who regularly worked with members of the King's information service. There the body would be able to be properly identified and disposed of.

Despite the death of the suspected arsonist Russell,

security remained tight in the capital. Stephen was forced to spend all his time in meetings with high ranking members of His Majesty's government, all the time doubting whether they could really be trusted. He had not been able to see William more than twice over the last few weeks.

William's condition weighed heavily on Stephen's already shattered nerves. Lack of sleep and the added responsibility of reporting to the King gave him little patience for the calm assurance of the doctors. He found it increasingly difficult to focus on the extra tasks placed upon him. His thoughts frequently wandered to the state of his injured friend. It had been three days since he was last able to visit. For all he knew, William could be drastically worse than the last time he saw him.

Stephen found himself constantly trying to find positives in what had occurred. Though terrible, the fire did not seem to have achieved its aim. The King had actually come out very well from it. Charles had been down on the streets, commanding the fight against the advancing flames. Seen by many of the inhabitants of the city, public opinion had grown increasingly favourable. The community spirit within London was as tight-knit as it had ever been. If anything, the chances of a popular uprising had decreased dramatically. The city would bounce back, it always did.

A sharp rap on the office door brought Stephen's attention away from his erratic thoughts.

"Come in."

The building next to Westminster had been deemed unsafe. For the time being, Stephen had set up in one of the small rooms inside the main government building. To call it an office would have been an exaggeration. It was really nothing more than a large cupboard or storage area, with just enough apce to squeeze in a desk and two chairs. With Stephen inside, it became very claustrophobic. He had to remind himself regularly that it would only be temporary.

The door slowly swung open. Stephen stood to receive his unexpected guest, before almost collapsing back into his seat in shock. William stood before him, barely recognisable from the unconscious figure he had been days before. Last Stephen had seen of him, though evidently very ill, he had still maintained some semblance of his healthy self. Now, the many days of near-death were clear on William's face. His cheeks were drawn up into his face, bones pushing against ivory white skin; giving him a gaunt, skeletal look.

"I'm here to meet the new head of King's intelligence." The stretched skin broke into a disconcerting, wide grin. "I hear he could use some assistance."

"Will? How are you on your feet? You look like the reaper himself."

"I'll survive. Doctors seem to think I'm in the clear now, just need to put the weight back on. I love what you've done with the place by the way."

Stephen was lost for words. After so many days worrying over the fate of his friend, the man had waltzed in looking like a corpse but full of his old sarcasm.

"Stop gawping man, it's not that bad." William helped himself to a seat. "You must be busy?"

"Errr...yes, I am, very busy actually. The whole intelligence network needs to be redeveloped. We don't know who was working with His Lordship and who is a genuine asset."

"I suppose they told you I killed him?" William's eyes flickered around the room.

Stephen shook his head. "There was no one else there when you got picked up, we assumed he had left you for dead?"

"No, he was definitely dead." He grimaced. "I don't suppose you found the woman from Oxford? His Lordship, or John Fenneck I should say, was using Ana's name to taunt me."

Stephen replied carefully, selecting his words with caution.

"I found her, but the woman you loved died Will. That woman wasn't your Ana. His Lordship, or did you call him John, was just trying to get the upper hand on you in any way possible." He sensed the relief flood through his friend. It was true, the real Ana had died long ago. After a short pause, William returned to his previous topic.

"I was wondering if there was anything I could do to help? It must be rather daunting setting up an entire spy network alone. I have suspicions that His Lordship - and yes his name was apparently John Fenneck - I think his influence went deeper than we anticipated. He knew of our involvement when Greatrakes met the King."

"Fenneck eh? We'll have to see if that helps us at all. Well, Robert has been helping as much as he can. But his talents are still very raw. I would be delighted if you would help. Truth be told, I have no idea where to start."

"Lunch seems like as good a place as any." William adopted a toothy grin, responding to the beaming face of the giant man sitting opposite him.

"Perfect."

THE END

∞

COMING SOON

Book Two of the Aeternitas Trilogy

RISE OF THE PHOENIX

Read an excerpt now

PROLOGUE

Wheels clattered along the well-worn road, throwing up clods of dirt as they bounced along the uneven surface. At the sound of his pursuers, the driver cracked his whip above the horses' heads in encouragement. He could still hear the ominous drumroll of many hooves fast approaching in the wake of the carriage. Their heavy breathing became audible as they drew closer.

It had been a long chase. Whoever was following him had appeared out of the trees miles back, but his trusty horses were the pride of the postal service. He had managed to hold a lead and he knew, if only he could stay ahead a little longer, he would get his cargo to safety.

The driver dared not look over his shoulder. The dark nights that only deep winter could bring had taken full effect, leaving the path ahead only visible by the faint light of the oil lamps that were swinging frantically from the side of the carriage. It was taking all his vast experience to remain in control. Such conditions were navigable, but normally not at such reckless speed. He could only guess at the number following him. From the sound of their mounts, he reckoned on somewhere between six and ten. They must have been accomplished riders to keep pace with him for so long.

As they rounded a corner in the road he felt his pursuers fall back. Deciding it was finally safe to glance over his shoulder, the driver saw them spreading across the width of the road. The thick trees on either side would mean there was no turning back. But that could mean only one thing – something lay in wait ahead. They had never meant to catch him at all, just to push him further up the road.

Wrenching his head back to what lay before him, he immediately saw it. Flames danced in the dark night, revealing many silhouetted figures blocking the road. Some held torches, illuminating strange masks that covered their faces. Behind them lay a fallen tree, dragged across the road in case the coach attempted to burst through their ranks. There would be no escape that way.

His flight had been valiant, but he knew there would be no way out now. Bringing the carriage to a standstill, he remained seated, steeling himself for whatever was about to take place.

The figures in the road parted to allow the approach of a lone horseman. A tall figure, dressed from head to toe entirely in black, steered the mount forward. The horse was as dark as the rider, only a thin streak of white between it's eyes preventing it being entirely swallowed by the night. A wide brimmed hat sat low on the rider's head, making the mask they wore below it almost unnecessary. A thin sliver of pale skin, all that was not covered, highlighted a pair of dangerously pale green eyes that flashed in the lamplight.

"I believe you have something that belongs to me." The voice was forced and rasping, as if the owner had been deprived of water for too long and it caused them pain.

"I'm just a post-" The driver was prevented from finishing as lead shot burst through his knee, shattering the cap. Falling from the carriage, he clutched at the mangled remains of the joint, screaming in agony as he lay in the cold dirt.

The rider in black lowered a smoking pistol, placing it in a sheath on his mount's saddle.

"I'm not in the mood for games Jack. I know who you are, and I know what you were tasked to carry. Where is it?"

"I'm a postman." Jack managed through gritted teeth.

Dismounting slowly, the rider paced over to the fallen man as if contemplating his next action. A booted foot came to rest on Jack's knee, gradually increasing the pressure until all the rider's weight was on the shattered limb. Jack screamed.

"Where is it Jack?" The question was a venomous whisper. "I have the carriage now so I will find it eventually. You lost. You can make this quick by telling me what I want to know."

"No." It was all the fallen man could manage before the pain sent him retching over the cold floor.

The boot stamped down, cracking the remaining shards of kneecap.

"Where is it?" The rider's voice was vile, high pitched.

Even if he'd wanted to, Jack was incapable of replying, too consumed by the pain to realise what was being asked of him. Losing patience, the rider pulled a second pistol from their belt, sending a second shot at Jack, this time into his skull. With a thud, the carriage driver's limp head met the floor. His blood was already beginning to freeze in the grass nearby.

Remounting, the rider motioned to one of the torchbearers.

"Bring the whole carriage. Leave the body."

∞

Printed in Great Britain
by Amazon